## of Special Importance to our American Readers

### The Case of the 24 MISSING TITLES ...

Over the years many of our American readers have been distressed that Harlequin Romances were published in Canada three months ahead of the United States release date.

We are pleased to announce that effective April 1972 Harlequin Romances will have simultaneous publication of new titles throughout North America.

To solve the problem of the 24 MISSING TITLES (No. 1553 to No. 1576) arrangements will be made with many Harlequin Romance retailers to have these missing titles available to you before the end of 1972.

Watch for your retailer's special display!

If, however, you have difficulty obtaining any of the missing titles, please write us.

Yours truly,

The Publisher
HARLEQUIN ROMANCES.

OTHER
*Harlequin Romances*
by BETTY NEELS

but I don't speak Dutch – it was my fault,' and smiled with relief when he answered her in English.

'You were on the wrong side of the road.' He spoke curtly, but Emma was so relieved to hear her own tongue that she hardly noticed it and went on, 'I'm so glad you're English,' and when he gave her a sudden sharp look and barked 'Why?' at her, she explained cheerfully:

'Well, the Dutch are awfully nice, but they're not very – very lighthearted. . . .'

He laughed nastily. 'Indeed? Am I supposed to be lighthearted because I have been run into by a careless girl who has probably damaged my car? You are an appalling driver.'

'I'm not,' said Emma with spirit, 'I'm quite good, only they drive on the wrong side of the road and when I turned the corner I forgot – only for a moment.' She returned the icy stare from the green eyes with a cool one from her own hazel ones and added with dignity:

'Of course, I will pay for any damage.' Her heart sank as she said it; Rolls-Royces were expensive cars, doubtless their repairs cost a good deal more than the lesser fry of the motoring world. She blinked at the unpalatable thought that she would probably be footing the bill – in instalments – for months ahead and ventured uncertainly:

'Perhaps the damage isn't too bad.'

The man looked down a nose which reminded her strongly of Wellington's. 'Probably extensive,' he stated evenly, his eyes boring into hers. Emma drew a long breath – it wasn't any good trying to guess at the cost; she thrust the unpleasant thought to the back of her mind and remarked practically, 'Well, if we could undo the cars we could see. . . .'

A faint convulsion swept over the stranger's face. 'And how do you propose to – er – undo them?' His voice was too smooth for her liking. She shot him a doubtful glance and then walked past him to have a look. It seemed to her that the Ford had had the worst of the encounter, for its bumpers were dented and twisted and hooked under the Rolls' bumper. Emma, who knew very little about cars anyway, hoped that its engine was all right. She said now,

# WISH WITH THE CANDLES

by

BETTY NEELS

HARLEQUIN BOOKS    TORONTO WINNIPEG

Original hard cover edition published in 1972
by Mills & Boon Limited, 17 - 19 Foley Street,
London   W1A 1DR, England

© Betty Neels 1972

Harlequin edition published June, 1972

SBN 373-01593-3

The Harlequin trade mark, consisting of the word
HARLEQUIN and the portrayal of a Harlequin, is registered
in the United States Patent Office and in the Canada Trade
Marks Office.

Printed in Canada

# CHAPTER ONE

MISS EMMA HASTINGS closed her eyes and a shudder ran
through her nicely curved person; she opened them again
almost immediately, hoping, rather after the manner of a
small child, that what she didn't wish to see would be
gone. Of course it wasn't. The Rolls-Royce Cornische
convertible still gleamed blackly within a yard or so of
her appalled gaze. In other, happier circumstances she
would have been delighted to have had the opportunity
of viewing its magnificence at such close quarters, but
now, at this moment, she could only wish it on the other
side of the world, not here within inches of her, with the
bumper of her humble Ford Popular, third hand, locked
with the pristine beauty of the Rolls' own single
bumper.

Its driver was getting out and Emma made haste to do
the same, quite forgetting that the Ford's door handle on
her side could be temperamental and had taken that
moment to jam while she was fiddling with it. As she
tugged and pushed she had plenty of time to observe the
man strolling towards them. As magnificent as his car, she
thought, eyeing his height and breadth of shoulder, and
her heart sank as she saw his hair, for it was a dark, rich
copper, and red-headed people were notoriously nasty-
tempered. Her mother apparently thought otherwise, for
she said softly, 'Oh, Emma, what a remarkably handsome
man!' and Emma, cross because she couldn't get out
began tartly, 'Oh, Mother ...' and went on silent
fighting the door, which, to make matters worse, yield
instantly under the man's hand.

She got out then, all five foot three of her, feeli
little better because she was face to face with him
though her eyes were on a level with his tie. She st
its rich silkiness for a long moment and then lift
gaze to his face. His eyes, she noticed with someth
shock were green, unexpectedly cool. Probably
furious; she said quickly in her pleasant voice, '

5

'If we could lift your car off mine....'

The convulsion returned briefly. 'Have you ever tried to lift a Rolls-Royce, young lady?' His voice was silky and when she shook her head he went on, still very silky, 'You really are bird-witted, aren't you?'

He had come to stand beside her, now he lifted an elegantly shod foot and gently kicked that piece of bumper which the Ford had wrapped round the Rolls. It fell to the road with an apologetic clang and Emma, watching it with her mouth open, didn't wait for its last rattle before she burst into hot speech.

'How dare you – how dare you kick my car, just because it's old!' She could have been accusing him of kicking an old lady from her throbbing accents; her voice shook with temper; her quite ordinary face had acquired a fine colour, even her pale brown hair seemed to have taken on a more vivid sheen. The man turned to look at her once more, intently this time, as if he were studying something he had previously overlooked.

'And how dare you drive on the wrong side of the road?' he queried mildly, 'an offence which I fear in this country is frowned upon by the law.'

As if some demon god had been listening to his words, a small white car skimmed round the bend of the road, made as if to pass them, and then stopped. It had the word *Politie* painted on its sides and the familiar blue lamp on its roof, and if that wasn't enough to convince Emma that Damocles' sword really had fallen, its doors opened and two large square men in the uniform of the Dutch police stepped out, advanced with the deliberate step of their kind and then stood to look about them. After a minute one of them spoke, and Emma, supposing it to be the equivalent of 'Well, well, what's all this?' said apologetically, 'I'm so sorry, I can't understand ...!' and then turned to the stranger. 'Do you speak the language at all?' she wanted to know. 'Perhaps you could make them understand.'

He looked at her without expression. 'I'll see what I can do,' he told her shortly, and then turned to the two policemen and broke into crisp speech, not a word of which did Emma understand. The policemen could though, they listened thoughtfully, inspected his papers and smiled at him as though he were an old friend. They smiled at Emma too and the stranger said, 'They wish to see your licence.'

She produced it and then, upon request, her passport, and stood patiently while they studied it, but her patience wore a little thin when the man received the passport from the police and instead of handing it back to her, had a good look at it himself, thereby culling the information that she was Emma Hastings, single, Theatre Sister by profession, hazel-eyed and brown-haired, and that she had been born at Mutchley Magna in the County of Dorset on the first of May, 1945. She longed to tell him how grossly impertinent he was, but since he had apparently smoothed things over with the police, she didn't dare.

He handed it back to her without a word and turned to the police once more, who wrote in their notebooks for a while and then laughing with him in what she considered to be a quite offensive manner, went to ease the Rolls away from her car while the stranger, without so much as a glance in her direction, got into the Ford and reversed it until there was a space between the cars' bonnets once more. This done, the police saluted her politely, made some cheerful remark to her companion and shot away in their little car. As they disappeared round the bend of the road Emma said accusingly, 'You're not English – you're Dutch! Why didn't you say so in the first place?'

The green eyes twinkled even though he said gravely enough:

'I imagine that I wasn't feeling lighthearted enough. I trust you will forgive me?'

He was laughing at her behind the blandness. She went a fiery red and said stiffly, 'I'm sorry I was rude. Thank you for – for . . .'

'Getting round the law? Think nothing of it, young lady, although I feel sure that you would have managed very well for yourself – our policemen, while by no means lighthearted, are kind.' His voice was mocking; Emma shot him a look of annoyance which he ignored as he walked over to the Ford and leaned through its open

8

window to speak to her mother. She stood uncertainly watching him and listening to her mother's pleasant, still youthful voice mingling with his deep one. Presently her mother laughed and called from the car, 'Emma dear, do come here a minute.'

Emma went, reluctant yet dying of curiosity to know what they were talking about.

'Just fancy,' said her mother, 'this gentleman knows Oudewater very well. I was just telling him that we intend to be weighed on the Witch's Scales there and perhaps spend the night, and he tells me that there is a very comfortable little hotel there. We might do better than one night and stay a day or two – we could reach Gouda and Schoonhoven very easily from there.' She glanced at the stranger for collaboration and he smiled with a charm which Emma found strangely disquieting even though the smile was directed at her mother.

'You like castles?' he asked. 'You have of course heard of the performances of Son et Lumière at the castle of Wijk bij Duurstede?' He spoke to Mrs. Hastings and didn't look at Emma. 'It is only a few miles along the river from Schoonhoven – you could perhaps visit it; there is a pleasant hotel there too – old-fashioned but comfortable, and the service is most friendly.'

'It sounds just the sort of thing we're looking for,' exclaimed Mrs. Hastings, and Emma sighed quietly; there really was no need for her mother to take this man into her confidence as she was obviously going to do. A man who drove a Rolls worth several thousand pounds and wore silk shirts and hand-tailored suits wasn't likely to be interested in the smaller hotels in out-of-the-way villages; probably he was just being polite. She caught her mother's eye and frowned slightly, and that lady gave her the innocent round-eyed look she adopted when she didn't intend to take any notice of her daughter. 'We've three days left,' explained Mrs. Hastings, 'and not much money.'

'Mother!' said Emma in a repressive voice, and avoided the man's amused eyes.

Her mother looked unworried. 'Well, dear,' she said reasonably, 'anyone looking at our car can see that for

9

themselves, can't they? Besides, we aren't likely to meet you again, are we?' She smiled at the man, who smiled back so nicely that Emma instantly forgave him for looking amused. She loved her mother very much, but now that her father was dead her mother needed someone to protect her from making friends with everyone she met. She went a little nearer the car and said quietly, her voice a little stiff:

'If you will let me have your name and address – so that I can pay you for the repairs . . .'

She looked sideways at the Rolls as she spoke and couldn't see anything wrong with it at all, but that didn't mean to say that there wasn't something vital and frightfully expensive that needed doing under its elegant bonnet.

He, it seemed, wasn't going to give her either his name or his address. He said mildly, 'I'll contact you through the A.A. when the repairs, if they're needed, are ready – the police have all the particulars.' And when he saw her worried look, 'No, they'll do nothing more. I explained. And now allow me to make sure there is no damage to your car before you resume your journey.'

Emma went with him, to peer at the engine and watch while he pulled at a few wires, which, she had to admit to herself, she hadn't realized were of any importance at all, and turned a few screws with large hands – well-kept hands, she noticed, with square-tipped fingers. She took a good look at his face too and silently agreed with her mother that he was indeed good-looking in a rugged way. He looked up suddenly, gave her another cool stare and said unsmilingly, 'Try the lights, will you? and then switch on the engine.'

She did as she was bid and after a minute or so he observed, 'Everything seems all right – you've got a worn plug, though.'

He took out a pocket book as he spoke and scribbled a note and tore out the page and handed it to her. 'There's a garage in Oudewater, on the left of the road as you go into the town. Give this to anyone there and they will put it right for you – it's only a trifle, but it may cause trouble later on.'

'Thank you,' said Emma politely, 'you've been very kind.' She swallowed and went on quickly, 'I apologize for what I said about the Dutch. I like them very much.'

He smiled at her with such enchantment that her pulse galloped.

'But you were quite right; we aren't lighthearted. I hope you enjoy the rest of your holiday.' He nodded in a friendly way and went back to the car again, put his head through the window and wished her mother a longer and warmer goodbye, then he got back into his own car and sat waiting for Emma to go. She drove away, on the right side of the road this time and without looking at him, although she would have liked to very much. Mrs. Hastings, having no mixed-up feelings, stuck her head out of the window and waved.

When they had gone a mile or so along the road Emma stopped the car and in answer to her mother's inquiring look, said sheepishly, 'I just want to see what he's written,' and opened the note he had given her. It was, of course, in Dutch; even if it had been in English she doubted if she would have understood a word of its scrawled writing; a good thing perhaps, for he had written: 'Give this car a quick overhaul without the young lady knowing. Charge her for a new plug and I'll settle with you later.' It was signed with the initials J.T.

Emma folded the paper carefully and put it back in her purse and her mother said thoughtfully, 'He was nice, that man. Emma, why don't we know anyone like him?'

Emma's pretty eyes twinkled. 'Dear Mother, because we don't move in those circles, do we? Not any more.'

'You liked him?'

Emma chuckled. 'Mother, we spoke to him for about ten minutes, and you did most of the talking. As far as I was concerned I wasn't very friendly and nor was he.'

Her mother sighed. 'No, dear, I noticed. Never mind, perhaps we shall bump into him again.' She nodded cheerfully, unaware of her unhappy choice of words.

'Oh dear, I do hope not,' said Emma, and knew as she

said it that there was nothing she would like more than to meet him again. She steered the car carefully to the other side of the road. 'There's the garage,' she remarked, glad to have something else to think about.

The young mechanic she addressed in English grinned and disappeared to reappear a minute later with an older man who said, 'Good day, miss,' and when he had read the note she handed to him, looked at her with a smile and asked, 'You stay at the hotel?' and when Emma nodded, went on, 'De Witte Engel – by the canal in the *centrum*, you cannot miss. The boy will come for the car. O.K.?'

'Oh, very O.K.,' said Emma with relief. 'I think I need a new plug.'

The man smiled again. 'That comes in order, miss. Make no trouble.' Which she rightly surmised to mean that she wasn't to worry about it.

Oudewater was rather like going through a door into Grimms' Fairy Tales; the road was cobbled and narrow and there was, inevitably, a canal splitting it down the middle, reflecting the great variety of gabled roofs of the old houses lining it. Possibly because it was so small, the little town seemed full of people. Emma drove cautiously down one side of the canal, crossed a bridge and went slowly up the other side until she reached the hotel. It was small and dark and cool inside, although through an open door at the back of the hall Emma could see the May sunshine streaming on to a small garden. There was no one to be seen, but there were voices clearly to be heard behind several of the doors leading from the hall. Emma, obedient to a large placard which requested '*Bellen, S.V.P.*', rang the enormous brass bell standing beneath it, and one of the doors opened and an elderly man, not very tall but immensely thick through, appeared.

'We should like to stay the night,' stated Emma, who like everyone else of her race, was ever hopeful that everyone else spoke English. It was a relief when he said at once, 'Certainly, miss. Yourself and . . .?'

'My mother. How much is it for bed and breakfast?'

'Twelve *gulden* and fifty cents each, miss. Two rooms, perhaps? We are not yet so busy.' He turned round with surprising lightness for so large a man and took two large keys, each attached to a chain with a brass ball on its end. 'You would like to see them?'

The rooms were in the front of the hotel, overlooking the bustling street and its canal, and although they were sparsely furnished they were spotlessly clean with wash-basins squeezed into their corners.

'Plumbing?' inquired Mrs. Hastings, who liked her warm bath. They followed the landlord down an immensely long passage which ended in a door which he flung open with a flourish to reveal a narrow tiled room with what appeared to be a wooden garden seat up against one wall and a bath shaped like a comfortable armchair. 'Very nice,' said Emma before her mother could comment on the garden seat. 'We may stay two nights.'

The landlord nodded and led the way downstairs again and while they filled in their cards at the desk, fetched their bags and took them upstairs. When he came down Emma inquired hopefully:

'I suppose we couldn't have tea?'

'Certainly, miss.' He waved a hand like a ham in the direction of the coffee room. 'And perhaps an evening meal?'

Which seemed a splendid idea; the ladies agreed without hesitation and opened the coffee room door.

It was dark, just like the hall, but in an old and comfortable way, with windows overlooking the street and a great many little tables dotted around. There were large upholstered chairs too and a billiard table in the middle which sustained a neatly laid out collection of papers.

Over tea and little wafer-thin biscuits, they discussed their day.

'A very satisfactory one,' murmured Mrs. Hastings. 'How many miles have we done, darling?'

Emma said promptly, 'Only about ninety, but we did Utrecht very thoroughly, didn't we, and Leiden. I liked Leiden and all those dear little villages between.'

Her mother agreed a little absentmindedly; she was thinking about something else. 'Do you suppose that car was badly damaged, Emma? I wasn't very near, but I couldn't see a mark on it.'

'Nor could I,' Emma frowned thoughtfully, 'and I don't quite understand why he said we should hear through the A.A. That time I bumped into those cows – you remember? – it was the insurance firm, and I'm sure you're supposed to exchange names and addresses.'

Mrs. Hastings said brightly, 'Well, he knows ours; I saw him looking at the luggage labels. I suppose he'll send the bill to you.' She added not quite so brightly, 'Shall we be able to pay it?'

'Of course,' said Emma sturdily, stifling doubts, 'it won't come for ages, they never do, and it won't be much. Don't you worry about it.' She frowned again. 'But we didn't see him drive away, did we? Supposing he couldn't. Perhaps he's still there....'

'Nonsense,' said Mrs. Hastings. 'Now you're worrying; that sort of car never breaks down. Let's go for a walk.'

They explored the town first, and then, because it was such a pleasant evening, strolled along a country road which seemed to lead nowhere. 'A pity we have to go back,' remarked Mrs. Hastings. 'It's been such a lovely holiday, Emma dear, and so sweet of you to let me tag along with you. You might have had more fun with someone of your own age.'

'Fiddlesticks,' said Emma vigorously. 'I've loved every minute of it, too – I'm glad we chose Holland, and if I'd gone with someone else they might have wanted to do things I didn't want to do. We've seen a lot – besides, we like poking around, don't we?'

Her mother agreed. 'Shall we go to Gouda tomorrow?'

'Yes, and the day after, Schoonhoven and then we can go to that place Wijk something or other. There's enough money for us to see the Son et Lumière at the castle. We can go south from there in time to catch the night boat from Zeebrugge.'

'Ten days go so quickly,' remarked her mother on a sigh, 'but with Kitty coming home – and it wouldn't be kind to leave her alone. It's a pity Gregory and Susan couldn't have her, but with a new baby in the house ...'

'Well, I couldn't have had a longer holiday, anyway. Sister Cox is having her feet done as soon as I get back.'

'Poor thing,' said her mother, and meant it; she had only met Sister Cox at Hospital fêtes, on which annual occasions the Theatre Superintendent showed only the better side of her nature. 'Let's go back, I'm hungry.'

They dined at one of the tables in the coffee room with a sprinkling of other guests who were, however, not dining but drinking beer or coffee and when the mood took them, playing billiards as well. They greeted the two ladies with friendliness and then, with perfect manners, ignored them while they ate. The food was good although limited in choice, and Emma, who had no weight problems, enjoyed everything she was offered and then sat back watching the players while she and her mother drank their coffee. Perhaps it was because of her obvious interest in the game that she was asked, in peculiar but understandable English, if she played herself, and when she admitted that she did and was asked if she would care for a game she took it as something of a compliment, for in none of the other hotels they had visited had she ever seen a woman playing. She took a cue and gave such a good account of herself that there was a little round of applause when the game was finally finished, even though she hadn't won. Thinking about it in her little bedroom later she wondered if, despite the language difficulty, she should have told them that she had played with her father for years before he died, and was considered something of an expert even though she wasn't wildly enthusiastic about the game. She went on to wonder, for no reason at all, if the man they had met that afternoon played too; if so, she would dearly love to beat him. She smiled at the silliness of the thought as she went to sleep.

They went to Gouda the next day and spent a long time looking at the Town Hall, which was quaint and very old and being in the middle of the square, could be seen properly by just walking slowly round it. They went to Sint Janskerk too, because the guide book told them to and were very glad that they had because of its quiet spaciousness and lovely stained glass windows. When they came out at last, they wandered off into the little lanes and alleys around it and stared at the small ancient houses, huddled together as though to support each other through the centuries, and when they found their way back to the *Markt*, they lunched off a tremendous pancake in a restaurant which looked like a Dutch interior painted by Pieter de Hoogh. They spent an hour exploring the rest of the little town and looking at its shops and then got into the car again and drove the mile or so to the complex of lakes just outside the town, where they stopped at a café for cups of milkless tea which they drank sitting at a little table overlooking the water and admired the boats bowling along before the stiff breeze they had come to expect in Holland.

'The car's running well,' remarked Mrs. Hastings as they started back. 'I had no idea that one new plug could make so much difference.'

'Yes, I'm surprised – it's almost as though she's been overhauled – it's surprising what a new plug will do. They only charged five *gulden* too. I must get the bumper fixed when we get home.' Which remark led her to think of the stranger again.

The next day they travelled the few miles to Schoonhoven, along a charming country road with little traffic upon it and a warm sun shining down on the flat green land around them, and spent the whole day wandering in and around that little town. A great deal of their time was taken up with a visit to the Edelambachthuis on its main canal, watching the silversmiths for which the place was famous and so enchanted with their work that they spent more than they could really afford on some silver tea-spoons because Mrs. Hastings declared them to be exactly right for the Dresden tea-set she still cherished. They parked the car in the town and lunched at the hotel on the edge of the river and then crossed by the nearby ferry to walk along the dyke on its other bank until they remembered that they still had to be weighed on the Witch's Scales in Oudewater. They went back the way they had come, with the little river running beside the road the whole way and the car windows open to the afternoon heat of the sun. When they got back they had tea at the hotel, examining their diplomas guaranteeing them immunity from a witch's fiery end and then making their plans for the following day – their last day.

They left Oudewater the next day with regret. The regret on Mrs. Hastings' part was for the comforts of the little hotel and the cheerful bustle of the little town; Emma's was for quite another reason. The further they travelled from Oudewater the less likely it was that she would ever see the owner of the Rolls-Royce again.

They went slowly, admiring the trim little villas as they went; there were bigger houses too, not so easily seen from the road, but a mile or so from the town Emma slowed the Ford to a sedate pace so that they could stare their fill at a tall red brick house with a handsome double stair leading up to its massive front door and rows of enormous windows. It stood in full view of the road, but well back from it, and the big iron gates which led to it stood open.

'My dear, the curtains – it would take miles and miles,' said Mrs. Hastings, and then, 'I'd love to see inside.'

Emma nodded. The house attracted her in some way, it looked a little austere from the outside perhaps, but inside she imagined that it might be very beautiful. She said thoughtfully, 'I daresay some of the curtains are the original ones put up when the house was built.'

Her gaze shifted to the garden, very formal and full of colour, and she couldn't help but contrast it with the small cottage in which her mother lived, with its pocket handkerchief of a lawn at its front and the small stretch of garden behind, probably her mother was thinking the same thing. She patted her parent's hands lying on her lap and said comfortingly, 'Never mind, darling, the garden at home is very pretty.' And they smiled at each other, remembering the lovely garden they had had in the old house, before her father died. Emma missed it still; it would be even worse for her mother. She took a final look and put her foot, in its neat sandal, down on the accelerator.

They dawdled along the dyke road bordering the Lek and stopped for a picnic lunch by the water, watching the barges chugging their way up and down its broad water as they ate, and presently, when they resumed their journey, they caught their first glimpse of the castle as they approached Wijk bij Duurstede, its round red brick towers standing out amongst the trees, but the miniature town itself they didn't see at all untill they turned off the road on to a narrow street which brought them to a cobbled square, shaded by enormous trees and lined with tall old houses and a handful of shops. The hotel faced the square; an old building with a balcony on either side of its door and called, rather inappropriately, thought Emma, *'de Keizer's Kroon,'* for its homely appearance hardly justified its royal title. But even if the hotel wasn't royal, their welcome was. They went inside, straight into a vast room with a bar at one end, a billiard table in the middle and a number of tables around its walls; most of these were covered with the little woollen rugs Emma rather liked, but half a dozen tables were laid for dinner with starched white cloths and highly polished silver and glass. Standing proudly amid them was the landlord, a large, genial man who listened carefully to Emma's request for rooms and led them through a double door into a narrow passage with an equally narrow staircase. 'Two rooms?' asked Emma hopefully as they started to climb, then came to an abrupt halt as he shook his head and broke into regretful Dutch, holding up one finger to clinch his argument, and then beckoned them on.

The room was at the back of the hotel, with two enormous windows, a very high ceiling and large enough to house the vast furniture in it twice over. Emma stared fascinated at the bed with its carved headboard putting her in mind of the Coronation chair in Westminster Abbey, greatly enlarged, but this awe-inspiring piece of furniture was offset by a small but modern washbasin and everything in the room shone with soap and polish, besides which the landlord, rather in the manner of a conjuror producing a rabbit from a hat, flung open a door at the end of a little passage to disclose a very large bathroom containing a very small bath. They agreed most happily to take the room and presently, when they had tidied themselves, went downstairs, where over a cup of tea they made the landlord understand that they wanted tickets for the Son et Lumière performance that evening. It was disappointing when he shook his head and after some thought, said, 'Many people.'

'We'll go and see anyway,' said Emma. 'Perhaps there'll be a couple of cancelled seats.'

The castle wasn't hard to find, for the town was so very small and its roads few. There was a gate leading to the grounds around the castle with a hut beside it and a man sitting inside, and when Emma asked about tickets she was delighted to hear the beautifully pedantic English with which he answered her. She exclaimed warmly, 'Oh, how well you speak, and how nice for us,' and he smiled and replied, 'I'm the schoolmaster here,' as though that explained everything.

Emma said a little anxiously, 'They said at the hotel that there weren't any seats left for tonight. We're going back to England tomorrow and we were told by – someone that we really should see it.'

He stared at her as she spoke; now he asked slowly, 'Someone you met?' and when she nodded, went on, 'It just so happens that I have two returned tickets. How lucky you are, ladies.'

The price seemed very modest, but perhaps it wasn't a very lavish affair. Emma paid up cheerfully and after a few minutes talk she and her mother walked through the gateway; it seemed a good idea to see the castle now that they were so close to it. It was an impressive sight, even though partly ruined, and the trees and shrubs around it added to its impressiveness. They looked their fill, and very pleased with themselves, went back to the hotel for dinner.

There were quite a number of people dining and even more drinking coffee. They sat in the window eating a simple well-cooked meal and, because it was their last night in Holland, drinking a glass of wine with it. The performance was to start at nine o'clock, but long before then the little town came alive with cars and bus loads of people, and by the time Emma and her mother arrived at the gate to the grounds, there was a throng of people. It took them a little while to find their seats, but Emma, who had a persevering nature, showed their tickets to a successive number of people until they at length arrived at them. They were good seats; the man at the gate hadn't exaggerated when he had told them that they were in an excellent position. They sat down and Emma looked around at the sea of strange faces. Not all strange though, for coming towards them with an unhurried stride was the man in the Rolls-Royce.

Emma's first reaction was one of pure pleasure, the second, satisfaction that she had put on the coral pink silk shirtwaister, an ordinary enough garment, but the colour suited her, but it could have been mud-coloured sacking for all the good it did her. His glance was as brief as his polite greeting before he addressed himself to her mother. It was then that Emma saw that he wasn't alone.

A majestic middle-aged lady, beautifully coiffured and gowned, accompanied him, so did a tall willowy girl with glowing golden hair and an outfit which Emma would have sacrificed her eye-teeth to possess. He introduced them with a cool charm as 'My aunt, Mevrouw Teyliugen, and Saskia,' which did nothing to clear up the question as to who he was himself. The majestic lady smiled nicely, shook hands and sat down between Emma and her mother. Her nephew took a seat beside Mrs. Hastings, and Saskia, after more handshaking, sat beside him. 'And that,' thought Emma, sadly put out, 'is that.'

It was her mother who asked, 'May we know your name? You haven't told us, you know,' she smiled. 'I don't know what Emma calls you, but I think of you as the man with red hair, and that really won't do.'

He laughed. 'I must apologize. Teylingen, Justin Teylingen.' His voice sounded friendly enough, but Emma, from where she sat, got the impression that he had been reluctant to tell them and she couldn't begin to guess why. After all, they were leaving Holland in the morning, and they didn't even know where he lived. She wondered if her mother, who had no inhibitions about asking questions, would ask him that too and watched her framing the words on her lips, but Mijnheer Teylingen must have been watching too, because before her mother could get the question out he asked her a question of his own which presently led the conversation right away from the subject, and even if Mrs. Hastings had been clever enough to slip her inquiry in again, there was no chance now, for the performance had begun.

It was fascinating; Emma sat entranced even though she couldn't understand the words, but the programme had an explanation in English anyway, and to watch and listen was enough – besides, from time to time the aunt whispered an explanation or two which Mrs. Hastings passed on to Emma in a rather scamped fashion, but Emma hardly listened. She was back in the past, her pleasant face enrapt.

It was over too soon. She sat back, aware of the bustle of people around her preparing to go home.

'You enjoyed it?' Mijnheer Teylingen slid into the seat just vacated beside her, and Emma nodded. 'Lovely – just lovely,' she said inadequately, and since he was so close and it was really the first – and last? – opportunity of studying him, took a good look; older than she had supposed, even in the lamplight she could see that he was nearer forty than thirty, despite the hair and the alert green eyes, pale in the uncertain moonlight, and his nose was just as she had remembered it – perhaps not quite so formidable as Wellington's but certainly a very good copy of it. His mouth was a little too stern perhaps . . .

'I hope I come up to expectations,' said Mijnheer Teylingen gently, and when she jumped visibly, 'That's what you were doing, was it not? Assessing my points?' He smiled with real amusement. 'Let me help you. I'm forty, more or less, my teeth and my hair are my own, my nose is an unfortunate family appanage; I am ill-tempered at times, fond of children and animals, like pretty girls and am used to having my own way.'

Emma blushed and was glad that the light was poor enough for it to go unnoticed. She began. 'I – I – that is, I didn't mean . . .' She came to a halt, flustered.

'Don't apologize. Tell me, do you go home with your mother or return to your hospital?'

She wondered how it was that he was familiar with her profession and then remembered that he had looked at her passport. Feeling she owed him something, she replied, 'I shall take my mother home first and then go back to Southampton, where I work.'

'You enjoy your work?'

She supposed that he was making conversation. 'Very much,' she said, and wished she could have thought of something interesting to say; normally she was by no means so tongue-tied; she felt like a young girl, uncertain and shy, and wondered why he should have such an effect on her. Fortunately there was no need to strain her conversational powers any more, for his aunt joined them, to embark on a short conversation upon the evening's performance before wishing Emma goodbye. Saskia wished her goodbye too, casually but staring at her thoughtfully as she did so.

Mijnheer Teylingen made his farewells with a charm rather spoilt by its brevity, and marshalling his two companions before him, disappeared in the opposite direction to the one in which Emma and her mother were to go, without so much as a backward glance.

Emma, with her arm tucked into her mother's, walked back to the hotel listening to her parent's remarks about the evening and adding very little of her own. Nor did she have much to say later as they prepared for bed in the large old-fashioned bedroom, although it seemed to her that Mrs. Hastings dwelt with unnecessary length on Mijnheer Teylingen. The fact that she herself had almost nothing to say on the subject did nothing to alter the fact that long after her mother was asleep, her thoughts were still busy with him.

They left the next morning and began their journey home, making a leisurely trip southwards to Zeebrugge, and then because Emma lost the way, having to race the last few miles, to join the end of the car queue with only minutes to spare. They slept on board in a cabin to themselves because Emma wanted to push on to Dorset the moment they landed and there was no hope of getting any rest on the boat otherwise; it was crowded with young and boisterous students and a large party of elderly people who sang 'Knees up, Mother Brown', with a good deal of vigour and without showing any signs of settling down for the night.

They were last off the boat, of course, but still succeeded in getting away before a good many other cars owing, declared Mrs. Hastings virtuously, to their honest faces. 'The Customs men could always tell,' she added smugly as they started on the long trip home.

# CHAPTER TWO

Emma was in the theatre getting ready for the morning's list, while Sister Cox, the Theatre Superintendent, stood in the middle of the large tiled apartment, watching her. Emma had been back two days and despite the fact that her nice little face still bore the light tan she had acquired on her creamy skin and the dusting of freckles she despised upon her ordinary nose, her holiday in Holland already seemed like a pleasant dream. She had had a day at home getting her mother settled in once more, organizing her own clothes, fetching Flossie the spaniel from the kennels and getting Kitty's room ready for her return from medical school before getting the little car out once more and driving herself back to Southampton to plunge immediately into the strict routine of theatre work. And for once she had welcomed it, for what was to have been a perfectly ordinary holiday had been in fact turned into a dream – by Mijnheer Teylingen, who, to her great annoyance, she was having the greatest difficulty in dismissing from her thoughts. Which she had told herself repeatedly and soberly was ridiculous; she was no callow schoolgirl to lose her heart to the first handsome man she met, despite her lack of looks. She was neither dull nor dowdy and possessed a charm which did more for her than all the good looks in the world; she had never lacked for boyfriends even though their attitude towards her had been of a brotherly nature, and she had twice refused offers of marriage, so it wasn't a question of being swept off her feet. It was just, she admitted to herself, that he had seemed different.

She sighed as she laid up her trolleys, and Sister Cox, watching her, sighed too, but for a different reason. She was a cosy-looking woman, with black eyes which appeared to have no expression in them, but her disposition was by no means cosy. The regular theatre staff did their work and kept out of her way; the student nurses, sent to do their three months' stint in theatre, trembled and shook

24

for the whole of that period, counting the days until they could get away from her despotic rule. Emma, however, despite her quiet manner, had a disposition every bit as tough as Sister Cox. She had worked with her for two years now and was completely unworried by that lady, bearing with equanimity her bad temper without apparent ill-effects and taking care not to pass any of it on to the junior nurses. It was possibly because of this that the Theatre Superintendent occasionally showed her human side, something she was doing now. 'Two months,' she was saying in a voice which boded ill for someone, as Emma, having arranged her trolleys to an exact nicety, proceeded to lay them up with the instruments in the wire baskets brought from the autoclave. 'He'll eat you alive in a week.'

'More fool he,' said Emma with calm, and laid two rib raspatories neatly side by side, 'for then he'll have no one in theatre at all, will he? Don't worry, Sister, I'll not be gobbled up by some bad-tempered surgeon – though only rumour say's he's bad-tempered, doesn't it? Anyway, the longer you leave your toes, the worse they're going to get.'

Sister Cox looked down at her feet in their hideously wide shoes needed to accommodate her hammer toes. 'You're right,' she said, her voice sounding cross as well as resigned. 'I'll take the first case, you take the second; Staff can lay up for the third while we're having coffee, and for heaven's sake keep that great fool Jessop from under my feet. What possessed Matron to send her here. . . .' She started for the theatre doors, still talking to herself, and Emma, standing back to survey the first of her completed trolleys with all the satisfaction of a hostess decking her dinner table, asked idly, 'What's this horror's name, anyway – the one who's going to eat me?'

Sister Cox rotated her chubby form slowly to face Emma. 'He's a foreigner – brilliant at chest surgery, so I'm told, but I'll have to see it first.' She snorted disdainfully. 'He's got some technique or other – name's Teylingen.' She turned back to the door, saying as she went, 'Red hair, so I hear, so you'd better look out, you know what they say about red hair and bad temper.'

Emma stood quite still, looking astonished. It couldn't be the same man; on the other hand, why shouldn't it be? And if it was, what would he say when he saw her again? She shook out the sterile towel for her second trolley and holding it by its corners with the Cheatles forceps flipped it open with the ease of long practice, allowing it to fall precisely on the trolley before beginning the task of arranging yet another set of instruments upon it. This done to her satisfaction, she covered her handiwork with another sterile cloth, took one all-seeing look around the theatre and left it, casting off her gown as she went along to the tiny kitchen. Here the rest of the staff were gathered, drinking as much coffee as they had time for and wolfing down biscuits with an air of not knowing where their next meal would come from. They got to their feet as Emma went in and she said at once, 'No, don't get up – you'll need your feet this morning. Staff, will you scrub in time to lay up for the third case? – It's the oesophagectomy – I'll be taking it.'

Staff Nurse Collins, a small dark girl with large brown eyes in a pretty face, said simply, 'Thank God for that, Sister. Mad Minnie seems determined to hate this professor type before he's even got his nose round the door. She's as cross as two sticks already, she'll be really ratty by the time the morning's half over.'

'Sister Cox is preoccupied with her feet,' said Emma quietly, not wanting to snub Staff, whom she liked, but mindful that she really mustn't allow the nurses to call the Theatre Superintendent Mad Minnie – not in her hearing at any rate. She turned her attention to the other two nurses. 'Jessop, count swabs for the first case, please' – that would keep the poor girl out of Sister Cox's way – 'and, Cully, you see to lotions and take the bits when they're ready.' She turned back to Jessop, a large girl, naturally clumsy and rendered more so by Mad Minnie's vendetta against her, but who, in Emma's opinion, had the makings of a good nurse if only she could stop herself from dropping things and falling over anything within a mile of her awkward feet. Emma smiled at her now and said encouragingly, 'The third case will be a long one, Nurse Jessop. I shall want you to keep

26

me supplied, and be ready to fetch anything I may need. You'd better count swabs for the second case too, and be very careful, won't you, because I often get the total wrong.'

Which was a great piece of nonsense but served to inflate Jessop's sadly flattened ego. She left them with a little nod and another smile and went unhurriedly down the passage to the office where she and Sister Cox wrestled with the off-duty, the stores, the supplies of theatre equipment and the laundry and from where the Theatre Superintendent blasted, by telephone, the various ward sisters who hadn't conformed to her wishes concerning the arrival and departure of the various cases which had been sent up for operation. Occasionally one of the sisters, fuming over some new rule Mad Minnie had imposed, would come tearing in, to spend a tempestuous ten minutes in the office before Emma, if she was on duty, calmed the two ladies down with tea.

The office was small; it was also crowded. Sister Cox was sitting at the desk, looking more orbicular than ever, and most of the remaining space was taken up by the four men with her. Mr. Soames, the senior consultant surgeon of the unit, was leaning against the desk, apparently unaware of Sister Cox's cross looks at the pile of papers he had disarranged in doing so. With him were his senior Registrar, William Lunn, six foot two inches tall and naturally enough known throughout the hospital as Little Willy, and the senior anaesthetist, Mr. Cyril Bone, middle-aged, a natty dresser and known to chat up the nurses whenever he had the opportunity to do so – he was also very good at his job and popular with everyone, even Sister Cox, whom he could butter up in the most extravagant fashion. The fourth man was the owner of the Rolls-Royce, who dominated the scene by reason of his height and size and autocratic nose, not to mention the brilliance of his hair and the elegance of his dress and this depite the fact that he managed to convey the impression that he was of a retiring disposition. Emma, standing just inside the door, was aware of all this without having actually looked at him, she was also aware of an alarming pulse rate. It was Mr. Soames, who liked

27

her, who saved her from making any possible foolish and impulsive remark by saying at once, 'Ah, Emma, meet Professor Teylingen from Utrecht. He's here for a couple of months to show us some new techniques which I think we shall all find interesting.'

Emma advanced two cautious steps and held out her small capable hand. 'How do you do?' she asked politely, and added 'Professor,' hastily.

He took her hand briefly. 'How delightful to meet you again, Sister,' he remarked in such a mild voice that she gave him a faintly startled look, to find the green eyes staring into hers with a most decided twinkle. 'I have been looking forward to this,' he went on, 'ever since we met in Holland,' and explained to the room at large, 'You see, we are already acquainted,' which remark was met with a chorus of 'Oh, really?' and 'How extraordinary!' a chorus to which Emma didn't add her voice, being far too occupied in restoring her calm. It was only when she realized that five pairs of eyes were watching her that she managed weakly:

'Yes, it's a small world, isn't it?' and followed this profound remark with a more businesslike one to the effect that the theatre was ready.

Professor Teylingen said at once, 'Splendid. I look forward to a most interesting morning.' He smiled at Sister Cox as he spoke and to Emma's surprise that formidable lady smiled back and got out of her chair with a show of willingness quite unusual to her. Probably the old battle-axe was holding her fire until they got into the theatre, where the professor would only have to ask for something she either hadn't got or didn't want, for her to flatten him. Emma took the opportunity to look at him as he stood talking to Little Willy – no, he wouldn't be easily flattened; it would remain to be seen who would come off best. She slid away from the office, put on her theatre cap and mask and went to send the nurses into theatre. She found them bunched together in the anaesthetic room and said urgently, 'For heaven's sake – he's about to scrub up!'

'Not before he's met the rest of the theatre staff,' interposed the professor's voice from the door, and she wheeled round to encounter a smile which threw her quite off balance.

'Oh, well – yes,' she began inadequately, and then becoming very professional indeed, 'Professor Teylingen, may I introduce Staff Nurse Collins, Nurse Jessop and Nurse Cully – we have a nursing auxiliary too, but she's not on duty until this afternoon, and two technicians and the porters.'

He said with a little smile, 'Yes, I met them yesterday evening when I came round with Mr. Soames. I feel sure we shall enjoy working together.'

The smile became brilliant as he went away, closing the door quietly behind him.

Jessop spoke first. 'Golly, Sister, he's smashing – he doesn't look bad-tempered either – they said he was.' Her tone of voice suggested that if anyone thought otherwise they would have to settle with her first. And Cully, who was a little older and a little wiser, observed, 'He's quite old, isn't he, but it doesn't notice – it makes the medicos look like schoolboys.' And Staff, who was engaged to be married and should have known better, asked, 'Is he married?'

'I've no idea,' said Emma calmly, 'and since he's only here for a couple of months and doesn't live in England, there isn't much point in getting turned on, is there?' She added in a quietly severe voice, 'Now into theatre all of you, please – Sister will want us all to give a good impression.' She paused as she went. 'And Nurse Jessop, do try not to drop anything.'

The first case was a lengthy one and Mr. Soames did it with the professor assisting and Little Willy making himself useful. It was the repair of a hiatus hernia which involved a partial gastrectomy and some excision of the oesophagus. Mr. Soames was good at it; he did a great many week after week, and being familiar with his work was completely relaxed – as was the professor. The two of them talked as they worked, frequently including Little Willy and Mr. Bone in their conversation, and even Sister Cox, who didn't agree with talking in theatre unless it was strictly business, so that her answers were short and a little snappy.

'You don't like conversation in theatre, Sister?' asked the professor at his mildest. She shot him a darkling glance over her mask.

'No, sir, I can't say I do,' she said huffily. 'We're here to work.'

She snapped her Cheatles angrily above her head and Emma, interpreting their clatter, nodded to Cully standing ready with her receiver to take what Mr. Soames held dangling from his forceps. He flung it lightly, forceps and all, in her general direction and she caught it with a dexterity which would have done justice to a first-class cricketer in a Test Match, and disappeared in the direction of the sluice, acknowledging Mr. Bone's thumbs-up sign with a soundless giggle. The professor, without looking up from the little bit of sewing he was engaged upon, remarked:

'I must compliment you upon your dexterous staff, Sister Cox,' and when she gave an impatient grunt, went on, 'I hope I shall not put you out too much while I am here. I find I work much better if there is a certain amount of talk. It is relaxing, you know – so vital to our work, do you not agree?'

Emma could see by the look on Mad Minnie's face that she had no wish to agree but felt it expedient to do so. After all, the wretched man was important, though why they had to bring foreigners into the country to teach them something they could do better she did not know. Emma read her superior's mind like an open book and suppressed a smile as Sister Cox's eyes widened as the professor went on, 'I daresay you find it most vexing having to put up with a foreigner for even a short time. I'm sorry to hear about your – er – feet. I take it the operation is to be quite soon?'

She looked as though she would explode. 'In two days' time,' she handed him a grooved director which he accepted politely and didn't use. 'You'll have to manage with Sister Hastings – by the time I'm back you'll be gone.' Her tone implied 'and a good riddance too'.

'Regrettably,' said Professor Teylingen gently, 'but I am sure your operation will improve you in every way, Sister Cox.'

30

carry on, shall we?'

No one else had said anything – what was there to say at such a time? Poor Jessop, quite overcome, had fled out of the theatre, and Emma had let her go, for she would be worse than useless now, and a good wholesome cry in the kitchen would restore her nerve more quickly than anything else.

Professor Teylingen came back presently and Staff with him to relieve an uneasy Mr. Moore, and the operation was finished without further mishap with the men talking among themselves in a deliberate, calm manner which Emma felt sure that in the professor's case was assumed, for she could sense his rage, well battened down under his bland exterior, and felt sure that once he had finished his work he would make no bones about unleashing it.

He didn't, but not immediately. The patient had gone back to the I.C. Unit, the theatre had been cleared and got ready for the next, luckily short case and Emma was scrubbing up once more before he appeared beside her. He wasted no time on preliminaries, but, 'Sister, you will be good enough to see that Nurse Jessop remains out of the theatre while I am in it. I will not have my patients' lives jeopardized by a nurse who cannot do her work properly.' He picked up a nailbrush and gave her a cold look. 'Perhaps I should speak to Sister Cox.'

'Don't you dare!' said Emma before she could stop herself, and then remembering who he was, added, 'Sir,' and saw his lips twitch faintly.

'No one – I repeat, no one, Sister Hastings – tells me what I may dare to do or not to do.'

Now she had made him even more angry. Poor Jessop! 'Listen,' she said earnestly, quite forgetting to say sir this time, 'don't tell Mad M ... Sister Cox. You see she's ... she didn't want Nurse Jessop here in the first place and so she thinks she's no good, and Jessop's scared stiff of her. I know she's clumsy and slow, but if she's given a chance she'll be a good nurse one day. Give her that chance, I'll keep her on swab counting if you like ... but if only someone would tell her she's not a fool.' She sighed. 'People are so stupid,' said Emma indignantly, and glared at him

34

Mr. Soames made a muffled sound behind his mask and Mr. Bone and Little Willy dealt with sudden coughs, and the nurses, who had the rest of the day with Sister Cox to face, saved their giggles until they could get down to the dining-room, where they would recount the conversation word for word, together with a thorough description of the handsome Mr. Teylingen.

The professor accepted another needle and gut into his needleholder and began to stitch with the finicky concentration of a lady of leisure working at her petit point, while Emma nodded to Staff to go and start scrubbing, ready to retire to one corner of the theatre and lay up for the next case. The professor, she noted, was a meticulous worker but a fast one, something which he chose to disguise under a deliberate manner which could be deceiving. He had also, to confound rumour, remained perfectly good-tempered throughout the lengthy operation, though there had been nothing to arouse his ire – no dropped dressings, no lotion splashed on the floor by Jessop's too quick hand; nothing in fact to spoil the calm of the theatre's atmosphere, only Mad Minnie's tartness, of course. Emma had got so used to her that she had rather overlooked the fact that a stranger coming into their circle for the first time might find her a shade dictatorial. She picked up the dressing lying ready under the trolley and arranged it correctly around and over the drains and tubes which the two surgeons had stitched into the patient with all the care of a dressmaker stitching in a zip, aware as she did so of the close proximity of the professor to her.

They had coffee at the end of the case while the nurses bustled around theatre, readying it for the next case, and Staff, sterile in gown and gloves, waited patiently by her trolleys. The office, thought Emma, was hardly the place for the social drinking of coffee by five people. She perched uneasily on the second chair while Sister Cox sat behind the desk, looking murderous, and the men lounged around the walls, drinking coffee far too hot and eating biscuits with all the enthusiasm of schoolboys while they discussed the case they had just finished. That the talk was highly inappropriate to the drinking of

31

coffee, or for that matter, the drinking or eating of anything, didn't worry Emma in the least; for several years now she had reconciled herself to taking her refreshment to the accompaniment of vivid descriptions of any number of unmentionable subjects. Now she listened with interest while the professor explained why he had found his method of performing the next operation so satisfactory — something which he did with a nice lack of boasting. She went away when she had finished her coffee and started to scrub up and was almost ready when the three men sauntered in to join her at the sinks.

'Taking the case?' inquired the professor idly, and when she had said that yes, she was, she added, 'Are there any particular instruments you prefer to use, sir, or any you dislike?'

He gave her a thoughtful look. 'Very considerate of you, Sister Hastings. I like a blade and a blade holder — always. I like Macdonald's dissector, I take a size nine glove if you have them and I prefer Hibutane solution. There is no need to bother about these today, though I should be grateful if the gloves could be changed.'

Emma said, 'Yes, sir,' and went into theatre. She sent Staff for the correct size and stood quietly while Cully tied her into her gown and then opened the glove drum so that she could take her own size sixes. The operation would be a long one — the removal of an oesophagus in a patient with cancer; the man was still young enough to make the operation worthwhile, severe though it was, and as it had been diagnosed in good time, there was every chance of success. She went without haste to her trolleys and began the business of counting swabs and sponges, threading needles and checking the instruments before making sure that all the complicated machinery needed was in position and that the technicians were ready. Sister Cox wasn't in theatre; she had gone to see the orthopaedic surgeon about her feet, so that the atmosphere of the theatre was a good deal lighter than it had been, although there was no let-up in the strict routine. Emma reflected that it was nice to see Cully and Jessop so relaxed, and Jessop, by some miracle, hadn't dropped anything at all.

32

The patient was wheeled in with Mr. Bone at his and propelling his anaesthetic trolley with him. winked at Emma as the porters arranged the patien the table and she returned the wink, for they had friends for several years and indeed she was one of the who knew that his wife had been in a nursing home years and was very unlikely to come out of it — a w whom he dearly loved. The three surgeons walked in a behind them, Peter Moore, the houseman, who w coming to watch. Peter was young and awkward, ver clever and just about as clumsy as Nurse Jessop. Emm heaved a sigh as she saw him, for if Jessop didn't do some thing awful, he certainly would.

She handed the sterile towels and watched while the surgeons arranged them with meticulous care and then fastened them with the towel clips she had ready. The professor asked placidly, 'Is everything fixed, Sister?' — a question she knew covered not only the actual operation itself but the patient's immediate aftercare as well. She said briefly, 'Yes, sir,' and proffered a knife.

He took it without haste. 'Good — I take it we're all ready,' and made a neat incision.

The operation seemed to be going very well. The professor dissected and snipped and probed and cut again and after a long time he and Mr. Soames started to stitch the end results together. They were perhaps half-way through this delicate, very fast process when Jessop, about to change the lotion in the bowl stand beside the professor, made one of her clumsy movements and lurched against him, pouring a jugful of warn saline over his legs, and for good measure, touching him with her hand. Emma prayed a wordless little prayer as she said calmly:

'Another gown for the professor, Staff. Nurse Cully, fetch another set of bowls. Mr. Moore, be good enough to stay by me in case I should need anything.' She handed tetra cloth to Mr. Soames, and the professor, after or short, explosive sentence in his own language, stood ba from the table so that Staff could take his unsterile gov He nodded to Mr. Soames before he went to scrub ag and Mr. Soames said, 'Right, old chap, Will and I over her mask.

'And I am included amongst these – er – stupid people?' He sounded interested.

Her 'Yes' was a mumble. She had got herself into a fine mess. Probably he would request Mad Minnie to keep her out of the theatre too and that would leave only Staff to scrub ... and serve him right. She began to scrub the other hand with her usual thoroughness and had the brush taken from her as he twisted her round to face him.

'I don't seem to be starting off on the right foot, do I?' he asked mildly. 'I don't make a habit of making girls cry, you know – but the patient comes first, don't you agree? Would it help if we were to go and find this nurse and endeavour to calm her down? You say she is going to be a good nurse – who am I to dispute your opinion?'

They found Jessop in the kitchen, squeezed behind the door with reddened eyes and a deplorable sniff. Emma said at once, 'Ah, there you are, Jessop. I shall need you in theatre in a minute or two, so stop crying like a good girl. No one's angry – here's Professor Teylingen to tell you so. Now I'm going to scrub and when the professor goes to scrub too go into theatre and make sure everything's ready, will you?'

She walked away, leaving him to deal with the situation, and presently when she went into theatre, evinced no curiosity as to what he had said to Jessop, who was standing, gowned and masked, waiting for her. The operation was to be a comparatively simple one. The patient had suffered a stab wound some weeks previously, had recovered from it, and now was back in hospital with an empyema. Now he was going to have an inch or so of rib removed and a drainage tube inserted – a fairly quick operation which Jessop should manage to get through without doing anything too awful. Emma counted her swabs, signed to Jessop to tie the surgeon's gowns, checked the contents of the Mayo's table and handed the first of the sterile towels to Little Willy.

A quarter of an hour later she was clearing up her instruments once more and Jessop was carefully unscrewing the sucker jar. The men, with a brief word, had gone, Staff and Cully would be back in twenty minutes or so and Mrs. Tate, the auxiliary, would be on duty in a couple of minutes. Emma put the last of the instruments into one of the lotion bowls and said, 'All right, Nurse, you're off at one, aren't you? Mrs. Tate can finish that,' and bent to do her sharps as Jessop said: 'Thank you, Sister,' and ploughed her way to the door, narrowly avoiding two electric cables and a bucket, and then turned round and ploughed all the way back again. 'He's lovely, Sister,' she breathed. 'He told me that when he was a medical student he forgot he was scrubbed up and turned on the diathermy machine and everyone had to wait while he took off his gown and his gloves and scrubbed up again and on his way back he touched the surgeon's gown. He says he's never forgotten it, and he said,' she went on rapidly, 'that you have to do something awful like that just once and then you never do it again, so I'm not to worry.'

She looked rather imploringly at Emma. 'He is right, isn't he, Sister?'

'Yes,' said Emma firmly, 'he's quite right, and he's been very kind too – you realize that, don't you? You could have done a lot of damage to the patient. Supposing Professor Teylingen had jerked his hand – he was stitching, remember?'

Jessop looked crestfallen. 'Yes, I know, Sister. I – I thought I had – that's why I ran away. I'm sorry I did. He said I must never run away again because we're a team and we can't manage without each other. I thought . . . that is, Sister Cox said I was a nuisance. . . .'

Emma started on the needles. 'No, you're not – you'll do quite well, especially if you remember that bit about one of a team. And remember too that Sister Cox has had a lot of pain with her feet and she's been in theatre so long, she's forgotten just a little how difficult it is at first.' She smiled. 'Now go off duty, Nurse.'

Jessop went to the door again. At it she said, 'Good-bye, Sister – you're nice.'

And let's hope I stay that way, thought Emma, and don't get like Mad Minnie. The prospect was daunting; she closed her mind to it and began to think about Little Willy's invitation to go with him to see the latest film that evening. They had been out together on several occasions, but although she liked him, that was as far as it went and she suspected that it was as far as it went with him too. She supposed she would go, and along with the thought came a speculative one as to what the professor intended to do with his evening, and where he was living, and with whom.

In the Sisters' dining-room, where she went a short time later, she was greeted with expectant faces and a great many questions.

'You lucky devil,' remarked one of her closer friends, Madge Freeman from Men's Surgical. 'I saw him in the distance this morning – that hair – and his smile!' She groaned in a theatrical manner. 'A trendy dresser too. What's he like, Emma?'

Emma looked resignedly at the cold meat on her plate and helped herself to two lettuce leaves and a radish. 'Very neat worker,' she stated. 'He's here to demonstrate his theory about. . . .' She was stopped by a concerted howl from her companions.

'Cut it out, Emma,' one of them begged. 'Who cares about his theories? Is he married – engaged? What's his voice like? Does he speak with an accent? Is he . . .?'

Emma peered at the potatoes; being late, there wasn't much choice. 'Cold,' she pronounced, 'and hard,' and seeing the astonishment on her friends' faces, hastened to add, 'The potatoes, and it's no good asking me. I don't know a thing about him, I really don't. He's got green eyes,' she offered as an afterthought, 'and a deep voice.'

'Dark brown velvet or gravelly?' someone wanted to know.

'A bit of both,' said Emma, having thought about it, 'and he's got almost no accent.'

She applied herself to her dinner amid cries of discontent from her table companions. 'Well, don't carry on so,' she advised kindly. 'He'll be going to the wards to see his cases, won't he?'

She looked at Madge, who brightened visibly and asked, 'What's he got this afternoon – something for I.C.U., I suppose.' She looked round the table. 'Margaret isn't here – she'll get it.'

'There's a lobectomy at half past two; he'll be using his new technique, so there'll be an audience in the gallery and the patient will go to Margaret – she's got the others. Why don't you go up and see her? You might be able to meet him, he's sure to be in and out of there for the next few hours after theatre's finished.'

Several pairs of suspicious eyes were turned upon her. 'You're very casual, Emma. If I were you I'd keep him to myself,' remarked Casualty Sister, a striking girl with corn-coloured hair and enormous eyes.

Emma helped herself to treacle tart and gave the speaker a considering look. 'If I were you, Sybil,' she said reasonably, 'I jolly well would.'

The afternoon's work went perfectly, probably because neither Sister Cox nor Jessop were there. The professor worked smoothly, his quiet voice detailing every stage of the operation he was performing to the audience in the screened-off gallery. When he had finished he thanked Emma nicely and left, closely followed by Little Willy and Peter Moore. Little Willy came back after ten minutes or so and asked Emma if she had made up her mind about going to the cinema. It was, he pointed out, a rather super film and if she could get away in time. ... And Emma, who, for some reason she didn't care to name felt restless, agreed to make the effort. Two hours later, as they were leaving the hospital by its main entrance, they passed the professor coming in. His 'good evening' was casual, but his green eyes rested thoughtfully for several moments upon Emma.

The next day he wasn't operating at all; Mr. Soames did a short list and then an emergency on a stoved-in chest. The professor, Emma was informed at dinner, had spent most of the morning in I.C.U. getting to know the nurses ... a most unfair state of things, someone remarked, for Margaret, who was in charge, was happily married. Madge had had a visit from him too, which had caused her to go all dreamy-eyed and thoughtful.

'He turns me on,' she sighed. 'I know he's quite old, but he's got such a way of looking at you.' She added complacently, 'I think he likes me. Is he nice to you, Emma?'

'He's very pleasant to work for,' said Emma sedately,

'but he can be quite stern – Mad Minnie didn't stand a chance with him; a good thing she's going off to Sick Bay tomorrow. By the time she gets back he'll be gone.'

She suffered a pang as she spoke which was almost physical.

Kitty was waiting for her when she came off duty that evening, sitting on the bed reading the latest book on theatre technique which Emma had just bought herself. She got up to embrace her sister, observing:

'Darling, what a conscientious girl you are – this is only just out.'

Emma cast her cap on to the bed and started to take the pins out of her neat topknot. 'Yes, I know, but things change all the time. How are you, Kitty?'

She smiled at her sister as she divested herself of her uniform. Kitty was four years younger than she was and by some quirk of nature, although they were alike, Kitty had been cast in a more vivid mould. Her eyes were brown and fringed with extravagantly curling lashes whereas Emma had to be content with hazel eyes and lashes of the same soft brown as her hair so that she had recourse to the aid of mascara when she had the time and patience to use it. Kitty's hair was a rich glowing brown and her nose was small and straight, while Emma's tilted at its end. They had the same mouths, though, rather large and turned up at the corners, and they both had the same sweet smile.

'How did the exams go?' inquired Emma. Kitty was a second year medical student at one of the London hospitals and doing well.

'I passed. I telephoned Mother yesterday. She seems to have enjoyed herself in Holland. Who's this man she babbled on about?

She went to the mirror and began to re-do her face. 'She said you had an accident and you'll have to pay for the repairs – poor you! Look, Emma, I can manage without the money you send me for a month or two, perhaps that would help to pay it off.'

Emma was struggling into her dressing gown and her voice was muffled in its folds. 'That's decent of you, Kitty, but I think I'll be able to manage. I haven't any idea how much it is – I suppose I shall have to ask him.'

'How can you do that?' Kitty wanted to know.

'Well, it's quite a coincidence; he's working here for a couple of months – he's a cardiac-thoracic man and they invited him over to demonstrate some technique he's thought up – he's had a lot of success with it. He's in our theatre.'

Kitty put away her compact. 'Well, well, darling, how nice for you – or isn't it?'

Emma was doing up buttons. 'I don't know yet,' she sounded composed. 'Wait while I have a bath, will you? I shan't be two ticks.'

They went out presently and had a meal in the town and then went back to the hospital car park where the Ford Popular stood rather self-consciously among its more modern fellows. 'For heaven's sake, go carefully,' Emma besought her sister. 'I'll need it when I go home next week-end. Leave it here on the way back, as usual, will you? I'll try and pop down for a minute.'

Kitty got in and started the engine and said yes, she'd be very careful and took the little car out of the hospital forecourt with a spurt of speed which caused Emma to close her eyes. Kitty always had the car when she went home unless she herself was using it. One day, Emma promised herself, opening her eyes again to watch her sister go round the corner, she would have a new car – something low and sporting, a Sprite perhaps. She went back into the hospital, passing the consultants' car park as she went and pausing by the professor's Rolls to see if she could make out any signs of damage on its polished perfection. She could see nothing at all, but probably Rolls-Royces were inspected for damage with magnifying glasses. She patted its bonnet and then rubbed where she had patted in case she had spoilt the polish. As she turned round she found Professor Teylingen standing behind her watching, so that, taken by surprise, she said weakly, 'Oh, hullo. I – I was looking to see if anything showed, you know – from the bump I gave you.' She gave him a direct look and went on in a carefully matter-of-fact voice, 'I should like to have the bill, so that I know how much . . .?' Her voice tailed away under his cool stare.

'I've no idea at the moment, Miss Hastings, I imagine it will reach you in due course.' He smiled suddenly. 'Who was the pretty girl who drove away in your car?'

And where was he hiding to see us? thought Emma crossly. 'My sister,' she told him shortly.

'Oh? Also a nurse?'

'No – she's a medical student. She's very clever as well as being pretty.'

'And she borrows your car?

'Well, of course,' explained Emma patiently. 'She comes down from London and drives home from here, then brings the car back on her way to catch the train.'

It sounded a little complicated, but all he said was simply, 'Why?'

She wasn't going to tell him it was cheaper that way, so she said, faintly irritated at his persistence, 'It's easier that way,' and glared at him in case he should dispute the explanation. 'Besides,' she said with finality, 'it means she's free to go where she likes or take Mother out.'

'And so you walk until the car is returned?'

'I have good legs,' observed Emma rashly, and went pink as he said quickly, 'Yes, you have, quite delightful,' and when she made a small sound, said in the most casual way imaginable, 'Don't let me keep you.'

She wished him good night rather stiffly and walked through the hospital and out of a small door at its back, crossed the inner courtyard to the Nurses' Home, where she joined her fellows round the T.V. and drank tea she didn't want, and tried not to think about Professor Teylingen.

They met a good deal during the following days, but always in a professional capacity. If they had exchanged half a dozen words of ordinary conversation during that time, it would have been a generous estimate. Margaret and Madge had fared better – he had lingered for tea with each of them when he had visited his patients during the afternoons and they had gleaned, between them, quite an amount of information about him, none of which, however, cast any light upon his private life. Nor did he show any sign of dating Madge or Sybil, who had contrived to meet him too. Consultant staff weren't in the habit of asking members of the nursing staff to go out with them, but it didn't seem quite the same with the professor; he was a foreigner for a start, which for some reason made a difference, and as far as they knew, he was unmarried – but there again, they weren't sure. It was annoying; it also gave them an unending topic of conversation.

It was a couple of days later that Emma, not on duty until one o'clock, decided to go out and buy herself a dress. She had no money to speak of and the need for a new dress wasn't actually pressing – it was merely that she wanted to cheer herself up. She had tried telling herself that there was no reason why Professor Teylingen should take an interest in her; she was perfectly aware that she was neither particularly exciting as a companion or even passably good-looking, which was probably why she was on such excellent terms with most of the men she worked with, all of whom were prone, if they talked to her or took her out, to spend a great deal of time telling her about their girl-friends. Even the occasional outings she had with Little Willy were like going out with a brother and just about as exciting, and she had never forgotten that on one occasion when she had listened sympathetically to some minor upheaval in his day, he had told her that although she was a homely little body, she was one of the nicest girls he knew. He had said it so nicely that she hadn't had the heart to be annoyed. She had taken a good look at herself in the mirror when she got back to her room and been forced to admit to herself that he was probably right about her being homely – a detestable word, she raged, tearing her clothes off and bouncing into bed – just because she hadn't got great blue eyes and masses of curly hair; but her rage hadn't lasted long, for Little Willy so obviously liked her.

She walked across the hospital forecourt now, trying to decide what colour she should have and how much she could afford to spend, and half-way over the Rolls overtook her and slowed to a halt.

'May I give you a lift?' Professor Teylingen's voice was casually friendly and when she said, 'No, thank you,' surprised her by asking her why not.

42

'Well, you don't know where I'm going,' she stated, rather at a loss.

He opened the car door. 'Naturally not. You can tell me as we go.' His voice sounded patient, but Emma still hesitated. 'The thing is,' she said at length, 'I'm not sure where I'm going myself – it's shopping.'

He nodded in an understanding way. 'Ah, no, of course not – how could you? Suppose I take you into town and you can tell me where to drop you.' He added suavely, 'Unless you dislike my company?'

Emma's usually serene face became animated with surprise so that she looked suddenly pretty. 'Dislike you?' she repeated parrot fashion. 'Why should I dislike you? Of course I don't.'

'Then get in.'

It seemed foolish to waste any more time; she got in and he leaned across her and shut the door, and without bothering to say any more, guided the car sleekly through the gates and on to the main road. They were well into the city before he spoke again.

'Could you spare time for a cup of coffee? I'm going to the Dolphin, I can leave the car there.'

It seemed churlish to refuse – besides, suddenly the new dress didn't seem important any more. Emma thanked him nicely as he turned the car into the arched entrance to the hotel and allowed herself to be led into one of the large bow-windowed rooms facing the street. Afterwards, thinking about it, she was unable to remember what they had talked about while they drank their coffee, only that the professor had maintained a steady flow of easy talk which required very little answering. When she at length rose with a garbled little speech in which thanks were rather wildly mixed with a quite unnecessary description of the shops she intended to visit, she was interrupted by his quiet, 'I shall be in town myself until midday. I'll wait for you here.'

'Oh, will you?' asked Emma, astonished. 'But I can go back by bus – they run every ten minutes.'

'I daresay they do,' observed the professor, not very much interested in the local transport service. 'I shall wait for you here.'

She arrived back at five minutes past the hour, without the dress because she had been unable to put her mind to the task of searching for it with the proper amount of concentration such a purchase deserved.

'I'm late,' she began, breathless, to which the professor replied with calm, 'For a woman who has been shopping, I imagine you are remarkably punctual. Where do you lunch?'

She hadn't given lunch a thought – she would make a cup of tea in the Home and there were biscuits in a tin somewhere or other. She didn't answer as he wove the car like a gleaming black silken thread through the fustian of delivery vans and long-distance transports.

'No lunch?' he queried. 'We must arrange things better next time.' He glanced at her sideways and she caught the gleam in his green eyes. 'And where's the shopping?'

'I wanted a dress,' said Emma, 'but I didn't see one I liked.'

'Hard to please?' He sounded mocking.

She heard the mockery and was stung into replying, 'Of course I'm not. I saw plenty I should have liked. . . .'

'You have just said you hadn't seen one you liked,' he reminded her silkily.

'Well,' explained Emma patiently, 'it's no good liking something you can't afford, is it?' and added hastily in case he should pity her, which was the last thing she wanted, 'I don't really need a dress, anyway.'

He laughed at that, but it was kindly laughter and presently she laughed with him. It was as they were turning into the hospital forecourt that he asked, 'When does your sister return your car?'

'Saturday morning, so that I can go home for the weekend. It's a bit of a scramble really, for she has to get the midday train up to London.'

'What does she do? Leave the car at the station?'

'No, she brings it here and parks it and leaves the key at the lodge unless I can manage to slip down.'

'Box and Cox, I see.' He opened the door for her to get out and smiled and she smiled too. 'Yes, it is rather, but it works quite well. Thank you for the lift.'

44

It wasn't until she was scrubbing up for the first case that afternoon that she began to wonder why he had asked all those questions about Kitty. Perhaps he wanted to meet her – he had had a glimpse of her when she had fetched the car. A sharp pain pierced her at the thought so that she stopped scrubbing for a moment to wonder at it. The pain was replaced by a dull ache which, when she thought about the professor, became worse. It was still there ten minutes later when, already in the theatre laying up the Mayo's table, she watched him stroll in with Little Willy, gowned and gloved and masked. There was nothing of him to be seen excepting his green eyes and the high arch of his preposterous nose, but that didn't matter. She realized all of a sudden that she knew every line of his face by heart, just as she knew every calm, controlled movement of his hands when he operated or drove the car or picked up a cup of coffee; she knew every inflection of his voice as well. She clashed two pairs of tissue forceps together as the realization that she had fallen in love with him hit her like a blast from a bomb. Such a foolish thing to do, she chided herself silently as she laid the necrosis forceps down with precise care, especially as she still owed him for the repair of his car – it didn't seem right to fall in love with someone to whom one owned money. He wished her good afternoon with pleasant friendliness and she replied in like vein, glad of her mask to cover the flush which crept up her cheeks. They plunged into their work after that and there was no more time for thoughts other than those to do with the job on hand. And when the afternoon was over, he went away with a careless good-bye, scarcely looking at her.

# CHAPTER THREE

THERE was no theatre on Saturday morning; at about half past eleven Emma slipped down to the car park to see if Kitty had got back with the Ford. She had; she was standing by the little car with Professor Teylingen on one side of her and Little Willy on the other and they were laughing together like old friends, but the moment Kitty saw her she started to meet her, her pretty face alight with pleasure.

'Emma darling, how lovely! I hoped you'd escape for a minute or two. I was just standing here doing nothing when these two—' she turned a smiling face to the men, 'came along and they knew who I was at once because we're so alike. Have you been busy? Mother's looking forward to seeing you.'

They had joined the two men as she was speaking and Emma said in her pleasant voice, 'Hullo, Willy,' and then, 'Hullo, sir.' She gave him a friendly glance as she spoke and tried not to notice how hard her heart was beating.

'Gosh,' said Kitty, 'do you call him sir? He said his name was Justin.' She turned to look at the professor, standing with his hands in his pockets, a half smile on his face. 'Do you mind?' she asked. 'Of course you're some-one important, aren't you?'

'None of us is important on our own, I imagine,' he observed mildly, 'and I very much prefer to be called Justin.' His green eyes flickered across to Emma, who went a little pink because they held laughter in their depths and she suspected that he was amused because she was always so careful to call him sir with the formality due to him. She said hastily, 'Kitty, shouldn't you be going? I hate to hurry you, but if you miss the bus you'll miss the train too.'

'No, she won't,' the professor's answer was prompt, 'I'll run her down.' He glanced at his watch. 'Only it had better be now.'

Kitty flashed him a dazzling smile. 'Oh, good – I did

hope you'd think of that. Good-bye, Will – I hope we meet again. Emma, you've a long weekend in a fortnight, haven't you? I'll come down and meet you here and we can go home together.'

She embraced her sister with loving speed. 'The keys,' she added breathlessly, and thrust them at Emma, 'and thank you for the car, Emma.'

Emma stood beside Little Willy watching her sister skip along beside the more dignified professor to where the Rolls was parked, then waved as they got in and drove away. When she looked sideways at Little Willy she was surprised to see a look on his face which she had never seen before – excitement, disappointment and determination all mixed up together.

He turned to face her. 'I didn't know,' he began, 'your sister – what a lovely girl she is. I've never met anyone like her, only you.'

Emma understood him very well. 'We're not really alike,' she said kindly, 'only the shape of our faces and our mouths. I'm – I'm a kind of dim copy of Kitty, aren't I? She is lovely, and she's very clever too.'

They started to walk slowly back into the hospital while she told him just how clever Kitty was, because it was obvious to her understanding eye that he wanted most desperately to know.

But he wasn't the only one who was interested. On Monday morning as she was wrestling with the off-duty in the office while Staff got the theatre ready, Professor Teylingen strolled in, bade her a good morning, made a few brief remarks about the day's work ahead of them, and then without further beating about the bush, began to talk about Kitty. It was apparent, after a few minutes, that Kitty had talked to him like an old friend, and Emma, sitting quietly in her chair listening to him, wondered uneasily just what she had said, for Kitty, although a darling, was a chatterbox. But presently Emma relaxed a little; it seemed that her sister, while disclosing their ages, likes, dislikes and various childish episodes, had remained reticent about their finances. Emma, for some reason which she didn't care to define, didn't want this man who had come so suddenly into her life to know how they had to count every penny and what an effort it was for her mother to live on her tiny income even with Emma's help – and least of all did she want him to know how much both her mother and sister depended on her earnings.

She looked up to find him watching her narrowly. 'Did you never want to be a doctor?' he asked.

But she wasn't going into all that. 'Goodness me, no,' she lied briskly, 'I've no brains to speak of,' and hoped she had sounded convincing because he smiled non-committally. But he couldn't have known – Kitty wouldn't have told him, and anyway it was all water under the bridge a long time ago.

She allowed a small sigh to escape her and he said, 'You make a very good Theatre Sister, anyway. Now that Sister Cox is no longer with us, you must be rather over-worked. How do you manage about off-duty?'

She explained carefully about long weekends and short weekends and Staff taking the short lists.

'So this was your short weekend?' he wanted to know, and when she nodded, asked, 'And how long is a long weekend?'

'Thursday evening, if I can get away, until Monday afternoon. Staff takes the morning list and we plan – that is, you plan, if you don't mind – all the heavy stuff for the afternoon so that we're both on. It works very well. Now Sister Cox isn't here, Staff will alternate with me so that theatre's covered, and we've a part time staff nurse too, who's on with Staff. Collins and I try to be on together for the heavier lists.'

'But surely with Sister Cox away, you're working short-handed?'

Emma gave him a level look. 'Yes, but it's not for ever and Staff's very good indeed.'

He smiled at that and got to his feet. 'As long as you can manage.'

'Of course we can manage,' her voice was stiff, 'but if you have any doubts. . . .'

She was interrupted by his quiet, 'Don't get me wrong. I believe you to be capable of running the theatre with your hands tied behind you if you had to, but you should have adequate staff.'

He smiled again, this time quite differently so that her heart gave a lurch despite her outward composure. 'That's kind of you to think about us. If I find I can't manage, I'll tell you, Professor.'

'Please do. Now I must find Lunn and have a word with him – I'll see you later.'

He was gone. She listened to his unhurried footsteps going down the corridor and presently the gentle swish of the theatre unit doors as they closed behind him. But instead of picking up her pen again, she allowed her thoughts to idle; she would have to get used to seeing the professor each day, drinking coffee with him, listening to his quiet, deep voice, watching his face and the way he smiled, seeing the little wrinkles come at the corners of his eyes when he laughed, steel herself to meet their penetrating green when he looked at her. She supposed it would be possible to do all that and it wouldn't be for long. She was a sensible girl, she told herself it had been coincidence that had thrown them together – what else could it be? as her mother had been eager to point out when she went home that weekend. Kitty had told her all about their meeting by the car and Mrs. Hastings had been full of carefully put questions – almost, Emma thought with wry amusement, as if her mother had expected something of the sort to happen; certainly she had seemed to think that this unexpected meeting would be the beginning of friendship. Indeed, she had suggested to Emma that she might like to invite the professor for a weekend, 'So that he can see something of the country, dear,' observed Mrs. Hastings guilelessly. 'Besides, I could give him some good wholesome food with our own eggs and vegetables.'

'I think he gets enough to eat, Mother,' Emma had observed dryly. Men who could afford to drive Rolls-Royces weren't likely to eat anything but the best. 'Besides, dear, it isn't quite . . . that is, I couldn't very well ask him. I don't know him well, you see. I know we work together and I see him almost every day, but it's difficult . . . he's a consultant.'

Her mother had nodded. Emma's father had been a

country G.P.; the niceties of the hospital hierarchy had meant very little to his wife. Emma explained carefully until she was satisfied that her mother understood that consultant staff weren't really in the habit of spending weekends with lesser fry. She had added consolingly, 'Never mind, darling, Kitty's sure to bring some boy-friends home,' and had been stricken into silence when her mother said, 'Yes, dear, but I should like it very much if you brought a nice man home from time to time.'

Emma smiled at the memory of her mother's words and looked up as Staff put her head round the door and said, 'Theatre's ready, Sister. Shall Cully and Jessop have their coffee – the others have had theirs.'

Emma nodded. 'Yes, Staff, and get yourself a cup and come in here and drink it. You'll have to scrub and get ready after the first case – it'll be a long one and they'll want their coffee after it. I'll take the first and second and you scrub for the lobectomy, will you?'

Staff nodded, disappeared and reappeared a minute later with her mug of coffee. 'Sit down, do,' said Emma. 'There are some biscuits in that tin – Jessop and Cully both want the same day off this week, isn't it tiresome? I wonder if it would help if I offered one of them a week-end? It's yours too, isn't it? I shall be all right with one of them, and Mrs. Tate's on with one of the technicians – Bob, isn't it? Mr. Soames is on holiday for a week, too. Let's have them in and see if we can persuade one of them to change her mind.'

The promise of a weekend was excellent bait. Cully immediately gave up her claim to Jessop's days; they went away happy, leaving Emma to do the next two weeks off-duty without any more difficulties. She had just finished when Mr. Soames, closely followed by the pro-fessor, arrived, and Emma, having wished them a brief good morning, went away to scrub.

The first case was going to be lengthy; the removal of the outer coat of the heart, thickened by pericarditis – a highly successful operation in the hands of a skilled sur-geon, even though full recovery would take some months. The patient was young too, Mr. Bone had told her, and had excellent chances of a normal life again. Emma checked her trolleys, laid up the Mayo's table and started to thread her needles, a task she had just completed when Mr. Soames, the professor, Little Willy and Peter Moore came into the theatre and she emptied her mind of every thought save those to do with her work.

The days slipped one into the other, some overfull, some not so busy, and it was on one of these quieter days that Emma went to the Orthopaedic Ward to see Sister Cox, poking her head round the office door as she entered it to address the Sister sitting at her desk with, 'Hi, Angie, how's life?' and went into the little room to sit on the edge of the desk.

'Lousy,' said the girl behind the desk. She looked up and smiled as she spoke. 'I've a nurse off sick and I can't get a replacement.'

'Hard luck. How's Mad Minnie?'

Her friend raised blue eyes heavenwards. 'The worst patient we've ever had. It's a wonder she didn't do the operation herself. The carry-on we had! She snaps and snarls all day and most of the night, and we've got her here for at least another week. Whoever gets her next has my sympathy – however you can work with her, Emma. . . .'

Emma chuckled. 'Poor Mad Minnie! You've no idea how quiet it is in theatre. Do you know Nurse Jessop was actually singing while she was doing the washdown? and she hasn't dropped anything for days.'

'I can believe it. Have you come to see Minnie? I'll give you ten minutes and then put the kettle on. There's nothing much to do for half an hour – visitors.'

Emma nodded understandingly. Visitors meant holding up all but the most urgent ward chores, with the consequence that everyone had to hurry a little more after they had gone.

Sister Cox was in a room to herself, sitting up in bed in a no-nonsense nightgown and looking belligerent.

'So there you are,' she began, 'and high time too.'

Emma offered the flowers she had brought. 'Hullo, Sister Cox. They asked me not to come until today because you needed a rest. I'm glad to hear everything's so satisfactory – I hope you're not feeling too bad.'

She sat down by the bed and Sister Cox said grumpily,

'I'm perfectly all right. That Sister Emmett – you're all far too young to be Sisters. In my day we worked at least five years as staff nurses. . . .' She enlarged upon this topic for some time and Emma made soothing little noises from time to time because it was no use explaining to Mad Minnie that times had changed. At length Sister Cox asked:

'Well, how's that new man? Rude, I suppose – all foreigners are – and wanting things we haven't got.'

'No, he's not rude at all,' said Emma composedly, 'nor does he ask for anything we haven't got. He's brought some of his own instruments with him anyway. He and Mr. Soames get on famously – they've had several demonstrations.'

'Huh, tramping housemen all over my theatre!'

Perhaps, thought Emma, when you've been theatre sister for twenty years or more, it became yours; the thought depressed her. She said quickly:

'Oh, no, they haven't tramped anywhere, only in the gallery, you know.' She didn't add that quite a few local doctors had been in too, not to mention a dusting of nurses.

'That man,' the Theatre Superintendent sounded suspicious, 'do you like him?'

'Yes,' Emma got to her feet, 'as a matter of fact I do. I must fly. I'm on in ten minutes and I mustn't be late because Staff's got a train to catch.'

Sister Cox glared at her. 'What do you mean? You know very well that you should be off this evening. It's Friday, isn't it?'

'And Staff's weekend – I've given her the evening off to add to it.'

The Theatre Superintendent frowned heavily. 'Now look here, Sister Hastings, I'll not have my careful routine altered just because I'm not there to see it carried out. You should . . .'

'Yes, I know,' interposed Emma soothingly, 'but we're working shorthanded, and Staff's done more than her share. She deserves a little reward.'

'Oh, well, I suppose you're right,' Mad Minnie conceded. 'She's not a bad worker.' She added surprisingly, 'Come and see me again, Hastings, it's a bit lonely.'

Emma went to the door. 'Yes, of course I'll come. Can I do anything for you? Shopping? books?'

'Not at present, but next time bring some notes of this man's work, will you?' She sounded reluctant. 'I suppose Mr. Soames intends to use his new-fangled methods, though I can't think why.'

'I'll bring them along with me when I come tomorrow. 'Bye, Sister.'

The older woman smiled reluctantly and Emma waved a small capable hand as she went.

There was nothing much to do in theatre that evening. Cully was cleaning instruments, the technicians had gone home and the porter was helping out in the Accident Room. Emma sat down at the office desk and started to write out the professor's techniques and special foibles in her neat handwriting. She had covered a carefully written page when there was a gentle tap on the door and the author of these came in.

'A case?' asked Emma instantly. She had gone a delicate pink at the sight of him and prayed that it didn't show – apparently it did not, for the look he gave her was neither long nor searching. He said mildly, 'No, Mr. Soames and I came in to see that first patient.' He sat himself down on the other side of the desk and went on, 'What are you writing?'

Emma explained and he said kindly, 'So I am giving you a great deal of extra work, am I not? It would be a better idea if I went to see Sister Cox myself and explain what she wishes to know.'

Emma gave him a startled look. 'Well – yes, I suppose so, but I'm not sure. . . .'

He interrupted her suavely. 'I am aware that she doesn't like me. I am a foreigner, am I not? She feels that I have no right to be here with my new-fangled notions. Nevertheless I will pay her a visit.' He smiled at her. 'When do you plan to go again?'

'Tomorrow, after I go off duty in the evening.'

'Good – if I may I will come with you.' He got to his

feet and she thought for the hundredth time what a very large man he was.

'Don't work too hard, Sister Hastings,' he said as he went, leaving her to do no work at all but sit and think about their conversation. She went over it word for word several times, and finally and a little crossly admitted to herself that he had said nothing at all which she could construe as interest in herself – not even the faintest interest. She told herself that she was being ridiculous, for there was nothing about her to invite his interest in the first place. Emma, not prone to envy, found herself wishing for her sister's good looks.

She went off duty presently, ate her supper in the company of the other Sisters, watched T.V. with them for an hour and then, with the excuse that she had a headache, went early to bed. Contrary to her expectations, she went instantly to sleep.

She was awakened just before one o'clock by the senior runner – a senior student nurse who filled the urgent spots which occurred on and off all night – who begged her in an urgent voice to get up immediately and take an emergency case in theatre.

'Here's a cup of tea, Sister,' said her unwelcome visitor, 'and Night Super says she's ever so sorry but Night Theatre Sister's busy in the main theatre and there isn't anyone else who can take the case.'

She looked anxiously at Emma, who was sitting up in bed in a rather beguiling nightie and with her hair streaming round her shoulders, looking quite incapable of taking the cup of tea she was being offered, let alone a case in theatre.

'You did hear me, didn't you, Sister? I'm going along to the theatre now to put the general set in and get the gowns and gloves – could you manage ten minutes?'

'Make it seven,' said Emma, gulping tea, 'and get both autoclaves going.'

She was as good as her word. She swung the theatre doors open just six and a half minutes later, every button of her neat navy blue dress done up, her cuffs on, her petersham belt fastened by its silver clasp, only her hair had been bundled up into a hasty knot under the pristine whiteness of her cap. She was passing the half-open door of the office when she heard the professor say from behind it, 'In here, Sister.'

He was sitting in her chair behind the desk, but he got up as she went in and pushed her gently into it. Willy was there too, leaning his length against one wall, wearing the grey slacks and old sweater he reserved for rising at night. The professor, however, had quite obviously not yet been to bed. Emma, eyeing the elegance of his dinner jacket, wondered where he had been and with whom, to have her errant thoughts recalled by his quiet voice.

'I'm sorry we had to get you out of bed, Sister, but the case can't wait. A man – an attempted suicide. He jumped from a half-finished block of flats somewhere near the harbour. His fall was broken by some railings – miraculously he has only a slight concussion, although his chest injuries are multiple and severe. I'm not even sure what we're going to find until we have a look.' He smiled at her and looked at his watch. 'He'll be up in fifteen minutes – does that suit you, Sister?'

Emma was already half-way to the door. She had a great deal to do in that time – she wasn't going to waste any of it in unnecessary speech. She said 'Perfectly, sir,' and started off briskly theatrewards.

The man was in a bad way, but he was young and strong and had a well-built body; he had three penetrating wounds in his chest which had in some miraculous way missed his heart.

'Double fracture of three ribs,' observed the professor, 'with a shift of the mediastinum – air in the pleural cavity and a good deal of free bleeding and, I imagine, almost certain lacerations of both lungs.'

He took the knife Emma was holding ready and asked, 'Ready, Sister – Lunn? We'll take a look at that left side first, I think.' He made a neat, very precise incision and said to Mr. Bone, crouching over the patient's head, 'Let me know if you're at all uneasy, old chap,' and not waiting for an answer, became immediately absorbed in his work.

Two and a half hours later the patient, minus some pieces of rib and a portion of lung, went back to the

I.C.U. That he would make a good recovery was due to the professor's patient and meticulous mending and stitching. The men yawned in the empty theatre and dragged off their gloves, then stood patiently while the runner untied their gowns and Emma, already busy clearing her trolley, asked 'Tea?' as they made for the door.

Little Willy paused briefly. 'Rather! I'll get it, Emma – we'll give you a call when it's ready.'

She had cleared both trolleys and the Mayo's table when the professor, still in his theatre shirt and trousers, appeared in the doorway.

'Tea, Emma,' he said cheerfully, and because he had called her Emma she dropped the forceps she had been counting and was glad of the mask she was still wearing to hide her face. She had to take it off when she left the theatre though, and followed him to the office where Little Willy was waiting, and although she was very tired she had to laugh at the sight of the tea tray. They had used the largest teapot – the one Sister Cox kept for her occasional tea parties of six or more; they had left the saucers off the tray too and there was only one spoon. And instead of the sugar bowl the week's supply of sugar, in its tin, graced the table, as did the milk bottle. Moreover, there was a plate of sandwiches.

'Wherever did you get those?' Emma wanted to know.

It was the professor who answered. 'One of the nurses on the floor below – she had just prepared her tea, but she kindly offered them to us.' He smiled a tired, charming smile which she knew would have charmed the patients' breakfast bread and butter upstairs too if he had so minded. She sat down and accepted a cup of tea while Little Willy spooned sugar into its rich strength and took one of the sandwiches the professor was offering. They munched contentedly for a few minutes, and then, her mind still on the patient, Emma asked, 'Will he do?'

'I don't see why not,' the professor lowered his cup, 'provided we get no pneumonia, sinuses or infection. He'll have to stay on the machine for a day or two.'

She nodded. 'Does anyone know why he did it?' She was busy pouring second cups.

The professor's green eyes rested briefly on hers. 'He loved a girl who didn't love him any more; it broke his heart. What is it your John Donne said? "Ah, what a trifle is a heart, if once into love's hands it comes".'

Emma stared back at him. 'Poor man,' she said softly, 'and of course you know the last line – "But after one such love, can love no more". He must have loved her very much.'

The green eyes didn't waver. 'Men do – most men. A woman – their own particular woman – is so woven into the tapestry of their lives that she can't be cut out.'

'And the mystery is,' remarked Little Willy, 'how the devil she ever gets into it in the first place.'

They all laughed and Emma put her cup down and stood up. 'I must go and do the sharps and needles. It's almost time to get up and I haven't been to bed yet.'

'Then don't let us hinder you,' the professor's voice was mild and held laughter. 'Good night, and thank you, Emma.'

She flew back into the theatre where the senior runner was just finishing the washdown. 'Go the minute you're clear, Nurse Appleby,' said Emma, and fell to work once more, her heart absurdly light because the professor had called her Emma twice within a few hours.

There was little of the night left for sleep. She got up at her usual time, feeling terrible and promising herself an early night. She would be off at five; she could see Sister Cox on her way over to the home, make a pot of tea and persuade the Home maid to find some sandwiches, then retire to a hot bath and a long sleep. She had forgotten completely that the professor had invited himself to go with her to visit Sister Cox.

But if she had forgotten, he had not. At the end of the long day, when the last patient had gone and Staff was back from tea, he suddenly appeared beside her as she hurried through the hospital towards Orthopaedics.

'You forgot,' he accused gently, and she stopped and looked up at him guiltily. 'Yes,' she said contritely, 'I did – I'm so sorry.' And in case he felt hurt she added hastily, 'I should have remembered once I got Mad M— Sister Cox, though.'

'From which remark I take comfort. I'll be very quick.'

He was. Presumably he lectured a great deal, for he was brief and concise and very clear. Sister Cox, who would have liked to find some fault with him, was quite unable to do so; within half an hour she was forced to admit that she understood everything he had said perfectly and what was more, she could offer no obstacles to the new techniques being carried out. It was of course for Mr. Soames to do as he wished, but she could make life very unpleasant for everyone in the theatre. Emma was astounded to see Mad Minnie smiling at the professor and even agreeing with him, and once she laughed out loud. Emma left with him presently, with Sister Cox's unexpected invitation to that gentleman to return whenever he wished, ringing in her ears. On the stairs she paused.

'But she doesn't like anyone, you know – I can't think what you did.'

He had stopped beside her. 'No? Never mind. If you aren't too tired we're going out to dinner. I don't seem to have had a decent meal for quite a time and I daresay you haven't either. I'll be outside in half an hour.'

Emma, torn between annoyance at his highhandedness and delight at the invitation, hesitated. 'Thank you, but – but I'm going to bed early.'

'So am I,' he agreed placidly, 'but I intend to eat first.' He smiled and she found herself smiling back at him. They went on down the stairs and at the bottom he repeated, 'Half an hour, Emma,' and left her.

Emma put on the pink dress; it was a warm evening, she wouldn't need a coat. She put on her new sandals too and did her hair twice as well as wasting a great deal of time over her face. At first she gave it the full treatment, but her nice hazel eyes looked, to her at any rate, odd with their lashes heavily mascaraed and the eyeliner added. She scrubbed her face clean again and applied the mascara once more, thinly, left her expressive eyebrows alone and used only a hint of cream and lipstick. At least, she conceded to her reflection, she looked the same as usual and her kind of face wasn't improved by elaborate make-up. And anyway, the professor wouldn't notice.

58

He was waiting for her when she went down to the forecourt and her heart lifted absurdly when he said, 'Ah, I'm glad to see you wearing that dress. I thought it suited you admirably.'

Emma got into the car, saying a trifle incoherently, 'Oh – did you notice? I didn't think – it's such a warm evening.'

To which disjointed remark he was kind enough not to reply to at all, but embarked on a gentle monologue about nothing in particular, which gave her time to recover her aplomb.

They were travelling out of the city southwards and after a few minutes she ventured, 'Where are we going?'

'To Hamble – Hamble Manor – I'm sure you know it. Being by the river we shall be able to get some air as well as eat. Did you have a pleasant weekend at home?'

'Yes, thank you,' answered Emma, surprised. 'It's only a small village, but I like pottering in the garden and seeing to the hens and taking the dog.'

'It sounds delightful.' He sounded sincere; she was encouraged to go on.

'It is – we haven't lived there very long, not in the cottage, but of course Mother's lived all her married life in the village – in another house. We three were born there.'

'Three?' The question was so casually put that she was barely aware of it.

'Kitty and my brother Gregory and I. Greg's married and has a practice in a village near Dorchester. They – that is, his wife Sybil too – have just had a baby. A boy, he's got red hair.' She stopped and looked at him, adding, 'We all like red hair.'

'A fortunate circumstance,' murmured her companion, 'for I have a strong feeling that there will be others of your family with hair of that colour.'

Emma made no sense of this remark; red hair wasn't all that common in the Hastings' history. She decided to ignore it and went on, 'Well, it makes a nice change, you know. Greg and I are both a very ordinary brown and so's Mother. Kitty's the lucky one, we're all rather proud of her.'

'I'm sure you have reason to be – she is indeed a most

attractive girl. Let us hope she will finish her studies before she gets snapped up and married out of hand.'

'But she will,' said Emma seriously, 'finish, I mean – she promised. Even if she married first, otherwise it would be such a waste.'

She didn't explain what the waste would be and he didn't ask, and Emma went on talking about Kitty for some minutes because it seemed to her at that moment that she had known the professor all her life and could tell him anything she wished. It wasn't until they were sitting over their Campari that he asked quietly, 'Won't you tell me why you didn't train to be a doctor too? Your brother did, your sister is, why are you the odd one out?'

She forgot that she had never meant to tell him anything, certainly nothing about herself. 'Gregory qualified before my father died and I was all set to start, but if I had Mother wouldn't have had enough money to live on and educate Kitty as well, even with a grant – so I decided to be a nurse and I can't say I'm sorry now. I've a good job and . . .'

'Kitty is able to go to medical school,' finished her companion smoothly.

Emma put down her glass, suddenly aware of how much she had told him. 'I had no intention—' she began severely.

'You didn't,' his voice was placid, 'I said it for you. In any case I think I had guessed something like that.' He sounded so understanding that she smiled despite her discomfort and he said at once, 'Let's eat – I'm hungry.'

The dining-room was pleasant and not too full, and the professor, although most unassuming in manner, was one of those men to get instant attention from waiters. Emma settled in her chair and confronted by the menu wondered what to order. If she had been out with Little Willy she would undoubtedly have asked him without embarrassment how much he intended to spend on their meal – indeed, in all probability, he would have already warned her to choose something not too expensive. But she hardly thought that the professor was a man to tolerate such an action on the part of his dinner companion, so it was a relief when he asked:

'Shall we start with iced melon? I think I'll have a carpet-bag steak, but I daresay you would prefer something a little less hearty. If you like chicken I can recommend the Suprême de Volaille Richelieu, and I think a bottle of burgundy would suit us both – Chambertin '52 should do nicely. We can decide on a sweet later, can we not?'

Having thus smoothly disposed of their meal he steered the conversation back to Emma and her family, but this time she was on her guard; she had, she thought uneasily, talked far too much about herself already. She countered his gentle questions with some of her own, which he answered with deplorable vagueness, so that she knew no more about him than she already did. She had more success when she turned to another subject though, he was more than willing to talk about his own country and proved an amusing talker as well as an informed one. She ate her chicken with a nice appetite and when offered Fraises Romanoff ate those too, but she declined the brandy he suggested with their coffee, leaving him to drink his. She wasn't overfond of it anyway and she had already had two glasses of Burgundy as well as the Campari, a combination which had made her surprisingly lighthearted, but not so much so that she didn't realize that her tongue had been loose enough for one evening.

They sat for a long time over the meal and when at length Emma said with regret, 'I should go back now if you don't mind – it's theatre cleaning day tomorrow,' which remark naturally enough led to the list on Monday.

'A valve replacement, isn't it?' queried the professor. 'A nice child – I hope we can do something for her.'

Emma got into the car, liking him even more because he always said 'we' and not 'I'. They talked in a friendly, desultory fashion for the rest of the journey back to the hospital, and when they arrived there he got out of the car too and walked with her to the Nurses' Home front door, took her key and opened it for her and held her hand for so long that for one exciting moment she thought that he would kiss her. But he didn't; he gave her back her hand and said merely, 'A delightful evening, sleep well, Emma.' So she said 'Goodnight and thank you' quietly and went into the home, through the rather bare hall and up the stairs and into her room, where she sat on her bed, just as she was, going over every second of the evening; remembering every word he had said and every smile and the way his eyes crinkled at their corners and how bright those eyes were when he looked at her. At length she got up and undressed slowly, for all the world as though she wasn't getting up at seven o'clock the next morning, and even when she was in bed she didn't at once go to sleep, for every time she closed her eyes he was there, behind their lids.

Sunday was a dull day on duty; books to write up, stores to check, instruments to examine and clean and the laundry to check for mending. Monday was a relief although the morning got off to a bad start – Jessop, within minutes of the first case starting, tripped over a swab bucket and, because the little group round the operating table were sterile, none of them could stretch out a hand to save her fall, and Tom, the technician, who could have helped, was in the sluice. She was a big girl and she fell hard, letting out an ear-splitting 'Ow!' as she did so, so that what with her protest and the bucket rolling around the tiled floor, the noise was enough to justify the surgeons making a protest of their own. In the silence which followed Emma waited for the professor to say something, but beyond a grunt and a few muttered words in his own language which didn't sound too wrathful, he said nothing at all, and Little Willy and Mr. Bone remained silent too. Emma lifted a gloved hand and Jessop lumbered to her feet breathing heavily and came carefully close.

'Get the swabs back in the bucket, Nurse,' said Emma, carefully calm, 'and make certain you've got them all, then go outside and make sure you're not hurt anywhere – Tom will cover for you.'

'Yes, Sister – sorry, Sister,' said poor Jessop, and Emma, hearing the misery in her voice, said kindly, 'Never mind, there's no harm done, just try and be very careful for the rest of the list.'

An injunction which Jessop obeyed to the letter so that by the end of the first long-drawn-out case, Emma's usually calm nerves were on edge from Jessop's painful efforts to be a model theatre nurse. When at last the patient was borne away and the men had stripped off their gowns and gloves and gone along to the office for coffee, Emma, leaving the readying of the theatre to Staff, followed them with some misgiving. Only a saint would operate with someone like Nurse Jessop puffing and blowing around the theatre and the professor, she felt sure, was no saint. He was sitting back with his eyes closed when she went in, but opened them at once to give her a long stare so that she said hastily:

'I'm sorry about that, sir – I'll put Nurse in the sluice for the rest of the list, but if I hadn't allowed her to stay for the rest of the case she would have lost her nerve.'

'Quite so, Sister,' agreed the professor gravely. 'I almost lost mine,' and when Emma gave him a guilty look, he smiled at her. 'Don't worry, I won't banish her, I daresay that one day she will prove her worth.'

Emma poured the coffee. 'Oh, thank you,' she exclaimed in a relieved voice. 'I'm still sure she'll do well once she's found her feet.' An inept remark which set everyone laughing.

The day went badly all the same, for the next two cases proved to be ones which, however great the professor's skill, weren't going to profit very long from it. But the last case was better; the patient would have a good chance of recovery and the results, if he did, would be entirely satisfactory. The professor took off his mask and gown for the last time that morning and left the theatre, tiredness creasing lines between his magnificent nose and his firm mouth. 'Can we manage to start in half an hour, Sister?' he asked over one shoulder as he went, and Emma, already frenziedly at work on the instruments, nodded cheerfully, knowing that her lunch would be a hastily snatched cup of coffee and a sandwich in the office.

She organized the work, sent Staff and Cully and Mrs. Tate to a hurried dinner and turned back to her own work. Jessop, who worked far better on her own, was clearing theatre with a will as Emma finished the instruments and went into the scrubbing room to put out the gowns and gloves then back again to pick out what they would need for the afternoon's list. Not very much, thank heaven; they had got through the heavy cases, so the afternoon should be a piece of cake. She went into the sterilizing room, added the instruments to those already in the wire baskets ready for the autoclave and went back to see how Jessop was faring. She had finished and Emma sent her to her dinner as Staff and the others returned and she was able to go herself to the office with her coffee and sandwiches. She had just over ten minutes, time to fill in the book as she ate. She was wolfing down the last sandwich and pouring her second cup of coffee when the professor, with the merest pretence of a knock, walked in.

'Why aren't you at dinner?' he wanted to know.

'No time,' said Emma, her mouth full, 'and I must get the book written up. Besides,' she added truthfully, 'I hate Irish stew.'

He laughed. 'If I fetch a cup may I share your coffee?'

She pointed with her pen. 'There's one in the wall cupboard. Do you want some sandwiches? Haven't you had lunch either?'

'Nothing to eat. I came back to see if we could fit in a repair of diaphragmatic hernia this week. How about Wednesday?'

Emma leafed through the tidy heaps of papers and notes on the desk. 'Yes, if you don't mind starting an hour earlier or work an hour later.'

'Wednesday then. We'll start early if you can manage that. Now, if you'll let me have those case notes I'll get them started.'

She handed them across the desk and he pulled up the chair and sat down opposite her, taking up far too much room, his vivid head only inches away from her. She studied his downbent head covertly. There was no sign of a grey hair and there really should be; he was forty, after all. He looked up suddenly to surprise her and there was a gleam in his eyes which she imagined to be laughter as she bent her head hastily over her own work and kept it so until Staff put her head round the door to tell them that the theatre was ready.

The afternoon, unlike the morning, went with incredible smoothness so that she got off duty punctually and after changing, went to meet Little Willy in the forecourt. As he had followed the professor out of the theatre that afternoon he had hesitated and then returned to where she was bending over a trolley.

'How about a meal out?' he had asked, and looked so beseechingly at her that she had instantly agreed. Now she got into his Austin Cooper waiting in the forecourt and exchanged a casual greeting as he turned out of the gates, where they passed the Rolls, whispering past them in the opposite direction. The professor lifted a hand in greeting and Emma longed to stop and run after him and tell him that she was only going with Little Willy because he had looked so lonely – a ridiculous impulse, she chided herself, for Professor Teylingen wouldn't care tuppence who she went out with.

Little Willy turned the car towards the city's centre. 'That man works like an ox,' he remarked. 'This afternoon after I'd asked you to come out he asked me if we had a date this evening and when I said yes, he said he'd got nothing much to do; he'd go in himself and have a look at the valve replacement.' He crossed a square and shot down a side street. 'Will Pip's suit you?'

Pip's was a small restaurant where one could eat substantially for a moderate sum. 'Fine,' said Emma, and wondered if the professor imagined that she and Little Willy were keen on each other. The idea annoyed her so much that she frowned and Little Willy, settling himself opposite her at a small table by the window asked her if she felt ill, then without bothering to wait for a reply wanted to know if ham salad would suit her. His manner was so absentminded that she was constrained to ask, 'What's the matter, Willy? Do you want to tell me something?'

His answer was far too quick. 'Lord, no, whatever made you think that? It's your weekend, isn't it?'

'Yes,' said Emma, and waited patiently.

'Your – that is, Kitty's coming down again, I suppose?'

So that was it. 'Yes, she is,' said Emma kindly. 'She'll be here on Thursday evening about five and I never get off until at least half past. If you see her as you leave theatre will you rush her over to the Home and tell her to go to my room and make herself some tea?'

He brightened visibly as she had known he would. He was twenty-eight and she suspected that he hadn't had a great deal to do with girls. He had told her once that he liked her because she didn't frighten him and she had wanted to laugh then, but since that time she had come to know that he was fiercely shy, but once that shyness had been breached, he was a very nice man. She started, in the most casual way imaginable, to talk about Kitty.

It was Thursday afternoon at last, the last case had left the theatre and Emma was bustling about, clearing up in a hurry so that she could get away on time for once. Staff was back from tea, so were Cully and Mrs. Tate, she only needed to get the needles sorted and Staff would take over. Little Willy had gone half way through the last case and Peter Moore had taken his place; he had left the theatre too, walking importantly because he had done the skin stitches and was still glowing from the professor's 'Very nice, Moore.'

Five minutes later Emma left the theatre and made for the office to collect her cloak and bag. The professor was sitting at the desk writing and without looking up, said quietly, 'Ah, Emma, do sit down a minute.'

She sat reluctantly. Kitty would be there by now and time was precious.

'Relax, Emma,' said the professor, still not looking up. 'You have plenty of time; you're going with me.'

Emma's nicely shaped mouth dropped open. She closed it firmly and said with equal firmness, 'No, I'm not. It's my long weekend – I'm going home, Kitty's waiting for me.'

'I know. Your mother has been kind enough to invite me for the weekend too – I had a letter from her, I can't think how I overlooked telling you about it.' He looked vague. 'We've been busy, haven't we, and it slipped my mind. It seems sensible that you should both come in my car, does it not?'

66

Emma goggled at him, nodded wordlessly and then frowned. 'However busy we were I can't think how you came to forget,' she said severely, and then was quite disarmed when he said:

'To tell the truth, I wasn't sure if you would like the idea, but I very much wanted to meet your mother again. It seemed wise to say nothing until it was – er – too late.'

'Well, really,' said Emma, quite exasperated, 'anyone would think that I was a – a—' She paused, at a loss for words.

'I'm sure you're not,' interposed the professor in a soothing voice, 'and I hope you will forgive me.'

'Why ever should I forgive you for coming to stay the weekend?'

'No, for dissembling,' he corrected her, looking so humble that she burst out laughing.

'What nonsense you talk,' she remarked. 'I'm going over to the Home to change. What time do you want to start?'

'I take it Kitty is already here? Shall we say half an hour? Less if you can manage it. I'll be in the car.'

There was no sign of Kitty when Emma got to her room, only a scrap of a note on the bed cover to tell her that Kitty had gone to tea with Willy and would be back in good time. But by the time Emma had changed into a neat blue linen dress and re-done her hair and packed an overnight bag, there was still no sign of her sister, and Emma, knowing her, decided that she had forgotten the time and went in search of her. She hadn't far to look. Kitty was with the professor and Little Willy. They were all in the forecourt beside the Rolls and when Emma joined them Kitty cried happily, 'Hullo, Emma darling – look, I've had a marvellous idea, Willy's free on Sunday from ten until the evening, why shouldn't he spend the day with us? I've already asked him,' she added. 'Justin thinks it's a marvellous idea too. You'll come, won't you, Willy?'

Willy cast an uncertain look at Emma, who said at once, 'That's splendid – do come, Willy,' and turned from his beaming face to catch the professor's eye and wonder if despite its blandness he was annoyed at not getting Kitty to himself for the whole weekend. But that, she thought fiercely, was something he could sort out for himself. At least it was nice to see Willy so happy at the prospect of Kitty's company. He looked even happier when that young lady, about to get into the car, put a hand on his arm and thanked him warmly for her tea.

'Willy found a dear little café,' she explained, 'and we had a nice talk.' She flashed him a brilliant smile and allowed herself to be ushered in by the patient professor, saying at the same time, 'See you on Sunday, Willy, and don't forget.'

It had seemed natural for Kitty to sit in front; Emma sank back into the leather luxury of the back seat and watched the professor stowing their bags in the boot. She would have liked to sit beside him, but he hadn't even given her the opportunity of refusing. She watched him from the back window as he stood talking to Willy and wondered what he was saying; something to do with his patients, she supposed, and looked away quickly when he glanced up and caught her staring.

The journey home, after the rather laboured efforts of her own elderly car, seemed very short. Emma sat quietly, watching the two in front laughing and talking as though they had known each other all their lives, and although Kitty tried to draw her into a three-cornered conversation, it wasn't very satisfactory, for the professor was driving fast enough to have to keep his eyes strictly on the road ahead. He drove well, taking no undue risks but never wasting time. Even when he turned off at Dorchester and had to rely on their directions through the country roads, he didn't slacken his speed; only as they approached Mutchley Magna did he slow down to look around him. The village was pretty, with most of its houses grouped round the small green before the church. It was in a hollow, so that the little community discovered itself with unexpected suddenness to the traveller, and although it was no size at all, several lanes led back into the hills around it from its centre.

'The first lane on the left,' instructed Emma. 'The cottage is on the right.' She waved to old Mrs. Beech leaning on her garden gate, as they passed. Mrs. Beech was in charge of the post office and general stores; before night-fall, Emma guessed that the village would know that the Hastings girls were home for the weekend with a man. Mrs. Beech, who had a great eye for detail, would have noted the colour of his hair and the number of his car and the more obvious fact that it was a Rolls-Royce. Emma smiled. It would give everyone something to gossip about for days!

# CHAPTER FOUR

THE cottage stood, small and sturdy under its thatch, by the side of the lane, from which it was separated by a nicely cut hedge, its open gate to one side of the small garden giving any passer-by a glimpse of a riot of flowers, colourful if a little untidy. Professor Teylingen turned the Rolls skilfully between the wooden gateposts and brought it to a silent halt before the cottage's stout front door – a door which was immediately flung open to reveal Emma's mother, a spaniel dog and two cats. The animals rushed out to investigate the visitors, but Mrs. Hastings contented herself with a welcoming:

'There you are – how clever of you to get the car through the gate. Emma has to try twice, don't you, dear, quite often.'

Emma got out of the door the professor was holding open for her and caught his eye; the gleam in it compelled her to say at once, 'I'm considered quite a good driver,' a remark which did her no good at all, for the gleam brightened wickedly and he murmured, 'But I haven't disputed it, have I?'

They stood in the porch for a moment while Mrs. Hastings embraced her daughters and gave her hand to the professor, who took it and said,

'It's most kind of you to invite me, Mrs. Hastings.'

'Ever since Emma told me you were at the hospital, I've wanted to, but Emma said that consultants didn't mix with the nurses and it just wouldn't do, but when I thought about it I decided that it was a load of rubbish – not you, Emma darling, just the silly idea. Why shouldn't you mix if you want to?'

The professor smiled down at her. 'Why not indeed? I quite agree with you, Mrs. Hastings, and I hope for a start that you will call me Justin.'

'Of course I shall. Now do come inside. You can fetch the cases presently and I daresay you can manage to get the car into the garage, though it'll be a bit of a squeeze.'

She led the way down the small flagstoned hall and into the sitting-room, warning the professor to mind his head because the doorways were low and the ceiling dipped alarmingly here and there.

The room was charming. It had been furnished with the smaller pieces of furniture from the doctor's house when it had been sold at his death. Most of them were Regency period, but there was an oak chest of considerable age and a Carolean worktable as well as a comfortable, rather shabby sofa and a pair of old-fashioned easy chairs flanking the inglenook. There was a good deal of china too and some nice little pieces of Nailsea glass on the inglenook shelf. The room ran from front to back of the cottage and french windows opened on to a small garden behind the cottage, its lawn in need of mowing, the surrounding beds full of flowers of every sort, giving a most pleasing picture.

The professor raised himself cautiously to his full height and looked about him with interest. 'Delightful,' he said softly, and Mrs. Hastings said, 'Yes, isn't it? It seemed small after the house – you passed it as you came through the village – Queen Anne, opposite the church, but I'm alone a good deal of the time. Sit down, do,' she waved him into one of the easy chairs, 'and have some sherry. Emma brought a bottle back from Holland.' She sat down too, rattling on about the holiday they had had while Emma poured the sherry and handed it round and then sat herself down by the open window, a little apart from the others, joining in the conversation pleasantly enough but not making any attempt to draw attention to herself. Presently her mother exclaimed, 'Supper – I must go and see how it's getting on,' and Emma got to her feet and said, 'I'll go, Mother – is it anything special?'

'No, darling. There's a chicken in the oven and a trifle. While you're looking at it I'll take Justin upstairs and he can put the car away.'

Emma, once in the kitchen, stayed there. She had made sure that everything was cooking as it should, and there was little enough to do, but if the professor had come in order to see more of Kitty, she must give him the chance to do so. Little Willy wanted to see more of Kitty too and Emma couldn't really blame either of them; Kitty was pretty and gay and great fun to be with and she loved her far too much to aspire to rivalry – besides, it wasn't very likely that the professor, or Little Willy for that matter, would bother with a second glance in her direction while Kitty was around. She sighed and began to dish up, draped in her mother's apron and with her hair a little wispy from the warmth of the little kitchen.

She was kneeling before the oven, gingerly removing the chicken on to a plate she was holding with one hand, when the door opened and the professor walked in. 'Why do you disappear?' he wanted to know.

'I'm not,' replied Emma, and frowned at the chicken, which was proving tiresome. 'I'm dishing up.'

He got down on his knees beside her, took the kitchen fork from her and speared the chicken neatly on to the plate, took the plate from her, transferred it to the plate warmer and closed the oven door.

'Thank you,' said Emma politely.

'Justin,' he prompted.

'Justin.' They were still kneeling side by side. 'Though it really won't do, you know – on Monday I'll be calling you sir again.'

'Only in public,' he suggested mildly. He got to his feet and pulled her to hers. 'And I shall call you Emma – after all, I have thought of you by that name ever since I saw your passport, and I can see no reason why I should not, can you?'

Emma was struggling with the apron. 'No, not if you want to.' She made her voice sound matter-of-fact, and went on fumbling with the apron strings which had got hopelessly knotted, and he turned her round to untie them, then turned her back again and before she could do anything about it, kissed her on her mouth.

'Well,' said Emma, 'I never did!'

'No? In that case allow me to repeat the action.' Which he did with an expertise she might have expected from a good-looking man of forty.

'I didn't mean that,' she said sharply, hiding delight and disquiet hopelessly entangled. 'It's an expression of –

of surprise,' she went on rapidly. 'I've been kissed before, you know.'

He gave her a smile, faintly mocking. 'But of course. Are not all girls kissed, just as all men kiss?'

She said, incurably honest, 'Well, some girls get kissed more than others. If I were a man *I'd* only kiss the pretty girls.'

He shook with laughter. 'But you're no man, my dear Emma. What is that most wise saying in your language? Beauty is in the eye of the beholder. Men do not share the same tastes, you know.'

'No – well, I wouldn't know. I'm going to dish up the vegetables,' Emma stated firmly, and lifted a saucepan from the stove and was thankful that at that moment her mother came in, saying, 'Justin, as you're here, will you carve? You must be an expert.'

His eyes narrowed with amusement. 'I imagine you could describe my work as carving,' he commented dryly. 'I shall be glad to offer my talents, such as they are.'

Emma escaped then, up to the bedroom she would have to share with Kitty because the professor was in hers. She did her hair and re-did her face in an effort to cool her cheeks down a little and presently descended the tiny staircase to present a serene face to the other three – a serenity which she managed to preserve for the rest of that very pleasant evening.

She was up really early the next morning and crept down in her dressing gown to the back door, to fling it wide and let the animals out and then put on the kettle. She made tea, had a hasty cup, then went back upstairs to dress in old slacks and shirt while Kitty slept. In the kitchen once more, she drank a second, more leisurely cup and went into the garden and thence to the small paddock where the hens were. Emma liked the hens, she knew them all by name and they were as much part of the family as the dog and the cats, so that there was never any question of killing and eating them; they were allowed to die of old age, which, while not being very profitable, gave both Emma her mother, and of course, the hens, satisfaction. And the hens repaid them by laying eggs with commendable regularity so that Mrs. Hastings was able to add to her tiny income by selling them to various people in the village.

Emma rolled up her sleeves, let the hens out into the paddock, and started to clean the henhouse, a task which she disliked, but it saved having to pay someone else to do it. It was a delightful morning, giving the promise of a warm day, and Emma paused to look around her as, finished at last, she turned her attention to a chicken coop on the grass and allowed its occupants, mother and eight chicks, to wander into their wired-in run while she moved the coop to a fresh patch. She had bent to do this when she became aware of the professor standing beside her, in slacks and an open-necked shirt into which was tucked an eye-catching scarf. He said cheerfully, 'Good morning, Emma. Where do you want this thing put?' and moved it for her under her rather breathless direction. She hadn't expected him to be up so early and she had been thinking of him in a dreamy fashion while she worked, and to be suddenly confronted by him now made it seem as though he had known that she had hoped – hopelessly – that he would come and find her. She said stiffly because she felt foolish, 'Thank you. Couldn't you sleep? It's very early still.'

He raised an eyebrow, but his voice was placid. 'I slept all night. I heard you go down and put on the kettle and when I looked out of the window and saw you going down the garden my curiosity got the better of me. You don't mind? What do we do next?'

'I was going to collect the eggs, but I'll come and get you some tea first.'

'No – let's get the eggs while I'm here, we can always drink tea later.'

She gave him one of the baskets she had brought from the kitchen and they went around the henhouse without haste, picking up the good brown eggs until they had a dozen or more, and then carried them back to the cottage where Emma added them to those already in the big basket in the old-fashioned pantry.

'You can't eat them all,' observed Justin as he added his quota.

'No, we sell them. People like brown eggs, you know.'

74

She didn't look at him. 'Come and have your tea and I'll take some up to Mother and Kitty.'

He was sitting on the kitchen doorstep when she got down again, drinking his tea and smoking a pipe. He waved it at her as she went in and said, 'You don't mind?' and when she shook her head, continued, 'What a nice easy person you are, Emma. I've only seen you in a temper once – when we met.'

'You kicked the bumper.' Which remark reminded her. 'You haven't told me yet how much I owe you – for the car.'

'Nothing – and before you say you don't believe me, let me assure you that it is true.' He went on quickly before she could argue about it, 'Tell me, how long has your father been dead?'

'Eight years.'

'So you were eighteen – you started your training then?'

'Yes.'

'And Kitty was at school?' His questions were gentle and persistent.

'Yes – she's only twenty-two now – she was taking her "O"-levels.'

He turned to look at her, a steady probing gaze which disconcerted her. 'So you had no fun – no trips abroad, no parties, no pretty clothes.'

She went a vivid and highly becoming pink. 'I always wear old clothes when I clean out the hens,' she began defensively, and then stopped because he was laughing.

'Dear Emma, I didn't mean . . . you look nice in anything you wear, even that shapeless theatre gown. But you must have missed a lot of fun. The kind of fun girls have when they grow up, before they settle down to a job or marriage. Have you never wanted to marry, Emma?' His question was unexpected, his voice urbane. She turned away to the sink so that he shouldn't see her face and said in a matter-of-fact voice which cost her quite an effort, 'Well, yes, of course. I imagine most girls do. But I – that is . . .' She thanked heaven silently as Kitty joined them to sit on the doorstep with Justin and make him laugh at her gay chatter.

He mowed the lawn after breakfast and then, when

Kitty had made the beds, joined her on the lawn with a pile of books, lying companionably side by side in the sunshine while he explained some of the knottier points about chest surgery to her. They all had coffee together later on and then Emma, dressed once more in the blue linen and with her hair tidily pinned up, went off to the village with a loaded egg basket. She hadn't many calls to make, but as she had known the customers all her life, the calls were lengthy.

Finally, she had only one more visit to pay; she crossed the village green from the vicarage where she had wasted half an hour chatting to the vicar's wife and climbed the hill past the church. The lane was narrow and winding and was called Badger's Cross. It meandered up the hill and down the other side, to join a more important road a mile or so from the vicarage, and there were only three houses in it. The first two were close to the village, but Mrs. Coffin's little cottage was half a mile further on, tucked sideways into the road where it reached its steepest pitch. Mrs. Coffin was turned seventy, and had lived alone there for the best part of ten years, going down to the village twice a week, once to order her weekly groceries, once to go to church. She was a brisk little woman, who wore sensible country clothes which never varied from year to year, although it was reputed in the village that she had money and to spare although no one really knew because although she was well liked she was reserved too.

Emma walked slowly up the hill, for it was by now quite warm, pausing to pass the time of day with the occupants of the two cottages as she went. Ten minutes later she pushed open the gate to Mrs. Coffin's well-kept garden and walked unhurriedly to the front door. The door stood open, but there was nothing strange about that; people in Mutchley Magna didn't hold with shut doors. Emma beat a cheerful tattoo on its brass knocker, calling at the same time, 'It's me, Emma, Mrs. Coffin!' This information was met with silence and after a minute or so, Emma pushed the door open and went inside, where she stood in the sitting-room and called again, and when no one answered this time either, she put the egg basket down and went through the house, puzzled because Mrs. Coffin had obviously risen from her chair in the sitting-room quite recently, for there was a cool cup of coffee on the little table beside it and the kettle was boiling its head off on the stove in the kitchen. Emma prudently removed it and went upstairs. There was no one there either, so she went out of the back door and down the garden as far as the hedge which separated it from the field where Mrs. Coffin grew her vegetables.

She called Mrs. Coffin by name once or twice, getting a little worried, but there was no sound other than the birds and some bawling calves in the field on the other side of the lane. She turned to go back to the house and called once more as she did so, and this time there was a reply – a faint one, coming from the field and sounding somehow hollow. She started to run and then pulled up short when Mrs. Coffin's voice came again from somewhere under the ground and quite close. Emma stood still and called urgently, 'Mrs. Coffin – where are you?' and began to cast about her, and when Mrs. Coffin's voice came again, she saw where she was. Down a disused well, its rotted lid splintered and lying on the ground around it, and poor Mrs. Coffin's elderly hands grasping its edge with desperate strength.

Emma went down on her knees, peering down as she did so. 'How long have you been there?' and not waiting for a reply, 'Hang on for just another moment.' She took a firm grip of Mrs Coffin's wrists and tried to lift her, but Mrs. Coffin, although small and slight, was tired and afraid and could do nothing to help Emma. She mumbled, 'I've been here about twenty minutes, I don't know any more. I caught my feet on a ledge as I fell and managed to hold on to the rim, but I can't hold on much longer.' She lifted a white strained face to Emma's, several feet above her.

'Don't worry,' said Emma cheerfully, desperately worried. 'I'll take the strain for you – I don't think I can lift you, but I can certainly hold you up for a long time, and someone's sure to come sooner or later.'

Which remark she knew was optimistic in the extreme. There was no reason for anyone to come up Badger's

Cross on a Friday – the butcher came on Saturdays, so did the baker. Emma swallowed an hysterical bubble of laughter at the thought of holding Mrs. Coffin's wrists for another twenty-four hours, and told herself that her mother would certainly wonder where she had got to before very long. It was a pity that Emma had said as she left the cottage, 'If I'm not back for lunch, don't worry, Mother, if Carol's at the vicarage I expect they'll ask me to stay.' Carol was an old friend and they had gone in and out of each other's homes ever since she could remember. Emma, recalling this remark with painful clarity, knew that her mother wouldn't suspect anything amiss until some time after lunch, and as far as Emma could guess now, it wasn't much past noon.

She took a firmer grip and told Mrs. Coffin that she had taken the kettle off the stove. Mrs. Coffin thanked her politely, her voice thin and hollow, then went on, mumbling a little, 'I remembered I wanted some beans and I thought I'd just pop and get them before I forgot.' Her voice died away and Emma felt her shudder, and plunged into an aimless monologue about her work, her holiday and all the village gossip she could remember – anything to keep Mrs. Coffin's mind off her predicament. After a few minutes she said, 'Mrs. Coffin, you couldn't hang on for a few minutes while I run down the lane to Tom's house and get help? I know he's home, I spoke to him on the way here.'

Mrs. Coffin's voice came very clearly up the wall of the well. 'If you leave me, I shall fall. It's a deep well, I shall – I shall . . .'

'No, you won't,' said Emma hastily. 'I won't leave you, don't worry. We shan't have to wait much longer.'

False cheer, she knew as she said it, but what else was there to say?

The sun got warm on the back of her head, the strain on her wrists was intolerable, and her knees ached as well as her back. And although she kept up a cheerful one-sided conversation, Mrs Coffin's monosyllabic replies got fewer and weaker. Emma stopped her chatter and listened, as she had been listening at intervals ever since she had found Mrs. Coffin. Birds, she thought wearily,

78

and those calves and the trees rustling gently in the almost still air and now, this time, the clock in the church striking two. . . . There was another sound too – footsteps and the creak of the gate opening and shutting. Emma drew a long breath and let out an ear-piercing whistle and then, on another desperate breath, a shout. She had hardly finished the shout when the professor dropped to his knees beside her and without saying a word clamped his hands below hers on Mrs. Coffin's wrists and said in a curiously harsh voice:

'Let go, Emma, I've got her. How long have you been here?'

'Almost two hours,' Emma was rubbing her wrists, unaware of their pain because she was so happy to see him. 'Mrs. Coffin fell in about twenty minutes before I arrived – she thinks. Her feet are on a ledge. The well's dry, but it's deep.' She continued, common sense taking over once more:

'She's quite a small woman, about eight stone, I should think, but she's tired and can't help.'

Justin nodded and when Emma looked at his face she was surprised to see how white it was. He said quietly to Mrs. Coffin, 'I'm going to pull you up in a moment. Just hold fast to my wrists and don't be frightened, we'll have you out in next to no time.'

He bent lower and Emma saw his broad shoulders brace. She asked, staring at his still strangely white face, 'Justin, can you manage – are you all right?'

He turned to look at her, very briefly. 'My dear Emma, now that I've found you, I'm capable of moving mountains.' He smiled with the quiet confidence of a man who had no doubt as to his capabilities. She supposed it was his relief in finding that he could rescue Mrs. Coffin fairly easily which had made him say that.

'Do you want me to do anything?'

'No, not at the moment.' He turned back to the well, said, 'Now, Mrs. Coffin,' and began to draw her up with steady strength.

He carried Mrs. Coffin back to the cottage with Emma hurrying on ahead to open doors, and laid her carefully down on to the oversized chesterfield which took up one entire wall of the sitting-room, and she opened her eyes to smile at them both and murmur, 'How kind,' and as she spoke she fainted. Five minutes later she was still unconscious, despite the professor's and Emma's efforts to revive her, and her colour, which had been poor in the first place, had become livid. The professor sat back on his heels beside her and took her pulse once more.

'Any idea of her medical history?' he inquired.

Emma shook her head. 'No – Dr. Hallett looks after her and she told me once – ages ago – that she had high blood pressure.'

The professor grunted. 'Run down to the village, dear girl,' he invited her, 'and telephone Dr. Hallett – ask him to come up here. I should think Mrs. Coffin might need hospital treatment. There's not much I can do without my bag.' He added unhurriedly, 'Run, Emma.'

Emma ran. She went very fast because it was downhill all the way and perhaps Mrs. Coffin's very life depended on her speed and because Justin had called her his dear girl. She arrived at the Post Office in a very short time indeed and Mrs. Beech, sensible body that she was, took one look at her face and swept her through the little shop to the telephone at the back, and when Emma said 'Dr. Hallett' rather breathlessly, got his number at once for her, so that she had a few seconds to get her breath, and was able to give her message without a lot of huffing and puffing. It was a relief to hear Dr. Hallett's voice saying:

'I'll be there in ten minutes, Emma, I've been expecting this for some time. She'll have to go to hospital – get an ambulance organized like a good girl, will you?'

She was waiting outside the shop when he drew up a few minutes later and going up the hill, sitting beside him, she filled in the bare bones of her message, then jumped out as he drew up beside Mrs. Coffin's garden gate and went in with him. Mrs. Coffin didn't look any better and the professor was doing artificial respiration. Emma left the two men to their work and went upstairs to pack a few necessities for the hospital, and when she got down again Mrs. Coffin's cheeks had the merest tinge of pink in them.

'I'll follow her in,' said Dr. Hallett. 'Emma, go in the ambulance, will you? You can come back with me – it shouldn't take too long. Sorry to spoil your day off.' He looked at her and then at the professor; a shrewd glance over the top of his pebble glasses. 'Not breaking anything up, I hope?'

'No, of course not,' said Emma hastily, wishing with all her heart that he were. 'We're only having a lazy day at home.' As an afterthought she added, 'Shall I introduce you, or did you do that yourselves?'

She was assured that she had no need and as there seemed no point in mentioning that she had missed her lunch she fell silent, and presently looked up to find the professor's green eyes inquiringly upon her. She frowned at him and he smiled very faintly and said nothing – probably he hadn't had lunch either, she thought guiltily, and was about to suggest that he might like to go back to the cottage when he anticipated her by saying, 'No, Emma, I'm not in a hurry. I daresay Dr. Hallett will be good enough to give me a lift back to the village as he goes.'

The ambulance arrived then and bore Mrs. Coffin and Emma away to Dorchester, where Emma waited with what patience she could muster, reading last year's copies of *Woman's Own* and *The Lady* while the patient was borne away to a ward and Dr. Hallett talked to the house physician. It was almost four o'clock by the time she got into the car once again and the doctor turned for Mutchley Magna.

'Nice chap, that friend of yours, Emma,' Dr. Hallett remarked as he pointed the car north. 'Do you fancy each other?'

Emma went pink, but she had known Dr. Hallett since she had been a very small girl indeed and she was used to his outspoken remarks.

'He's only here,' she declared, 'at Southampton, that is, for a little while – to demonstrate some techniques. He's a chest surgeon. He's Dutch.'

'None of which answers my question, though perhaps you have answered it after all, Emma. There's some chocolate in the glove compartment – you must have missed your lunch.'

Emma gave him a grateful look, as much for not persisting with his awkward questions as for the chocolate. When they arrived at the cottage she said, 'Thank you for the lift. Come in and have tea, you must need it and I'm sure Mother will have some ready.'

They went into the cottage together, straight through its little hall and out of its back door because everyone was in the garden with tea spread out comfortably around them. Mrs. Hastings and Kitty greeted them with cries of welcome and the professor got to his feet, but beyond a smile and a quick word he had little to say to Emma, contenting himself with a long and earnest conversation with Dr. Hallett, so that Emma was left to answer her mother's and Kitty's questions. 'And I promised to go back to Mrs. Coffin's house this evening and make sure everything was safe and lock the front door for her. I'll go when I've had tea.'

'No, I'll go, darling,' said Kitty. 'You've had a rotten afternoon – you lie here in the sun for an hour. I've made a huge pile of sandwiches for you, for you had no lunch, did you?' She rolled over the better to look at the professor and called, 'Hi, Justin, I'm going up to Mrs. Coffin's presently to lock up – she asked Emma to do it, but Emma's due an hour of peace and quiet. Come with me?'

He smiled at her. 'Yes, of course, but don't make it too late, I thought we might all go out to dinner – there's a nice little inn at Cerne Abbas. That's if you would all like to come?'

His inquiring eyebrows swept the little circle and Kitty and Mrs. Hastings answered at once that it sounded lovely and Emma said, 'How nice,' more slowly. She would rather have stayed home and gone up to Mrs. Coffin's with Justin, but he was obviously glad to be going with Kitty and, she reminded herself firmly, it would be delightful to lie on the grass and do nothing for an hour or so. The only thing was, when she did nothing she had time to think, and nowadays the only thoughts she had were of Justin.

All the same she went to sleep, with the dog curled up

close beside her and the late afternoon sun beating down warmly on to her untidy head. She didn't wake up until Kitty came back into the garden; it was her laughter which roused her and she rolled over on to a protesting Flossie to see her sister and Justin standing by her. Kitty said at once:

'Hullo, Emma, did you have a good nap? Justin telephoned the hospital and Mrs. Coffin's O.K. – isn't that nice? We locked up – I've hung the key over the door in the eaves. Are you coming in to change?'

Emma got to her feet. 'Yes, of course. Is there going to be a run on the bath?' She didn't look at the professor.

'No, Mother's already dressed and Justin's goodnatured enough to say he doesn't mind if the water's not hot. You go first, you're quicker than I am.'

They all three went into the house and the two girls went upstairs and the professor went into the sittingroom to join Mrs. Hastings. It was while Emma was doing her hair that Kitty, tearing into her clothes, declared, 'What a dear he is, Emma! I can't believe he's forty – I mean you expect men to be a bit stuffy by then, don't you, but he's not, and he doesn't try and behave like a young man either, and he knows exactly how to treat a woman, doesn't he?'

Emma raked a comb through her hair and winced with the pain. 'I wouldn't know,' she commented mildly; a direct antithesis of her true feelings. 'We don't get treated like women in theatre, you know – just automatons.'

Kitty gave her a piercing look which she didn't see. 'Emma, I know all about that, but you're not in the theatre all the time. What about coffee time and the odd chat before you start work – hasn't he taken you out?'

Emma got up from the stool before the dressing table. 'Well, yes. Once. But only because we'd been up during the night and we had a busy day after it and he happened to meet me after the list was finished. He was hungry,' she stated flatly. 'Does this dress do?'

It was a pretty dress, brown and white print with a smocked bodice and billowing sleeves. Its white collar was extravagantly large; the sleeves were held at the wrists by brown silk bands, and it somehow turned Emma into a pretty girl.

'Smashing – sometimes you look prettier than I do,' commented Kitty with sisterly candour.

Emma laughed. 'How nice, but not true, alas. Turn round and I'll zip you up at the back. I like this dress.'

Kitty looked down at herself. 'Yes, so do I, blue always suits me. What's Little Willy like, Emma?'

She leaned closer to the mirror and put on a little more lipstick while Emma watched her. 'Tops,' Emma said briefly, 'but a bit shy. He's a good surgeon.'

Kitty nodded. 'Yes, I noticed he was shy.' She smiled to herself. 'Rather nice in this day and age. He likes you.'

'In a casual sort of way. I don't make eyes at him.'

Kitty giggled. 'You've never made eyes at anyone, Emma, which makes you a very nice person to know. Let's go down.'

Mrs. Hastings, in the black and white printed silk she kept for bridge parties, the Church bazaar and the occasional visit to friends' dinner-parties, looked up as they went into the sitting-room. The professor was there too, elegant in grey suiting of impeccable cut and a tie in which good taste and high fashion mingled nicely.

'At last!' said their mother. 'Had you forgotten we're going out?'

Kitty blew her a kiss. 'Darling, no – we were talking, you know how it is.' She slipped across the room and tucked an arm into Justin's. 'I was telling Emma she was prettier than I was and she wouldn't believe me.'

Emma went pink. 'Kitty, how absurd you are. I can't hold a candle to you and you know it.' She turned to her mother. 'Sorry, dear, but we're ready now.' She smiled vaguely for the benefit of the professor and made for the door to stop halfway as Justin said quietly, 'Could we not settle the matter by saying that if Emma cannot hold a candle to you, Kitty, no one can hold a candle to Emma?'

Kitty laughed. 'Oh, nicely put, Justin. Trust a man of the world to think of something so satisfying for us both! Let's go, I'm famished.'

They dined in the pleasant restaurant of the small country inn with the evening sun casting a warm glow to mingle with the soft candlelight. They ate lobster cocktails and drank a very dry sherry with them, went on to sample the Coq au Vin with a white Bordeaux to accompany it, then a fresh fruit salad laced with Curaçao and veiled in whipped cream, and throughout the entire delightful meal the professor, without appearing to do so, led the conversation from one lighthearted topic to the next, never once touching upon his own private life, although he was willing enough to talk, in a somewhat reserved fashion, about his work. It wasn't until they were drinking their coffee that Emma came to the conclusion that they had told him a great deal about themselves, at least, her mother and Kitty had; she had been content to leave most of the talking to them, content to add a word here and there and watch unnoticed the professor's face with its high jutting nose and mobile mouth. Once or twice she hadn't been able to look away fast enough and he had stared at her, without smiling.

They drove back home through the quiet country roads in the still light summer evening and when they got back Mrs. Hastings said, 'If it won't spoil that lovely dinner, shall we have coffee?'

'I'll get it,' said Emma before anyone else could offer, and went through to the kitchen and started on the business of grinding the coffee and putting on the kettle. She was bending over the fridge looking for the cream jug when Justin walked in.

'I've come to carry the tray,' he observed pleasantly, and then sat down on the table and watched her so that after a few moments she grew uncomfortable under his look and felt compelled to say something.

'I enjoyed dinner,' she said at length. 'Thank you very much.'

'The pleasure,' he said with faint amusement, 'was mine.'

Emma tumbled brown sugar into the silver sugar bowl her mother liked to use, even when there were no guests. 'Oh, I'm glad. You see, it's not – that is, we lead rather a quiet life. You're not bored?'

His eyes narrowed. 'No, Emma, I'm not bored. Why do you imagine that I should be?'

'Well,' said Emma truthfully, 'I don't think this is the way you live.'

The professor put his hands in his pockets and asked with the air of a man about to be entertained, 'And in what way do I live?'

Emma banged the teaspoons into the saucers. 'You ask so many questions,' she snapped. 'How should I know? In Holland, of course, in one of those square houses. . . .' She remembered all at once the house they had stopped to look at. 'Like a house outside Oudewater,' she went on, talking more to herself than to him. 'It was tall and red brick, and it had a big double gate of wrought iron – very elaborate – and a great front door. There were rows of windows – I remember Mother said it would take hundreds of yards of curtains and I said that perhaps they were still using the ones which had been hung when the house was built.'

He gave her a look which defied her understanding. 'Most of them are. They're taken down and cleaned and repaired from time to time and of course they're faded, but I like them like that,' and in answer to Emma's openmouthed stare, 'You see, it's my home.' He smiled suddenly. 'You liked it, Emma?'

She nodded, the memory of her longing to see its interior strong inside her. As though he had known her thoughts, he said, 'It's very beautiful – a little severe from the outside perhaps, but inside – one day you shall see it, Emma.'

She still goggled at him, like an earnest child trying her best to understand. She said at last, 'Well, I don't think that's very likely. I thought – they said you worked in Utrecht.'

'So I do, but Oudewater is only ten miles or so away from Utrecht. I go to and fro each day unless I'm away lecturing or travelling.'

Emma took the milk off the stove just in time. 'Do you travel much?'

'Occasionally – not as much as I used to, and now I intend to settle down and shall hope to travel even less.'

Emma, longing to know more and afraid to ask in case

he would say in so many words that he was going to get married, said pleasantly:

'That'll be nice. Would you carry the tray? I'll bring the coffee.'

Later, in bed, she regretted her cowardice in not asking the one question she really wanted to know the answer to. It looked as though she would never know now unless she plucked up the courage to ask, for he was singularly unforthcoming about his own affairs. She sighed and turned over restlessly and Kitty asked, 'Emma, why are you awake? Are you worrying about Mrs. Coffin, dear? She's in good hands. It must have been horrid for you. Now go to sleep. I'll get up in the morning and see to the chickens and bring you a cup of tea. How's that for a noble deed?'

Emma smiled into the dark. 'Lovely – only don't let me sleep late, will you? Not in this gorgeous weather, it's such a waste of time.'

She didn't sleep late, but she didn't waken when Kitty went downstairs either. Not until her sister stood over her with the promised tea did she open her eyes. Kitty was in old slacks and shirt too and contrived to look bewitching in them. She perched on the end of the bed and said, 'Hullo there, here's your tea. I've done the henhouse – at least, Justin did it for me while I got the eggs. He's outside now mending that fence at the bottom of the garden. He's handy about the place, isn't he? It's a heavenly day – we thought we might take a picnic up on to Bulbarrow. He doesn't know Dorset – we could go to Blandford and out on that road to Sturminster Newton and turn off at Shillingstone, then go through Haselbury Bryan and across Blackmoor . . .' She rattled on while Emma drank her tea and listened with half an ear. A picnic would be fun, but they would have to come home after tea at the latest and what on earth would they do to entertain their guest in the evening? He had said that he liked a simple life, but wasn't their life just a little too simple?

She need not have worried. They spent the whole day crossing and recrossing the byways of Dorset, stopping to eat first a picnic lunch and then later boiling a kettle and having tea, accompanied by one of Mrs. Hasting's satisfying cakes, before they went home, and although the professor should by rights have sat reading a book or watching televison while they got the dinner, he did nothing of the sort, but laid the table and went down to the Brace of Pheasants for a bottle of wine, then settled himself in the garden once more to help Kitty sort out her notes. And after dinner he washed up while Kitty dried the dishes and Emma went to shut the hens up for the night and Mrs. Hastings pottered to and fro, happily doing nothing. They played Scrabble for the rest of the evening, and try as she would, Emma could detect no signs of boredom in the professor's manner.

Little Willy arrived shortly after eleven the next morning, which meant that he had either driven the whole way at ninety miles an hour or had left considerably earlier than ten o'clock, but no one, least of all the professor, asked him about it, and he joined the rest of them in the little back garden and drank his coffee rather shyly, although everyone was at great pains to put him at his ease. Presently their combined efforts had their effect and he was laughing and talking as though he had known them all, and not just Emma, for years, and when he made some remark to the professor and addressed him as sir, he was begged not to be a fool, but call him Justin like everyone else.

He grinned sheepishly and said, 'Thanks, I will, though I don't suppose it's the right thing to do, because I shall have to call you sir again tomorrow.'

The professor rolled over lazily, selected a blade of grass and began to chew it. 'That's what Emma says, and by all means call me sir tomorrow, but not, I beg of you, today.' He rolled back again and closed his eyes. 'Would it be a good idea to go somewhere for a swim? Is there anywhere quiet within fifty miles or so?'

Emma and Kitty said 'Lulworth' together and Mrs. Hastings added:

'You young things go, I'm going to laze about reading the Sunday papers. What do you want to do – take sandwiches, or come back for a late lunch?'

'Sandwiches,' said Justin promptly. 'If you'll tell us what we can have Will and I can see to them – he's handy with a knife too.'

There was general laughter at this and a concerted movement indoors where the sandwiches were cut, swimsuits found, and Mrs. Hastings, who was a good mother, gave advice about not lying about too long in the hot sun and not to swim immediately after they had eaten.

But the sea, when they reached it, looked too inviting for them to bother with lunch and they dispersed to change into swimming gear and plunged in. At least the professor and Little Willy and Kitty plunged, while Emma, who could swim, but only in an unspectacular way, advanced more cautiously and swam, with equal caution, not too far and then back again until the professor, who had watched her repeat her prudent sorties several times, came back to join her. He said in a matter-of-fact voice:

'You swim quite well, Emma – you could manage half a mile, you know. If we swim together, I'll help you if you get tired.' He was lying on his back in the calm water looking at the sky and not at her at all.

'That won't be much fun for you,' declared Emma. 'I've no nerve, you know: I'm liable to panic and drop like a stone.' She began to swim sedately away from him; she had watched him in the water – he swam with the speed and strength to make her own efforts appear ludicrous.

His voice came from close beside her and turning her head cautiously she saw that he was idling along beside her, keeping pace with her hardworking efforts.

'I'll be your nerve,' he promised, 'and if you feel like sinking, just mention it and I'll swim for both of us. It's just a question of you trusting me.'

Put like that there was nothing more to be said. She turned her face seawards and presently, when the professor said in her ear, 'Tired?' she nodded.

'We'll rest a bit then. Turn over on to your back.'

'You must be joking,' she said flatly. 'I've tried and I fold up in the middle.'

She heard him chuckle. 'Not this way, you won't,' and he flipped her over so that she lay beside him with his arm under her shoulders. 'Relax a little,' he besought her, 'you're as stiff as a poker. Turn your head and look at me, Emma.'

She did so, cautiously, astonished that nothing awful happened, and he smiled at her. 'See? Now I'm going to show you how to do the crawl, there's no earthly reason why you shouldn't.'

'No?' Emma felt uncertain and at the same time compelled to go on. 'Are we a long way from the beach?' She kept her eyes on his face because she was afraid to look and then panic.

'No. We'll turn and go back now.' He flipped her over and kept a steadying hand on her still. 'Now do as I say.'

She did, and incredibly, she neither fell like a stone nor panicked, although she was secretly much relieved to feel the ground under her feet once more.

She tried again before they left the beach and this time, when commanded by the professor to tread water and see how far she had swum from the shore, did so and was astonished and a little scared to see just how far it was.

'You see?' his voice was reassuringly calm. 'You swim very well, only you didn't know it. You must practise your crawl too.'

She said meekly that she would and thanked him and sat quietly beside him while he drove back, trying not to think about him and failing utterly.

It was after they had eaten the vast tea Mrs Hastings had ready for them, while they were all lying on the grass soaking up the sun and talking about nothing in particular, that Kitty remarked:

'Oh, lord, how awful to have to go back to London, and so early in the morning too. I can't bear it!'

'Why don't you go up with Will this evening?' asked the professor gently. He looked across at Little Willy, who had come erect and was staring at him. 'You have to go up this evening, don't you, Will? I'm surprised you hadn't thought of it before.'

He closed his eyes, apparently no longer interested in the subject, but Kitty exclaimed, 'Will, are you really going up to town? May I come with you, then? It'll be marvellous to go the whole way by car – the train's always packed on Monday mornings.'

Will said quickly – almost too quickly – 'Yes, I am. I – I should have asked you before, but I didn't think it would be any good. I'd love to have you. Would it be O.K. if we left about half past eight?'

'Smashing,' said Kitty, and she sounded very happy. 'Mother, you don't mind?'

Emma, sitting between Little Willy and her mother, glanced across at the professor, still lying prone. His eyes were shut, his handsome face turned up to the still warm early evening sun. He looked, she thought with sudden suspicion, extremely pleased with himself.

She gave vent to her suspicion the following morning as they drove back to Southampton. The professor had been unusually talkative about a variety of subjects, almost as though he didn't want her to introduce any other topic than those which he might choose, but she took advantage of a pause while he negotiated a particularly tricky snarl-up of the traffic and asked him, 'Did Willy really have to go to London? I found it very strange that he hadn't said a word to me.'

The professor, judging his distance to an inch, extricated the Rolls from the traffic around them, and gave her her head. 'And was there any reason why he should?' His voice was mild and only faintly interested.

'No, not particularly, only – it seems funny – I mean what could he possibly want to go to London for?'

'Not your business, surely, Emma.' Her companion's voice was silky and she flushed.

'No, of course it's not, it's just. . . .' She paused, unable to put into words something which was only a dim idea in her head.

The professor, still silky, went on easily, 'A suspicion? Quite right, Emma. He had no idea he was going to London until I told him so.'

'Why on earth . . .?' began Emma, thoroughly bewildered.

'My dear girl, surely you could see for yourself that Will is besotted with Kitty? It seemed a good chance to give him a helping hand.'

A helping hand or a clever move on the professor's part

to bring his rival into the open? Emma pondered the idea and discarded it as unworthy of him. She laughed instead. 'Well, what a thing to do – I thought he was interested, but not – not besotted. He's so shy, and nice,' she added fiercely.

If he heard the fierceness he gave no sign. 'I realize that interfering in such a matter is unpardonable. I must confess that it's something I wouldn't tolerate in anyone else.'

Emma stopped laughing. 'No,' she said, still fierce, 'you're too arrogant – you're the last man on earth to need it.'

'Meaning I'm an experienced philanderer?' the silk was back in his voice, so was laughter, 'able to conduct my own affairs?'

Emma peeped at him. Despite the laugh he was frowning, his brows jutting alarmingly above his haughty nose. 'No,' she said placatingly, 'that isn't quite what I meant. I think what I was trying to say was that you're more experienced and you've lived longer. . . .'

She stopped at his shout of laughter. 'Now I'm Methuselah! Oh, Emma, how you do cut me down to size!'

Which remark surprised her very much. She had tried not to think about it several hours later, when, in company with a remarkably cheerful Willy and the rest of the theatre staff, she was standing at the theatre table and the professor had given her a wholly impersonal look above his mask and asked in an equally impersonal voice, 'Ready, Sister?' and she had answered with a calm which by no means reflected her feelings:

'Quite ready, sir.'

# CHAPTER FIVE

It was while they were all – Emma, the professor, Mr. Bone, Little Willy and Peter Moore, having a quick, late cup of coffee after the list that the telephone rang, and when Emma answered it, Kitty's voice, gay in her ear, said, 'I bet you're surrounded by men.'

'Well,' said Emma cautiously, 'as a matter of fact, I am – we've only just finished.' She frowned at Will who was preparing to go as Kitty went on. 'Good, be a darling and let me speak to Will.'

Emma handed him the receiver with a brief 'For you, Will,' and was rewarded by a glowering look and a frown in his turn so that she felt constrained to ask, 'Shall we go?'

'Of course not.' He was listening to Kitty now and looked, as far as his rather craggy face would permit, excited. But the conversation wasn't the least exciting, it consisted of yes and no and then no again until he grinned suddenly and handed the receiver in his turn to the professor who took it without any show of interest and after saying, 'Justin here', listened without a word while Kitty talked at great length. His answers were as sparse and unilluminating as Will's had been, only he finished up by saying that he would be delighted before handing the receiver back to Emma, who, consumed by curiosity, was unable to forbear from asking, 'Kitty, is anything the matter?'

'Nothing – just something I wanted to ask.'

'Oh, surgical advice.' Emma felt relieved without knowing why.

'Something like that. 'Bye for now, darling.'

Emma put the receiver down and looked round the circle of faces deciding which one she would question first, but before she could speak Justin said smoothly,

'I should like to switch the first case to second place tomorrow if you could arrange it, Sister. Shall I warn the ward or will you?' And when she said that yes, she would see to it he got to his feet and the others got up with him. They filed out after him, echoing his polite, 'Good afternoon, Sister Hastings.'

When they had gone Emma sat on, idle behind her desk. They had wished her farewell in the same tones they used for Sister Cox; polite, impersonal and giving the impression that they really didn't care if they never saw her again. The grim thought that she might be getting like Mad Minnie crossed her mind, but when she asked Little Willy about it the next morning he told her not to be a fool and wasn't she getting too sensitive these days?

The days piled tidily one on top of the next and Emma, seeing Justin each day, tried to find the delightful companion of the weekend lurking behind his placid face, but failed. He was kind, pleasant and considerate and on only two occasions did he demonstrate any sign of the temper which was supposed to match the fieriness of his hair. The first time was when Peter Moore swore vividly when he dropped the retractors, using words which Emma, a broad-minded girl, winced at, and even the professor hadn't said very much, merely pointing out in an icy voice that Mr. Moore might contain his feelings until he was in more suitable company; but he had cast him a withering glance from his green eyes which had caused that young man to get scarlet in the face and tender a hasty apology. The second time had been Nurse Cully's fault, for she had considered that Jessop was being too slow in offering the receiver for that portion of the patient's anatomy which the professor had seen fit to remove and she had snatched the receptacle from Jessop's hand at exactly the wrong moment and just too late to catch the professor's offering, which had fallen messily to the floor as a consequence, and to make matters worse, Cully had giggled. Without pausing in the tying of ligatures, he had flashed her another withering look and remarked tartly that perhaps it might be as well if she were to attend to her own work and allow Nurse Jessop to perform her own tasks.

He had followed this up with an austere apology to Emma for encroaching upon her preserves, delivered so coldly that she felt, most unfairly, that the whole episode had been her fault in the first place. Her 'Don't mention it, sir,' was just as tart and delivered with great dignity, disconcertingly answered by a chuckle behind the professor's mask.

Later, when they were scrubbing-up for the next case, he apologized again, this time very handsomely, adding the opinion that it was a pity that Sister Cox hadn't been there so that she could have had proof of the ill-temper he was reputed to inflict upon those who worked for him.

'Oh, you're not ill-tempered,' said Emma generously. 'Why, we've had surgeons who threw instruments on the floor if they got put out – so time-wasting.'

'You will be relieved to hear that I don't, as a general rule, throw things about,' Justin replied. He stood upright and allowed Cully to tie him into his gown. 'Are you going home for the weekend, Emma?'

Her pleased mind registered the fact that he had called her Emma.

'Yes, but not until Saturday morning. I shall leave early, I like driving then – besides,' she added in a burst of candour, 'there's not so much on the roads.'

A remark which called forth a gentle smile from the professor and a hearty laugh from Little Willy, who, despite his retiring nature, became transformed when he got into his car and drove with a nonchalant *sangfroid* which Emma found quite unnerving, although she was at a loss to understand why Justin's driving, while just as nonchalant, left her completely at ease.

Friday was a busy day as well as being Emma's birthday. She had first of all thought that she would go home in the evening and celebrate the event with her mother, but one look at the day's list decided her against this; she would never get away in time, besides, she would be too tired. They would go out on the Saturday instead, lunch perhaps, or a trip to Dorchester or Yeovil and tea somewhere. She looked at her cards and the gifts she had received from her family and friends and told herself how lucky she was to have so many people to remember her. The wild, extravagant thought that it would have been

95

even more satisfactory if the professor, in some mysterious way, had known about her birthday and had given her some gift – a pearl necklace? a pair of diamond earrings? a mink coat . . . no, it was hardly the season for mink coats, they were more suitable for Christmas . . . she burst out laughing at her preposterous imagination and went to inspect the trolleys.

The day's list ended at last and the professor hurried away with a vague word or so about an appointment and Will hurried after him, to return half an hour later, just as Emma was beginning on the needles, to ask her to go out with him that evening.

She looked doubtfully at him. 'Oh, Will, it's half past six and I can't leave Staff to do more than she's doing at the moment. There's only Mrs. Tate on with her until eight and we must leave everything ready – supposing something came in?'

'I know all about that, Emma. It's not going to take you all that time, is it? Be a sport.'

She supposed he wanted to talk about Kitty. She inspected a round-bodied needle with care, frowned at it and threw it out. 'All right, I'll come. Where are you going – Pip's?'

'No,' Will sounded flurried, 'and wear that brown and white dress.'

Emma looked at him in puzzled astonishment. 'Brown and white dress?' she repeated. 'But you've never seen it.'

He avoided her eye. 'Kitty told me about it.'

'Well, that's a funny reason for wearing it, but I suppose it's as good as any.' She glanced at the clock. 'I'll be outside at half past seven.'

It was twenty past the hour when she reached his car, wearing the brown and white dress and smelling deliciously of *Quelques Fleurs*, but beyond a hurried, 'You look nice, Emma,' which was no more than she had expected, Will had little to say. It was only when he had driven rather too fast through the city that she asked, 'Where are we going? I thought you said Pip's.'

'I thought we'd go somewhere else.'

Emma nodded in agreement. 'Why not?' The idea that

Will might have discovered that it was her birthday crossed her mind, to be at once dismissed; even if he knew, he was unlikely to mark the occasion with an outing. Much more likely, she thought shrewdly, her first guess was the right one; he wanted to talk about Kitty. And it seemed she was right, for when she mentioned that young lady's name, he was disposed to talk at some length about her and only paused when they turned in at Hamble Manor. Emma peered round her. 'Look,' she said with all the freedom of an old friend, 'I'm not one to turn my back on a good dinner, but this isn't anything like Pip's.' She glanced at her companion. 'We're only going to eat,' she pointed out.

Will smiled, but not at her – over her shoulder at someone behind her, someone who was opening the car door and inviting her to get out. Justin.

He said, 'A happy birthday, Emma,' took her unresisting arm and helped her out and then stood smiling down at her, and Emma, staring back, had to admit to herself that she loved him more than ever before, quite unaware that despite the serenity of her face, her eyes were troubled – something the professor was quick to see, for his hand tightened on her arm and he began 'Emma?' then stopped and started again in his usual calm, almost lazy manner. 'Your mother and Kitty are here. I know you're tired, but . . .'

'Do I look awful?' Emma instantly wanted to know.

He shook his head. 'You look delightful. Come and enjoy yourself – you can sleep it off tomorrow.'

She was on the point of reminding him that she intended to leave very early the next morning, but that might seem ungrateful. She gave him a sweet smile instead and, urged on gently by his hand, entered the hotel.

Her mother and Kitty were having drinks, and so, surprisingly, was Mr. Bone, and as Will joined them, Justin said:

'I hate uneven numbers at table. Six seemed just right, don't you think?' and she agreed without really listening because she was still getting over her surprise. When there was a little pause in the general babel of talk she asked

Kitty, 'How did you arrange it? Who thought of it?'

Kitty laughed. 'I thought of it – I wanted Will to come up and fetch me, but of course he couldn't get away, so Justin came as far as Winchester and met my train, and a fine rush it was, I can tell you – we thought we'd never make it before you got here. Mr. Bone fetched Mother; that was Justin's idea too.'

'That's why you telephoned?'

'Yes – wasn't it a marvellous idea?'

'Lovely, Kitty. How are you going back?'

'Will's taking me all the way.'

'And Mother?' She glanced over to where her mother was sitting, talking to the professor and Mr. Bone.

'Mr. Bone's taking care of her. He says he likes travelling at night.'

'Yes,' said Emma, 'but what about . . .?'

She was interrupted by her mother who wanted a detailed account of the cards she had had and the presents she had received. She was only half-way through them when the head waiter came to whisper discreetly in the professor's ear, and they all went in to dinner.

The food was delicious and had been ordered beforehand. Emma discovered herself to be hungry and the champagne which accompanied it gave her a pleasurable if slightly woolly feeling. She sat between Mr. Bone and the professor, and probably because of the champagne, remembered to call him Justin.

She was half way through the dessert of chocolate soufflé, lavishly mantled in whipped cream and almonds, when she began to wonder how she was to get back to hospital. Perhaps Will would drop her off as he and Kitty went to London. She was on the point of leaning across the table to ask him when the waiter brought in the birthday cake, complete with candles, all twenty-six of them. It was set before her, the candles lighted and her health drunk before the professor said gaily:

'Blow your hardest, Emma. Remember you'll get a wish with the candles.'

She took a deep breath and blew and was aware as her breath failed that he was blowing gently beside her to douse the remainder.

'Now it won't come true,' she said sadly. Her wish had been an impossible one anyway.

'Oh, yes, it will,' Justin sounded quite convinced. 'You see, I wished the same wish.'

She picked up the cake knife with a hand which shook a little. 'That's impossible – I mean it was something that couldn't possibly happen.'

He smiled. 'We'll see,' was all he said.

The party broke up soon after that and her mother kissed her goodbye with a cheerful, 'See you tomorrow morning, darling,' before she went away with Mr. Bone, and Kitty embraced her briefly with the remark that she was glad she had thought of the whole thing and hadn't it been fun and she would let Emma know when she was free. Then she was gone too, with Will beside her, holding her arm as though she was fragile china. Emma turned round, rather at a loss to hear the professor say, 'If you're not too tired, how about going back at our leisure?'

Emma agreed that it would be nice, and for the second time that evening forbore from reminding him that she intended getting up early and it was already well past ten o'clock and that she hadn't packed so much as a hanky, let alone washed her hair. But it was certainly pleasant to be driven along the quieter roads while Justin talked placidly about a variety of unimportant subjects. They had been clear of the outskirts of the city for some time before she ventured to inquire where they were going and was shocked into sitting upright when he said calmly, 'The New Forest,' and then on a laugh, 'don't worry, Emma, I'm only working round the city. We should land up in Beaulieu eventually – we can turn back from there.'

It was a warm late evening, with a pale moon, almost full, battling with the last of the long daylight so that the countryside was etched in black and whitewashed with pale colour. They were running into the Forest now, not travelling fast, and presently Justin slid the Rolls on to the grass beside the road and switched off the engine.

'Your birthday's almost over,' he commented pleasantly.

Emma turned her head to look at him. The moonlight had turned his hair to no colour at all and had emphasized his nose – his face looked as though it had been engraved in steel, only his eyes were alive.

She said, 'Yes, but it was a lovely one, unexpected parties always are. We haven't had a family gathering like that for quite a time.' As she spoke she remembered the gay parties they had had before her father died and sighed. 'I expect you have a big family party on your birthday, don't you? The Dutch like to do that, don't they?'

'I have no family – no close family.' He turned towards her and slid an arm along the back of her seat without touching her. 'My father died ten years ago and my mother two years later. I had a brother and a sister – he was ten years older than I and my sister was eight years older. When the war broke out I was eight and they were teenagers. Towards the end of the war they joined the Dutch Underground. They were killed when I was eleven.'

Emma said with swift pity, 'Oh, Justin, I'm so sorry. How terrible for you all, and how lonely.' She went on impulsively, 'You should have married,' and stopped.

'Yes, I should,' he agreed blandly. 'It's unfortunate that I happen to be a man who is unable to put up with second best. I prefer to wait until the girl I want to marry is ready for me.'

So there was a girl. Emma remembered Saskia, who had faded into a comfortable dream and had suddenly become very much alive again. She swallowed sudden intense misery and said warmly, 'Well, as long as you've got someone, even if you do have to wait.'

'Are you waiting too, Emma?'

'No,' said Emma bleakly, 'I'm not.'

'Yet I fancy you must have had your chances to marry before now?'

'What makes you say that?'

He ignored her question. 'Am I right?'

'Yes, but only twice, and one was a middle-aged widower.'

'I'm middle-aged, Emma, and I may be a widower.'

Emma said instantly, 'No – you're not, are you?'

She tried to see his face, but the moonlight played

tricks; his eyes gleamed, whether with amusement or anger she didn't know.

'And would it make any difference if I were, Emma?'

She gave up trying to read his expression and stared out of the window instead. After a moment or two she said with perfect truth, 'None at all,' and all the same was extravagantly relieved when he replied:

'Well, I'm not. As I said, I have waited patiently and I think the years of waiting will be worth while.'

She was digesting this when he asked to surprise her, 'You don't mind that Lunn has fallen for Kitty?'

She gaped foolishly. 'Mind? Why should I? We aren't – that is, he's – I don't frighten him,' she finished, rather lamely.

'Ah, yes, I can understand that perfectly.' Justin's remark deflated poor Emma, for it could only mean that he thought of her in the same way, a kind of Universal Comrade, to fill a gap – quite safely and without fear of any feelings being involved. For a few moments she allowed herself the pleasure of hating Saskia and carried away by her feelings, asked before she had stopped to think, 'Who is Saskia?'

If the professor found her remark in any way extraordinary he refrained from saying so.

'A charming girl, isn't she? And pretty. She is a cousin.'

Cousin! thought Emma fiercely. Cousins could be thrice removed, or even further than that, so that they need no longer see each other as family. . . .

'Perhaps we should go back,' she suggested.

They talked a great deal going back to Southampton, safe topics which Emma introduced, guaranteed not to lapse into anything personal. She worked her way through Wimbledon, Test cricket, the growing of roses, touched lightly on small antiques, and when the pauses became too lengthy, the weather. In all of which the professor followed her with appropriate comments and observations. It was only as he was setting her down at the Nurses' Home door that he remarked, half laughing, 'I had no idea you were such a chatterbox, Emma – or were you afraid I might start a conversation of my own?'

She blushed in the dark. 'Oh,' she faltered, 'did I bore you?'

'On the contrary, you entertained me very much.'

Which hadn't been her intention at all. She thanked him again for her evening and went up to her room, where she made short work of getting into bed, determined not to think any more about her not entirely satisfactory birthday.

She was up betimes to find the morning grey and wet. She dressed quickly, drank a hasty cup of tea which she made in the little kitchen at the end of the corridor, packed a small bag, and enveloped in her raincoat and a head scarf, crept quietly through the Sisters' quarters and out to the forecourt. The Ford was where she had left it, and next to it was the Rolls, with the professor sitting at its wheel, smoking a pipe. Despite the earliness of the hour he looked well rested and exquisitely turned out. She made to pass him, but he knocked out his pipe, got out with unexpected dispatch, took her bag from her and said, 'Good morning – I should have mentioned last night that I would be taking you home this morning. Do jump in.'

He tossed the bag on to the back seat and opened the door a little wider for her to enter. Emma did no such thing, for although she would dearly have loved to go with him she wasn't a girl to give in tamely to high-handedness such as his. She said coldly, 'Good morning, I'm sorry, but I intend to drive my own car.'

She could have spared her breath. 'Jump in,' he invited, 'there's a good girl. You must see how ridiculous it is for us to use two cars when one would do.'

He smiled charmingly at her and put a large, persuasive hand on her shoulder and without meaning to in the least, she capitulated. When she was sitting beside him and he was on the point of starting, she declared, 'This is all very well, you know, but I have to come back tomorrow evening.'

'That has been taken care of. Have you had breakfast? I do hope not, for I thought we would stop in Dorchester – I noticed a place at the top of the town when we went through.' He idled the big car through the hospital gates into the almost empty street.

'Why are you going to Mutchley Magna?' demanded Emma. 'You never said a word – nor did Mother.' She added waspishly, 'I don't think I like being taken for granted.'

He slowed the car and pulled into the kerb and turned to look at her. His voice was bland. 'My apologies, I had no idea that you would object to coming with me. I'll take you back.'

He stretched out a hand to the ignition just as Emma stretched out a quick hand and gave his arm an urgent shake. 'No, oh, no,' she spoke very fast, 'I didn't mean that, really I didn't, not – not in the way you think I did. I like being with you.'

She stopped before she said something she might be sorry for later on, but she was honest not to look away from his level gaze. His smile changed subtly, enveloping her in its warmth.

'Now, isn't that nice?' said the professor mildly. 'I like being with you too, Emma, which clears up the matter very easily, doesn't it?'

He eased the car away from the kerb and when next he spoke it was merely to remark in an ordinary voice that with any luck they should be at breakfast within the hour. Which was true enough – they ate their way through eggs and bacon, large quantities of buttered toast, and consumed several cups of coffee before taking the road to Mutchley Magna, a journey which they completed in an atmosphere of great good humour and with the comfortable feeling on Emma's part that they had been friends all their lives, and when they reached the cottage her mother welcomed Justin with the ease of an old acquaintance, so that it was doubly surprising to Emma that having spent a bare ten minutes talking to them both, he got up to go, declaring that he had an engagement and would have to leave immediately. Only as he got into his car did he mention:

'I'll be back tomorrow evening for you, Emma – about eight.'

'Supper?' asked Mrs. Hastings. 'There'll be cold

chicken and salad and a custard tart.'

'It sounds delicious,' he both sounded and looked regretful, 'but I shan't be able to spare the time.'

Emma, standing beside her mother to see him off, felt a surge of temper. He was on the point of leaving when she poked her head through the window and said a trifle haughtily, 'In that case, there's no need for you to come for me. I can very well go back on my own.'

His eyes were only a few inches away from her own; she watched them narrow. He said, 'Stop being a goose, Emma – I can always spare time for you.'

He let in the clutch and the car slid silently down the lane and out of sight, leaving her standing there repeating his words to herself and wondering just exactly what he had meant. She would have liked to think that he had meant just what he had said, but it seemed unlikely. With the vivid mental picture of Saskia clouding her good sense, she turned back to her mother and went indoors.

It seemed a very long time until Sunday evening. Emma took her mother out to tea in Yeovil, went over to the vicarage for supper, and in between these two social events pottered in the garden, saw to the chickens and took Flossie for a walk. On Sunday she accompanied her mother to church, cooked the lunch and gardened again in a desultory fashion while Mrs. Hastings, from her garden chair, gossiped happily. Emma, rooting up weeds with awful ferocity, thought that she had far too much to say about Justin while at the same time listening with avid curiosity for any information about him, however small; afraid to say too much, though, in case her interest in him might show. Apparently it didn't, for her mother discussed his looks, his voice, his manners and the interesting fact that a man of his kind, obviously well blessed with this world's goods, should still be unmarried.

'Probably,' she hinted darkly, 'he's divorced or a widower.'

Emma said, 'No, he's not,' without thinking.

'How do you know, dear?'

'He told me.'

'And not engaged either?'

'He said that he was – was waiting for a girl. I'm not sure exactly what he meant.'

'That pretty girl we met in Holland, do you suppose?' asked Mrs. Hastings far too shrewdly, and Emma was thankfully saved from having to answer her by the appearance of Mrs. Marshall, whose husband had bought their old home in the village. She was a pleasant enough lady, a little given to gossip but kind and easy-going. She came down the side path from the gate exclaiming:

'Hullo, you don't mind if I come in for a moment? It's about the coffee morning next week, Mrs. Hastings. We wondered if you could manage a little before ten o'clock and help to arrange the produce stall – you know how everything comes at the last minute.' She smiled at Emma. 'No good asking you, my dear, is it? I suppose you'll be hard at work at that hospital of yours. Didn't I see you with that good-looking man again yesterday morning? He was here last – or was it the weekend before, wasn't he?' She wagged a finger in Emma's direction. 'Do I hear wedding bells?' she demanded coyly.

Emma said in a choking voice, 'No, Mrs. Marshall, you don't. He's one of the surgeons and happened to be coming this way and gave me a lift.'

'But the other weekend?'

'He was Mother's guest,' stated Emma woodenly.

'Well, I do call that a shame – when I saw him I said to James: "There's Emma with a boy-friend!" ' Her tone suggested that she had only just stopped herself in time from saying 'At last'. 'Still, I expect you find your work absorbing. I daresay he's very busy too?'

'Oh, very, Mrs. Marshall,' said Emma politely, and turned thankfully at the sound of footsteps. Footsteps she belatedly recognized as Justin's as he came round the corner of the cottage. She rose to meet him with a fine colour in her cheeks which she knew, vexedly, Mrs. Marshall was busy filing away for future reference.

He stopped before Mrs. Hastings and said with charm, 'I'm hours early, I'm afraid. Do you mind?' He took her hand and then advanced to be introduced to Mrs. Marshall, who smiled at him archly.

'Well, I am glad to meet you, Professor – I was just asking Emma about you and I must say I'm delighted to have the chance to talk to you. I thought from what Emma said that that would be extremely unlikely.' She looked archly at them both in turn. 'But although I'm a very old friend, I dare say she doesn't wish to discuss it with me – not just yet.'

Emma stood silent, trying to think of something to say and not succeeding; hoping that Justin wouldn't put two and two together and make five of Mrs. Marshall's hints. It was a relief when he made some noncommittal answer which Mrs. Marshall was unable to construe into anything in the least enlightening; a short-lived relief when she glanced at Justin and saw the laughter gleaming in his eyes.

Mrs. Marshall stayed another ten minutes and then departed, disappointed at the lack of response to her veiled inquiries. She shook the professor's hand, wished Emma a rather fulsome good-bye and disappeared down the little path to the lane with Mrs. Hastings acting as escort, leaving Emma and Justin together on the lawn.

'I am all agog,' he said as Mrs. Marshall's voice died away in the distance, 'to know exactly what it was you didn't want to discuss about me with Mrs. – er – Marshall.'

'Well, I shan't tell you,' said Emma forthrightly. 'It's of no consequence – you know what people are in villages.' She gave him a dark look.

'No, I don't,' his voice was smooth. 'Do tell.'

She heard the smoothness; it would be best not to answer. She said instead and severely, 'You're early.'

A remark echoed by her mother but in kindlier accents as she rejoined them, saying, 'How nice, Justin, and don't tell me you have to tear off again in ten minutes. What a tiresome woman Mrs. Marshall can be – all those questions! What about tea?'

The professor answered this muddled speech without confusion.

'No, I don't have to tear myself away, Mrs. Hastings. I had arranged to go over to Portsmouth this evening – there was a case they had asked me to operate upon, but

as it turned out, I went early this afternoon so I'm free.'
He smiled and went on easily, 'I daresay in a village of
this size any stranger causes comment – and yes, I should
like tea if you haven't already had it.'

'Just going to,' said Mrs. Hastings in a satisfied voice,
and waved Emma back when she would have gone to the
kitchen. 'Stay here, darling, it's all ready. We'll have it
here, shall we? You can come and carry the tray when I
call.'

So Emma was left alone with Justin once more. 'Do sit
down,' she invited him stiffly. 'I'll go and get the tray.'

He took no notice at all. He had come to stand beside
her and she took care not to look at him.

'I thought – I hoped that you would be pleased to see
me,' he spoke so gently that she forgot about not looking
at him and encountered a smile as gentle as his voice so
that her heart doubled its beat.

'I am. Why didn't you tell me you had a case? I
thought. . . .' She went bright pink because of what she
had thought and his green eyes twinkled.

'That I was going to spend the day with some gorgeous
dolly bird?' he finished for her. 'That's it, isn't it,
Emma?'

And when the pink turned scarlet under his amused
gaze, he added, still in that same gentle voice, 'I don't
mean to tease. Do you suppose your mother will invite me
to supper too?'

'Yes, of course. Was the case successful?'

'Yes – a crushed chest. They had hoped to get him a
little more fit for operation, but he started to deteriorate
and something had to be done at once, so I went over this
morning. With any luck he'll be out of the wood.'

Emma gave him a straight look. 'I feel ashamed and
mean,' she pronounced. 'All the while you were working
and I thought. . . .'

Justin said quietly, 'What a child you are, Emma,' and
smiled again and patted her arm in a sympathetic
fashion, then went into the cottage as Mrs. Hastings'
voice could be heard begging someone to carry the
tray.

Tea was a merry meal, for the professor could be amusing company and an interesting talker when he had the mind to be so; he was making them laugh now and Emma, who sometimes thought that her mother didn't have much fun any more, was grateful to him for making her look young and carefree again; just as she had looked when Emma's father had been alive. After tea, while they were washing up, Justin wanted to know how Mrs. Coffin was and Mrs. Hastings gave him the latest, satisfactory reports of her progress and added, 'There – I knew there was something I'd forgotten. She asked me to go up to the cottage and see if the currants were ready for picking. I said I'd make jam for her, otherwise it's such a dreadful waste.'

The professor hung the dishcloth tidily on its hook. 'Supposing Emma and I go up and have a look now?' he suggested. 'It will save you a journey, for if they aren't ready, you can wait a few days.'

'Splendid!' Mrs. Hastings glanced at Emma as she spoke. 'Do go now, both of you.' And when Emma was about to speak her mother cut her short with, 'No, dear, I can manage the supper very well on my own – it's all cold and only needs to be eaten.'

The evening was tolerably fine; they walked briskly down to the centre of the village and past the church and began to climb Badger's Cross. Here by common consent, they slowed their pace, strolling along as though they had the rest of time before them, and when presently Justin caught Emma's hand and kept it in his, she made no effort to remove it. They talked of nothing much; of what was going on around them mostly, and once they stopped and waited, motionless, while a stoat flashed across the lane and then came back to have another look at them.

'Are there any badgers?' asked the professor.

Emma, supremely content in an endless present, said comfortably, 'Oh, yes – but you have to come up here late at night to see them and even then you might not be lucky. They're difficult to discover, you know, but sometimes they cross the road if there's no one in sight.'

There was no one in sight now and it was quiet, with only the silky tremble of the leaves on the trees bordering the lane to make a constant accompaniment to the other country sounds; birds, the distant calves on the hills beyond, and below and behind them, the bells ringing the village to church. Mrs. Coffin's cottage, when they reached it, looked lonely and unlived-in. Emma took the unwieldy key from its hiding place under the eaves, saying, 'While we're here, we'd better make sure everything's all right, hadn't we?' and led the way indoors, where she left Justin to tour the small place while she collected the geraniums which filled its windows and placed them in the kitchen sink. 'Otherwise they'll die,' she explained, turning on the tap, and Mrs Coffin's rather proud of them.'

The professor sat on the kitchen table, smoking his pipe and watching her in a silence which made her feel unaccountably shy, so that she made short work of the geraniums and said with unnecessary briskness.

'There, they'll do – we'd better go and look at the currants, hadn't we?' and he followed her outside, still without speaking, down the garden path to the little field where she had found Mrs. Coffin.

The well had been covered in with stout new planks and fenced in besides. They stopped to look at it as they passed and Justin flung an arm round her shoulders and pulled her close as though he was afraid she might fall in. 'You looked very small,' he said. 'Your eyes were like saucers.'

Emma, conscious of his arm, moved on towards the currant bushes; she kept her voice deliberately light when she spoke.

'I daresay. I was dead scared, though I'm sure poor Mrs. Coffin was feeling even worse.'

They had reached the little patch of fruit bushes and she left his side to poke among them. 'They're ready,' she pronounced. 'Mother can come up tomorrow and pick the lot – I expect she'll bring someone with her – it's a bit much for one.'

Justin was eating redcurrants with a reflective air. 'A pity we can't pick them for your mother.'

Emma sent him a withering look. 'Have you forgotten the list for tomorrow? It goes on for ever – and Staff's got a half day.'

'Bad management?' he teased, and held out a handful of currants. Emma took them before she answered. 'Of course not. The poor girl has to have her off duty like anyone else. She's been on this weekend with only one nurse.'

'And what about your days off next week?'

Emma ate the currants and held out her hand like a child, for more. 'Well, I have to help at the hospital fête on Wednesday and the only way to do that is to have a day off – a half day if I'm lucky – in uniform, too.'

'You look charming in uniform, Emma.'

Emma experienced a delightful sensation somewhere deep inside her chest, all the same she looked at him uncertainly and contented herself by saying, 'Oh, do I? Ought we to be going back? Mother will have supper ready. I – I don't know what time you want to leave.'

'Since we are to have no leisure tomorrow,' he said gravely, 'as late as possible.' He caught her arm and strolled back towards the cottage, saying as they went, 'You know, dear girl, I wasn't wildly enthusiastic about coming to Southampton, but you have provided me with just the distraction I need. You really are a most agreeable companion.'

They went back through the garden and out of the gate into the lane once more and Emma watched him fasten the gate, choking back temper. He really was the most exasperating man and he had the power to send her spirits soaring and drooping like a yo-yo. Probably he had disliked the idea of coming to Southampton because it meant leaving Saskia behind and had found in her a kind of temporary stopgap to stave off the boredom of his loneliness. And she disliked being called an agreeable companion – a term which covered either sex and any age group; it was in fact no compliment at all. She started down the hill, not waiting for him so that he had to lengthen his stride to catch her up. He took her hand again, ignoring her surreptitious tug to get it free and with uncanny insight, said:

'I do believe you dislike being called an agreeable companion. Why?' He stopped, halting her too, and turned her round to face him. 'No, don't try and explain.' He smiled and bent and kissed her, gently, on the mouth, which action, although thoroughly enjoyable from Emma's point of view, did nothing to dispel her doubts.

They ate their supper in the cottage's tiny dining-room and Justin did full justice to it so that Mrs. Hastings declared:

'You poor man, I do believe you missed your lunch,' to which he replied that yes, he had, staring at Emma as he said it, making her feel remarkably guilty. For no reason at all, she told herself silently. He had said eight o'clock – if he chose to come earlier than that it was his own business, and then she denied the thought by pressing him to take another helping of custard tart.

It was after nine o'clock when they left, for Justin had insisted on washing up first, but the evening had cleared and the sky was deepening to a darker blue. The roads were almost free of traffic and even Dorchester seemed deserted. They slid through its main street, down the hill and on to the main road beyond and the professor sent the car surging effortlessly ahead, keeping up a steady flow of small talk as they went.

It was as they approached Southampton that Emma said diffidently,

'It was kind of you to fetch me back, especially as you had such a busy day,' and then a little crossly, 'If you hadn't insisted on taking me home in the first place you need not have come.'

His voice was bland. 'I sometimes wonder, my dear Emma, if you enjoy my society as much as I should like you to.' He slowed the car a little and sat back, very relaxed, smiling a little. He didn't look at her at all, for which Emma was thankful because she had flushed up finely at his words. Presently she found her voice, and it was a shade too matter-of-fact. 'Well, I do like it,' and she stopped. She had intended to say more, but she could think of nothing sufficiently nonchalant.

Hours later, when she was in bed and on the verge of sleep, a number of suitable answers popped into her head, far too late and therefore useless. She closed her eyes on the resolution not to get caught like that again.

# CHAPTER SIX

THERE was a list on Wednesday morning and Staff had a sudden and violent toothache which necessitated an urgent visit to the dentist, so that, at the last minute, Emma changed her whole day to half a day, which meant that by the time she had had dinner there was precious little time to do more than put on some fresh lipstick and push her hair back under her cap before going out into the hospital courtyard to join the other Sisters who had offered to run the bottle stall. The list had been an easy one and the professor had wasted no time on it, although he had been pleasant enough, but he had made no mention of the fête, and had made no mention of attending it, either, and it was only now, as she tore across towards the stall, that Emma admitted to herself that she had expected him to turn up. Most of the consultants did, even if only for a minute or two, although in all fairness there was really no reason why he should.

The stall was barely started for some obscure reason which everyone was far too busy to explain to her. In company with the others, she began feverishly fastening labels on the vast assortment of bottles which had been dumped in and around the stall. Presently, when the fête had been opened, they would be besieged by would-be winners of a bottle of whisky or sherry which the price of a ticket might entitle them to, although as there were only a few of these and a multitude of bottles of vinegar, lemonade, tomato sauce, bath essence, cooking oil and Pepsi-Cola, their chances of getting the whisky, let alone the sherry, were slight.

The fête was to be opened by a film star, reputedly even more beautiful in the flesh than on the screen, and she would presumably go from stall to stall, as time-honoured custom predicted, buying this and that and encouraging everyone else to do the same. Emma, arranging bottles in tidy rows at her end of the stall, wondered what it would be like to be famous and beautiful and have a great deal of money besides. It would certainly have its advantages, not the least being a much better chance of attracting – and keeping – the attention of equally famous, good-looking and wealthy men – such as the professor, for instance. She arranged some bottles of ink, which she considered a dull prize, even if free, at the back where they couldn't be seen very easily, and set an enticing row of eau-de-cologne, hair shampoo, lime juice cordial in the front with a half bottle of sherry in their exact middle.

The film star was beautiful all right, after a glossy magazine fashion. She opened the afternoon's proceedings with a speech in what Emma privately considered to be too girlish a manner and then proceeded to tour the stalls. A close-up of her as she bought a fistful of tickets from Emma revealed a make-up which must have taken hours to perfect and what was undoubtedly a really super wig, but Emma had to admit that even without these aids, she was a very lovely girl, and she sighed as she offered this mirror of beauty and fashion the bottle of Dad's Sauce she had won. With a face like that, one could attract anyone – anyone in the world.

Almost all the bottles had been sold when Emma caught sight of Justin at the flower stall and she wasn't really surprised to see that he was escorting the film star. She turned her attention to her bottles, feeling put out while acknowledging the inevitability of it, and to make matters worse, she was forced to hear her companions' comments on the striking appearance of the two people she had been watching.

'Made for each other,' observed Madge. 'The only snag is, she's been married twice and is contemplating a third go – what about him?'

She raised inquiring brows at Emma, who handed over a bottle of mustard sauce to a hard-faced woman in a terrible hat before she replied:

'Not married,' she answered briefly.

'Engaged?' asked someone, and Sybil from the Accident Room chipped in.

'Don't tell us you don't know, Emma – you must have prised something out of him, he's been to your home and you've been out with him. Oh, yes, you've been seen, ducky. Is he interested?'

Emma took a small boy's coin and although he drew a blank ticket she awarded him a bottle of fizzy lemonade because he was looking so hopeful; it gave her time to collect herself too.

'No, he's not,' she said lightly, 'and he doesn't talk about himself, but I believe there's a girl in Holland. I met her while we were on holiday – very dishy.'

'Aha!' Madge sounded triumphant. 'I knew he had a girl, and don't ask me how I know. There's something about him – he's charming and friendly and lovely manners, and all the time you're aware that you don't really matter to him. I wonder,' she went on, 'what it would be like if you did matter?' No one had a chance to answer this interesting question, for she added in a hurry, 'They're coming over.'

'Almost sold out?' inquired the professor pleasantly. He took a handful of change from his pocket. 'We'll try our luck, shall we?' He smiled at the film star, who smiled back, fluttering false eyelashes so skilfully applied that they looked real. He selected some silver and handed it to Madge while the film star clapped her hands and giggled:

'Oh, I do hope we win the whisky – you must come and help me drink it, Justin.'

'Justin!' thought Emma savagely, and choked back a laugh when he won a bottle of vinegar, followed by furniture oil and disinfectant. She handed the prizes over, longing to tell them to go away and share them together, but instead she gave the film star a bright smile and ignored the professor. The film star tinkled with laughter and said helplessly, 'Oh, dear, I don't even know what these are for,' and pushed her spoils across the stall to Emma. 'You have them, I'm certain you can use them.'

'No,' said Emma politely, 'I don't have much time for housework, but I'll put them back on the stall and we can use them again.' She turned away to give tickets to someone else and when she looked round they had gone. She could just see Justin's bright head over by the hoop-la stall. They were standing in a group composed of Matron and the hospital Secretary and several members of the Board of Governors, with a sprinkling of local philanthropists. She heard them all laughing as she turned away again to hand a triumphant gentleman in a bright pink shirt a bottle of tomato ketchup. There weren't many bottles left now and the crowds were thinning. 'I want my tea,' said Madge, 'and I'm going out at seven. What shall we do with what's over?'

They were debating this when the professor, by himself, joined them.

'Supposing you sell me the remainder of the tickets,' he suggested. 'How many are there left?'

Emma counted, did some arithmetic with the aid of her fingers and said, 'One pound, thirty-seven and a half pence,' and gave him the tickets without saying anything else. But when she went to give him change for the two pound notes he offered her and he refused to take it she had to thank him, but he cut her casually short, merely wanting to know what he could expect for his money.

The whisky, of course, the disinfectant and the vinegar and the furniture oil, besides two bottles of bubble bath, some unlikely-looking lemon squash and a very small bottle of eau-de-cologne, and lastly a bottle of soda water.

'The whisky for me,' said the professor coolly, and Emma, handing it to him, seethed. He would of course take it with him when he went to visit the film star – probably that very evening. 'We'll share the rest,' he continued pleasantly, and proceeded to hand her the bottle of soda water. The rest he presented to Emma's friends behind the stall and then, with a genial wave of the hand, strolled away.

They made short work of clearing up after that; it was barely half past six when they reached their sitting-room and, over a pot of tea, discussed the afternoon. They had done well at the bottle stall; now they felt free to go, each her own way, for the remainder of the day. They parted company, complaining a little at the lateness of the hour and what their boy-friends would say at being kept waiting, and Emma, lacking a boy-friend, went upstairs with them, intent on nothing more exciting than a hot bath.

She had been lying in it for perhaps five minutes when there was an urgent knocking on the door and Madge called, 'Emma? Come out, Emma – you're wanted!'

'Who by?' asked Emma with a sad lack of grammar and without any intention of doing anything of the sort.

'Professor Teylingen. He's down in the hall, looking quite immovable – he wants to speak to you.'

'Not a case? For heaven's sake, it's my half day!'

'I wouldn't know, he's hardly the man to shout his wants aloud in the Nurses' Home.'

Emma muttered crossly to herself, got out of the bath and wrapped herself in a towel. 'Oh, tell him I'll be ten minutes at least – and he needn't think I'm getting back into uniform, for I'm not – he can find someone else if he wants to open theatre. Staff's on call anyway, why couldn't he have gone to her?' She flung open the bathroom door and pattered damply past Madge into her bedroom. 'And you needn't laugh like that!' she snapped, and banged the door.

She didn't hurry. Almost twenty minutes later she went downstairs, looking rather pink and warm from her bath and wearing a green and white checked dress which made her look ten years younger than she was. Her hair she had tied back with a green velvet ribbon and the whole charming effect was a little marred by her heavy frown.

The professor was in the hall, just as Madge said, looking neither impatient nor annoyed. Indeed he had the air of a man very much at leisure and instead of the urgent request to open the theatre which she was expecting, all he said was, 'Hullo, Emma – have you got the soda water with you?'

Emma stood on the bottom stair and gaped at him. 'The what?' she echoed faintly, her mind still running on emergencies and who could be called back on duty because the night staff would never be on in time.

'Soda water,' he repeated patiently. 'I have the whisky; your mother may not have any soda.'

'Soda?' said Emma stupidly. 'Mother?'

'Who else should I have intended it for?' He gave a sudden crack of laughter. 'Emma, you imagined that I was going to spend my evening with our beauty of this afternoon – now I come to think of it she did suggest it, didn't she? Is that what you thought?'

Emma took a step backwards up the stairs and didn't answer.

'Is it?' He hadn't moved an inch, but she had the impression that he was looming over her.

'Well, as a matter of fact, I did think that – after all, she did invite you if you won the whisky, and you did.'

'So I did. I don't remember accepting her invitation, though.'

Emma took another step. 'I'll get the soda water for you,' she said, very red in the face, and turned and bolted back to her room.

Downstairs again she said, 'Here you are,' rather ungraciously. 'You said you wanted to see me and I was in the bath – I thought it was a case.' She scowled.

'Yes, I know – your hair's still damp. Now we have to look sharp; we can't get there and back if we don't start now.'

'There and back?' reiterated Emma, her powers of conversation sadly curtailed.

He put the bottle under one arm. 'I don't know when you will be free again this week,' he explained with patience. 'I thought it might be a good idea to run over to your mother's this evening – unless,' he added smoothly, 'you would prefer to spend it in the bath.'

Emma recognized it as one of the occasions where her spirits were allowed to soar. All the same, she said cautiously, 'It sounds nice.'

'It will be nice. No, don't go upstairs again, you don't need a handbag, if you want a hanky you can have mine and I've money enough for both of us.' He cast a leisurely eye over her person. 'You don't need to do anything else to yourself.'

He urged her through the door and she found herself sitting beside him in the car without having uttered a word. They were across the forecourt and out of the gates, heading west, before she said weakly:

'Mother's not expecting us.'

'No – a nice surprise for her, don't you agree? We'll

stop at the Compton Arms for a quick meal, shall we?'

Emma nodded, then said, at her most polite, 'It's very good of you – I can't think why. . . .'

'I feel like a run in the car,' he offered blandly, 'and this was the best excuse I could think of for taking one. How much money did the fête make?'

Emma digested the fact that she was an excuse, nothing more. 'We shan't know until tomorrow, but I believe everyone is very pleased. I – I thought the film star was very beautiful.'

'Yes? All those eyelashes, and I'll swear she was wearing a wig – such a pity, for I must agree with you that she was a most attractive girl. She didn't need them, she was pretty enough.'

And that's enough of that, thought Emma, launching into an account of what was to be done with the spoils from the fête. She hadn't quite finished when he brought the Rolls to a quiet halt in front of the hotel.

'I don't know about you,' said the professor silkily, 'but I shall be glad of the respite.'

She was mulling this remark over as she allowed herself to be led through the hotel to the bar at the back and out on to the paved terrace beyond it. It was still pleasantly warm and she sat down thankfully on one of the chairs lying around, to be joined presently by Justin carrying lager and followed by a barmaid with a plate of sandwiches. The sandwiches were of a delicious variety and she was hungry. They ate, talking little at first, and then, as their hunger was appeased, embarking on a rambling conversation which embraced most subjects but most of all themselves, their aims, their ideals, their hopes for the future. They had a great deal in common, Emma decided as they got back into the car, to continue the journey, still talking and in perfect harmony.

Mrs. Hastings flung the door open as the professor inched the Rolls through the gateway and allowed it to come to a dignified halt.

'There now!' she said happily. 'I was just wondering what sort of a day you had had at the fête, now you can come in and tell me all about it. I'll make some coffee.' She embraced Emma, gave a hand to the professor and ushered them into the sitting-room where Justin produced the whisky.

'Since you couldn't be there,' he explained, 'it seemed only fair to bring you some of the spoils.'

'Angel!' declared Mrs. Hastings. 'I shall treasure it against the winter, you dear kind man.' She put an arm on his well-tailored sleeve and gave him a kiss, and he kissed her back with a warmth which touched Emma's heart.

'That was nice,' said Mrs. Hastings with disarming frankness. 'Sit down and I'll get the coffee. No, Emma, you sit down too, darling – I shan't be above five minutes.'

But Emma didn't sit, she prowled round the room, picking up bits of china and putting them down again, rearranging flowers and generally fidgeting around, and Justin, still standing because she was, watched her from the open door leading to the garden.

'Restless?' his voice was casual.

'Me?' asked Emma. 'No.' She re-did some roses in a vase. 'Why did you want to come here this evening?' She gave him a quick glance and saw his eyes narrow with amusement. 'And you could,' she went on with asperity, 'have come without me.'

'So I could, my dear Emma, but I felt like company – besides, how selfish it would have been of me to leave you sitting in the bath when I could so easily take you with me.' He was laughing softly.

'I don't understand you,' said Emma in a vexed voice.

'I don't intend you to. Now sit down like a good girl and I'll go and get the coffee tray.'

She sat listening to them talking in the kitchen, and presently they came into the room together on excellent terms with each other. Over coffee Justin described the fête for Mrs. Hastings' benefit; when he came to the bit about the film star Mrs. Hastings remarked dryly that he had a very observant eye and he twinkled nicely at her and said:

'Of course, especially when there are pretty girls around.'

They all laughed, though Emma's laugh was a little hollow. 'It's time you settled down,' observed Mrs. Hastings forthrightly, and when Emma shot her a speaking glance across the little room, said, 'Don't look at me like that, Emma. Justin could have been married and had children these last ten years.'

The professor didn't appear to share Emma's horror at her mother's outspokenness. 'An omission I intend to rectify in the near future,' he remarked, at his most placid.

'Splendid,' Mrs. Hastings beamed at him. 'Who is she – or mustn't I ask?'

'You mustn't ask,' he answered her smilingly, 'but I promise I'll tell you before very long.'

'And I'll be the first to congratulate you.' Emma didn't see the lightning glance her mother flashed at her before she asked, 'More coffee?'

She filled his cup and then turned to Emma, sitting curled up on the sofa with Flossie and the cats. 'You, Emma?' Justin got up and took her cup for her and when he brought it back sat down beside her with Flossie between them and began to talk about a great many things, not one of which threw any light at all upon himself or his future.

It was almost ten o'clock when Emma said regretfully, 'There's a heavy list tomorrow morning – ought we to go, do you think?'

Justin got to his feet. 'So there is – I had quite forgotten we had decided to do those two cases. Poor Emma, I'm keeping you from your bed.'

He pulled her to her feet, waited patiently while she and her mother embraced, then kissed Mrs. Hastings in his turn, saying in his quiet way, 'I seem to be getting into a pleasant habit,' and smiled at her. 'I hope we shall meet again soon.'

'Oh, I expect so,' declared Mrs. Hastings airily. 'Emma comes home on her weekends, don't you, dear?' She turned a limpid gaze upon her daughter. 'Justin can always come with you – or by himself for that matter.' She smiled in her turn very sweetly at him. 'You know you're welcome.'

In the car, going back through the quiet by-roads to Dorchester he said, 'Your mother is a delightful woman, Emma, and a happy one despite her circumstances.'

Emma nodded into the semi-dark of the car. 'Yes, she's wonderful. She misses my father still – they were so happy. It's a good thing in a way that we had to leave our home in the village and move to the cottage. At least she hasn't got a constant reminder.' She stirred a little and turned to peer at his profile. 'Thank you for bringing me this evening – it was nice for Mother.'

'Nice for me too,' he commented placidly. 'I enjoy her company. I enjoy yours too, Emma. You fill a gap in my life.'

So that's it, thought Emma gloomily, I'm a stopgap, someone to keep him company while he's away from Saskia. She brooded over this unpleasant idea, so deeply that she failed to notice that the car had slowed down and presently stopped altogether. They were still some miles from Dorchester; the road was narrow, but the grass verges on either side were wide enough. The professor switched off the engine and turned towards her.

'You don't believe me, do you, Emma?' he queried mildly.

'No,' said Emma, longing to say yes, and was caught and kissed with a leisurely thoroughness which took her breath and left her speechless.

'Now do you believe me?' asked the professor.

She didn't answer him at once. For one thing, she knew that if she spoke at that moment her voice wouldn't be quite under control – her heart wasn't either; somewhere up in her throat, it was beating to deafen her. She took refuge in silence and after a long moment he drew away from her and said gently, 'All right, Emma – I'll not ask you that, not just yet, anyway.'

He leaned forward once more and kissed her again, but this time it was as gentle as his voice had been, and as though compelled by some force beyond her control, Emma kissed him back, her thoughts in a turmoil. She made no resistance either when he drew her head down on to his shoulder, but sat quietly listening to his voice, calm and friendly, telling her about his home and the family he no longer had, and presently, greatly daring, she mentioned Saskia by name, but he shrugged the question off with a casual air which she couldn't be sure wasn't deliberate, and then changed to the more lighthearted topic of the fête and after that, naturally enough, their work.

It must have been half an hour before he withdrew his arm and started the car again to go on to Dorchester and then tear through the quiet night, still talking with the easy casualness of an old friend. By the time they had reached the hospital, Emma had allowed her natural good sense to overrule the nonsensical ideas which had been swarming in her head and was able to wish him a friendly good night and express her thanks for the trip in a perfectly normal manner before going quietly past the closed doors in the Home to her own room. Once there, she undressed quickly and got into bed, thinking over her evening. An hour later she was still wide awake, having come to the conclusion that she might have enjoyed her evening much more if she hadn't loved Justin so much, for then she could have accepted his kisses in the lighthearted manner in which they had been given – there was only one thing wrong with this theory, however; his kisses hadn't been lighthearted at all.

It was obvious to her the next morning that Justin didn't share her doubts. He greeted her with detached friendliness, no more, and although she coloured faintly at the sight of him she answered his good morning in a sensible voice, aware of the tumult beneath her ribs and determined not to show it.

'Sleep well?' he wanted to know as he took his place at the sink beside her and started to scrub up, and when she nodded, went on, 'So did I – we should do that more often. When is your next evening off?'

'This evening,' said Emma quickly before she could have second thoughts.

'Good, keep it free for us, Emma.' He smiled at her and she said in a low voice, 'Very well,' and rinsed off carefully and went through to the theatre.

It was a busy day, but a pleasant one, too. Emma watched the professor at work, wondering how she would feel when he had gone, and put the twinge of pain under her belt down to this miserable thought. But the twinge came again, several times, and even the delectable thought that she would be with him again in a few hours didn't dispel it. She ate no dinner, but after several cups of tea she felt better and went back to the afternoon's list, telling herself that she would be more careful what she ate in future; perhaps the sandwiches they had eaten hadn't been quite fresh – she dismissed the idea at once. There had been nothing wrong with them at all, perhaps it was just excitement. But by the end of the list the vague feeling of discomfort had returned and didn't go away again, and when the professor and Little Willy left the theatre she went after them, and Justin, aware that she had followed him, stopped on his way down the corridor. 'I'll catch up with you in a minute or so,' he told Will easily, and walked back to meet her and then stood, relaxed and calm, waiting for her to speak.

'I think,' began Emma, a little wanly, 'if you don't mind, I won't come out this evening. I – I think I must have eaten something that didn't quite agree. ...' She gave him a beseeching look and despite the fact that she wasn't feeling too good, her heart leapt at the concern in his eyes.

'My dear girl, why didn't you say so earlier? Staff could have scrubbed for you. Are you sure that's all it is?' And when she nodded he smiled and said, 'Of course I mind, Emma. I was looking forward to being with you. Go off duty as soon as you can and go to bed. Is there someone to bring you some supper?'

Emma, in a little voice which sounded relieved, said, 'Oh, yes, thank you.' The thought of supper was nauseating, but it was kind of him to think of it. 'I'm sorry,' she added.

He said nothing to this, but gave her an avuncular pat on the shoulder.

'Don't come on in the morning if you don't feel like it,' he admonished her as he turned on his heel and strode off to where Will was patiently waiting.

Emma felt quite well again in the morning although she had wakened once or twice in the night, feeling queasy, and she had had no appetite for her breakfast. She was in the office making out the next day's theatre list when the professor, much earlier than usual, stalked in.

'Better?' he asked. He studied her narrowly. 'I can't see much wrong with you.'

Emma smiled up at him. 'I feel fine. I can't think what came over me.'

She watched the green eyes narrow. 'The cold wind of caution, perhaps?' His voice was silky, and she faltered, 'What – what do you mean?' while she sought for the right words and failed to find them. She was still cudgelling her brains when Little Willy walked in and put an end to any chance she had of succeeding. She wished him good morning and went quite unnecessarily to the linen cupboard to count the towels, a prey to a variety of thoughts, none of them pleasant.

There was a lobectomy, a second stage thoracoplasty and a couple of bronchoscopies on the morning's list; routine stuff, reflected Emma, wondering why everything seemed such an effort. She found it difficult to respond to the professor's tranquil voice and even then impossible to offer more than monosyllabic replies, and when they paused for coffee she sat in the office listening to the three men talking and taking no part in their conversation herself. She drank her coffee without any pleasure, left them to their second cups and went along to scrub once more, followed, after a very few minutes, by the professor. He made no attempt to scrub, however, but leaned against the tiled wall, watching her.

'Sulking, Emma?' he inquired, and his smile mocked her. It hurt her too, but she couldn't summon up the spirit to contradict him. She murmured, 'No, oh, no,' and escaped to the theatre.

When the list was finished and the men had gone, Emma went along to the office, thankful that Staff was there to clear up. She sat down feeling listless and debating whether to ask Staff to stay on and take the case that afternoon. But it was hardly fair to change her off duty at a moment's notice and probably, thought Emma hardily, she herself would feel well again presently. But when it was time to go to dinner she stayed where she was drinking the tea the theatre maid had brought her and nibbling dry biscuits which revived her to such an extent that she was able to tell herself that whatever it was had been unimportant and transitory.

There was only the one case that afternoon, but a difficult one; an oesophagectomy which would require all the professor's skill as well as the co-operation of his helpers. Feeling almost lighthearted because she felt so much better, Emma went along to the theatre to make sure that everything was perfection and then scrubbed up before the men arrived, determined to have no conversation with Justin for the time being. She was in theatre, quite ready, when Mr. Bone came in with his patient and the porters and by the time Justin, with Will and Peter tailing him, came in, she was entrenched securely behind her trolleys with everything ready for them, and beyond exchanging their usual pleasant 'Good afternoon,' there was no need to speak.

The case was half done when the pain began; a dull ache at first which she was able to ignore, but which increased with the slow minutes until it was almost past bearing. Emma worked mechanically, handing instruments with perfect timing; counting swabs with her usual care; rearranging instruments; threading needles, intent on hanging on until the end of the case. Any commotion which might disturb the surgeon's work could spoil the whole tricky operation – not that the professor was likely to lose his head in any circumstances, of that she was reasonably sure, but she didn't dare take the risk of getting the part-time staff nurse to scrub for her with all the consequences of a change-over, however smooth. Besides, she thought uneasily, Staff Betts hadn't taken an oesophagectomy before, she might get some of the instruments wrong and hinder the professor's concentration.

She saw with relief that he was beginning the deep suturing and handed the needleholder with its needle threaded and then clung to the trolley before her, feeling the sweat beading her forehead, doggedly watching the professor sewing precisely and all too slowly. Even when he had finished this there would be a minute or two while he checked his needlework and she must be ready to anticipate anything he might need at a moment's notice. At last he handed her back the needleholder so that she could remove the needle and put the holder in the bowl of saline on the trolley's shelf, aware that the pain had got out of hand; she would have to give in to it. She glanced at the clock; if she could hold out for another ten minutes that would see the crucial part of the operation over. She handed the probe he asked for with a hand that shook, something which he saw at once, for he paused for a split second and gave her a sharp glance. Emma looked back at him, that portion of her face which was visible a pale green, her eyes huge with pain. He said softly – urgently, 'Emma,' and bent to his work even as he was speaking with unhurried command.

'Staff Nurse, scrub and take over from Sister. Nurse Jessop, come behind Sister and stand so that she can lean back on you if she must, and if she faints for God's sake keep her away from the trolleys and us.'

He put down the probe and picked up some gut and started tying off.

'Peter, take over whatever Staff was doing. Tom,' – this to the technician – 'go and telephone Mr. Phillips and don't come back until you've got him. Get him to come here at once if he can manage that. It's urgent, Sister is ill.' He gave Emma another quick searching glance between tying off. 'Look sharp, man!'

He went on working then, without visible haste or worry, not looking at Emma at all, and she watched through a mist of pain as Will took off the retractors and the professor began to stitch the muscle sheath.

'Can you stick it, Emma?' his voice was very gentle. 'Just a minute more.'

The pain had receded. She said in an almost controlled voice, 'Yes, it's not too bad,' and then closed her eyes in relief as Betts insinuated herself beside her with an encouraging, 'O.K., Sister, I'll be all right.' Emma nodded and began to speak and then as the pain twisted through her again, the words turned to a small sobbing moan.

They were putting in the skin sutures now, working fast, one at each end of the wound. Emma, leaning against Jessop's firm support, kept her eyes on the professor's hands, her teeth clenched against the next scream bubbling in her throat. It was only seconds, but it seemed like as many hours when he said, 'Right, Will, take over,' and backed away from the table, pulling off his gloves as he walked behind the trolleys and scooped Emma up. 'Open the door, there's a good girl,' he said to Jessop, and lifted Emma clear, slowly and carefully so that nothing was touched. She felt his arms holding her close as he carried her out of the theatre and laid her on the anaesthetic room trolley. She felt his fingers too, cool and firm, as he took off her theatre cap and mask to expose her pallid face and Jessop, without being told, was cutting the tapes of her gown. Lightheaded with pain, Emma mumbled, 'Sister Cox wouldn't like that, Nurse,' and Jessop said comfortably, 'Don't you worry, Sister, I'll take care of everything,' and Emma felt a small thrill of satisfaction mixed in with the pain because Jessop was behaving very well in an emergency. She opened her eyes and saw Justin's face above her and whispered, 'I told you she would be a good nurse,' and then because she felt so ill, closed them again.

Mr. Phillips came then. Emma lay quietly under his gentle searching hands until the pain got worse again and she heard her own voice, very high and strained, beseeching someone to do something, and then, 'I'm going to be sick,' she said urgently.

It was Justin who held the bowl and then took her hand and held it while Jessop wiped her face. 'Dear Emma,' he said, and his voice sounded as calm and placid as it always did and for some reason that made her feel quite safe. 'You're going to have something now,' and as he spoke she felt the thin prick of a needle in her arm and in a blessedly short time the pain had melted away and presently she floated away into a quiet limbo of her own, not bothering to think any more, but still aware of Justin's hand holding hers in a firm, sure grip.

The next few hours were a timeless stretch in which she was vaguely conscious of being lifted and undressed, and voices which she was too weary to recognize came and went over her head. One of them asked her to sign a consent form and another one told her that she was going to have her appendix out and she murmured politely, not caring in the least. Only after a little while she felt less happy because Justin's hand wasn't there any longer, and though she longed to ask where he had gone, she couldn't summon the energy to speak, and by and by, when they took her to theatre, it was Mr. Phillips' face which floated above her when she opened her eyes, although the last thought she had in her head before she dropped off under the anaesthetist's skilful needle was of Justin.

# CHAPTER SEVEN

EMMA, working her way through layers of sleep-filled mist, heard Justin's voice before she opened her eyes, and it sounded reassuringly unworried. It was a pity that whatever he was saying made nonsense in her still bemused mind, but all the same, she forced her eyes open only to discover that the face looking down at her wasn't Justin at all, but Mr. Phillips' craggy visage. It grew large and then receded in the mist and she opened her mouth to tell him how funny he looked, then had no idea what it was she had been going to say, and in the same instant was once more enveloped in sleep.

The second time she woke up she knew where she was – Nurses' Sick Bay, off Women's Surgical, and Ann, her friend and Night Sister on the surgical side, was taking her pulse. Emma said in a woolly voice, because her tongue was still far too large for her mouth, 'Hullo, Ann,' and then, 'He's gone.'

Ann seemed to understand. 'Only just – he went to fetch your mother and they both went about half an hour ago. He's taken her to a hotel for the night.'

'Night?' asked Emma, faintly puzzled as to the passage of time but prepared to believe anything Ann said. 'What's the time?'

'Almost half past two. Go to sleep, Emma, everything's fine, you'll feel as fit as a flea in the morning.'

Upon which sound but inelegant advice Emma closed her eyes obediently and slept.

Her mother was there when she awakened for the third time, sitting by the bed with the *Daily Telegraph* on her lap but not reading it. Emma felt quite clear in her head, surprisingly hungry and only a little sore. She moved cautiously, found that the soreness was only a little worse when she did and said, 'Hullo, Mother.'

Mrs. Hastings got out of her chair and embraced her with warm caution.

'Darling – there you are again, how lovely! Everyone

told me you were perfectly all right, but you seemed a long way away, if you know what I mean. So very quiet, not at all like you.' She smiled her relief and went and sat down again. 'Does it hurt, darling – it must have been awful. Justin told me you were so brave.'

'When did Justin . . .?' began Emma, when her mother interrupted her with, 'I'm to ring the bell as soon as you wake, so I'd better do that, hadn't I? They said I could come back presently.' She kissed Emma again and went to the door, and as she went out Brenda, another of Emma's friends and Sister of Women's Surgical, came in. Brenda was tall, dark and beautiful, very good at her job, oblivious of her good looks and perfectly happy with her life. The story went that she had been dated at some time or other by every presentable man within a ten-mile radius of the hospital, and Emma, watching her as she walked towards the bed, decided that it was probably an understatement.

'Why aren't you married?' she asked as Brenda came to a halt by the bed.

Brenda's lovely face split into a grin. 'Hey, you're supposed to murmur "Where am I?" or moan gently about the pain, not put searching questions about my love life!' She whipped back the bedclothes and went on, 'If you must know, I'm having great fun as I am, thank you. Besides, there's that corny old type, a girlhood sweetheart, obligingly waiting until I want to settle down.'

She cast an expert eye over the small neat scar and remarked comfortably, 'That won't notice in six weeks or so – nice tidy job old Phillips does. Like a cup of tea? Nurse shall bring you one, then you'll be sat out, my girl, and like it.'

'It's the spoiling I've been looking forward to,' murmured Emma. 'Why's Mother here?'

'Professor Teylingen fetched her.' She rolled her expressive dark eyes at Emma. 'That car of his must travel – he was there and back almost before old Phillips could lift his scalpel. Came and looked at you the minute you were out of theatre, too.'

'Oh?' Emma's voice was carefully expressionless.

'Where is he now?'

'Operating, of course. It's gone ten o'clock, ducky, you've been snoring your head off all night.'

To which unkind remark Emma reacted naturally enough with, 'Do I look awful?'

Her handsome friend regarded her with a kindly eye. 'No, not in the least – a little like a mouse that's under the weather, perhaps – but mice are rather sweet.'

Emma sighed. Anyone could be rather sweet; a term applied to any age group from a day-old baby to an old lady of ninety. It would be wonderful to be pallidly beautiful with great blue eyes full of suffering and everyone falling over themselves to do things for you . . .

'Upsy-daisy,' said Brenda cheerfully, and sat her up in bed. 'Here's your tea – Nurse, put that bowl where Sister can reach it, just in case she needs it – the first cup of tea doesn't always stay down, you know. Ring when you've finished it, Emma, and one of the nurses will give you a bedbath, then we'll get you into a chair – can't have you lying around in bed, you know. You'll want some nighties – I'll send a nurse over to your room to get some.'

Emma sipped the tea with caution. 'Please – top drawer of the dressing table – two pink ones and there's one with blue daisies, and a dressing gown behind the door – the pink one with the ruffle.'

'Sounds nice,' commented Brenda. 'Can Nurse get in?'

'My uniform pocket; my keys,' said Emma, suddenly overcome by a great longing to go to sleep again.

She awoke half an hour later, much refreshed by her brief nap, to find her mother there. Mrs. Hastings smiled at her happily and said:

'Brenda told me to let you sleep – what a nice girl she is, and so pretty too. I must go again, darling, so that you can be bathed and got up, but I'll be back this afternoon. I'm not going home until Justin has finished his list.'

Emma nodded. 'That's nice. Poor Mother, what a rotten time you've had, sitting there while I snore my head off.' She gave her parent an affectionate glance, thinking at the same time that she wasn't likely to see Justin. She frowned, trying to remember what was down

131

for the day, and when she did, decided that he would be kept busy until five o'clock at least, perhaps later than that, and if he was going to take her mother home, by the time he returned, she herself would be in bed and asleep. She said, 'It was decent of Justin to fetch you, darling – thank you for coming.'

Mrs. Hastings looked surprised. 'But, Emma, I should have come anyway. As it was, Justin saw to everything – it made it all so easy.' She got up and kissed Emma. 'I'm going before that nice Brenda turns me out.'

It was refreshing to be bathed, even in bed, and have one of her own nighties on again. Emma, faintly apprehensive, swung her legs over the side of the bed and with Brenda beside her, was stood up on cottonwool legs, walked to a chair and sat in it, where she submitted to having her hair brushed and her dressing-gown put on, which done:

'There you are,' said Brenda encouragingly. 'How do you feel?'

'Hollow.'

'That wears off, ducky. I'll get a paper for you to read and here's the bell if you want anyone. There'll be a little light something on a tray presently.' She made for the door. 'Be seeing you!'

Emma read the paper slowly from front to back, not taking in a word because her mind was full of Justin. Surely he could have looked in on her before the list started, or even sent a message? She swallowed a ridiculous desire to burst into tears, telling herself it was because she felt so stupidly weak, and read, for the second time, the sporting page, not a line of which made any sense to her.

She had pecked without appetite at the little something on a tray, and the nurse had taken it away again when the door opened once more and because she was feeling drowsy Emma didn't open her eyes when she heard the crisp swish of Brenda's apron and her light laugh; but the laugh was echoed. Emma opened her eyes and saw Mr. Phillips and Justin following her friend into the room. They came and stood in front of her chair and Mr. Phillips said, 'Very nice – I like pink,' which was so unexpected a remark that a little of that colour washed over Emma's pale cheeks. He took her pulse, peered at her knowledgeably over his spectacles, asked a few questions pertinent to the removal of an appendix and then strolled back to the door, professing himself entirely satisfied. 'Busy,' he mumbled as he went. 'Talk to you later,' and went away.

Emma hoped that Brenda would go with him, but she stayed where she was beside Justin, who stood with his hands in his pockets looking down at Emma with a detached air. He inquired politely after her health and then stood silently while Brenda rattled on cheerfully, laughing a little at her because she was amusing as well as remarkably pretty. Emma, watching her, felt pale and uninteresting and a little peevish and talked hardly at all. Only as her visitors turned to go did she bring herself to say, 'It was kind of you to fetch my mother, Professor Teylingen. Thank you.'

He looked as though he was going to laugh. 'My dear girl, it was the least I could do – I had to make amends, did I not? Supposing your excuses to be merely excuses when all the while they were genuine. I apologize handsomely, if only to prevent you from calling me Professor Teylingen in that redoubtable fashion.' He didn't look amused any more, only concerned. 'You were very brave, Emma – it must have needed a great deal of courage to have stood there as long as you did. It certainly gave the patient a fair chance. I'm very much in your debt.'

He smiled, and Emma, fighting a second, much stronger desire to cry, stared at him wordlessly while he wished her a quick goodbye and made for the door, saying that he was already late.

He came again at five o'clock, when Emma was back in bed, looking washed out, half listening to her mother's soothing inconsequential chatter. He came alone this time, a pile of magazines under one arm and an extravagant bouquet of roses under the other, and laid his offerings on her bed, observing apologetically that he would have brought them sooner but that the list had been a heavy one. His voice was light, but Emma, looking at him, could see that he was tired, so that she, full of remorse for forgetting his hard day, said warmly, 'Thank you, Justin, how lovely and how kind you are.' She smiled at him rather tremulously and as he smiled back, the tiredness somehow disappeared.

'Feeling better?' he wanted to know, then picked up her hand and held it between his own, and although his voice hadn't changed, his touch was firm and comforting. Emma, her hand fast held between his, felt suddenly that everything was right once more and said cheerfully, 'Oh, yes – heaps better.'

'Good. I've come to take your mother home.' He glanced across to Mrs. Hastings, Emma's hand still in his. 'Unless you want to spend another night here?' he wanted to know.

Mrs. Hastings shook her head. 'Emma's all right now, isn't she? I can't thank you enough for fetching me, Justin, and I feel awful about you driving all that way now after a hard day's work. Are you sure . . .?'

'Quite sure,' his voice was unconcerned. 'I find driving relaxing after standing for hours in the theatre.'

'Then I'll just go and say goodbye to that nice Brenda and get these flowers into water.' She gathered them up as she spoke, smiled at Justin and then at Emma and disappeared.

'Still cross with me, Emma?' Justin asked as he seated himself on the side of her bed. He looked kind and friendly and she said at once:

'Have I been beastly? I've no reason to be – you've been so kind . . .'

'But I didn't come until after the morning list, did I?' he prompted, his eyes twinkling.

She pinkened. 'There wasn't any need – I didn't expect . . .'

'No? I'm disappointed.'

Emma eyed him warily; probably he was teasing her. He wasn't. The pink deepened delicately as he lifted the hand he had been holding and kissed it gently and she said a trifle breathlessly, 'I thought I heard your voice – before I was quite conscious – but when I opened my eyes you weren't there.'

'I came to have a look at you with Mr. Phillips after

they had put you back to bed. You were almost round, but I couldn't wait – there was a patient . . .'

'Oh, dear,' said Emma, and repeated without much originality, 'you're so kind.' Two tears trickled untidily down her cheeks and she wiped them away with the back of her free hand.

'Surely no reason for crying?' the professor wanted to know.

She swallowed at the tears crowding her throat and after a moment faltered, 'I don't know why I'm crying,' and managed a watery smile as her mother came back into the room.

She put the flowers on the bedtable. 'Aren't they gorgeous, Emma? I do hope you thanked Justin nicely.'

'I was just going . . .' began Emma when the professor interrupted with:

'On the very point of doing so, were you not, Emma?' and bent down, his eyes twinkling wickedly. She kissed his proffered cheek meekly under her mother's pleased eyes, submitted to a careful maternal embrace and watched them go through the door together, not sure whether to laugh or cry. She was still making up her mind when she fell suddenly asleep.

Being young and healthy, she slept with only the briefest of wakeful periods until the junior night nurse brought her an early morning cup of tea and then returned presently to escort her to the wash-basin in the corner of the room. Emma, walking a little gingerly still, decided that although she was still vaguely sore and uncomfortable walking wasn't too bad; all the same, she was glad to get back into bed and brush her hair – she had meant to do something to her face too, but the effort was too great, so she lay back thankfully against the pillows and picked up the first of the glossy magazines the professor had brought. She was still poring over it when Brenda came in at eight o'clock.

'Hullo,' said Emma. 'I do feel a fraud. I slept like a top, too – and I walked over to the basin.'

'Very nice too,' said Brenda cheerfully, 'but to save any further argument, you're here for eight days, ducky, and then you'll get at least three weeks' sick leave – and don't tell me that's too long, for remember, you'll be on your feet most of the day once you're back in that theatre of yours, working all hours, and no one will listen if you plead tired. You had a nasty appendix, you know, and for all your brave words, you look like skimmed milk.' She smiled widely. 'Now I must go and take the report – I'll come back presently and we'll have coffee together and that'll give me a chance to cast an eye over these.' She nodded towards the magazines. 'Who's the generous donor? The professor, I suppose – did he give you the roses too? I thought so. Nice work, little Emma – he must prize you highly.'

Emma bit her lip. 'As a theatre sister, yes, I think he does. He's nice to work for, you know.'

Brenda chuckled. 'I thought perhaps he was. I imagine he's just as nice when he's not working. I think I'll have a try for him – he might be fun. You don't mind?'

'Mind?' echoed Emma lightly, minding very much indeed. 'Why on earth should I mind? Go ahead and I'll study your technique from my bed, heaven knows I could use it.' She even managed a smile as Brenda, chuckling, went away.

The professor didn't come until after tea, with Brenda, looking magnificent, beside him, and Emma, her eyes sharpened by love, watched every look and gesture her visitors made and listened to every word which was said, twisting the most commonplace remarks into double meanings, an operation of doubtful value brought to an end by the professor saying suavely, 'Don't let me keep you, Sister, I'm sure you must be waiting to get back to the ward. I'll see you before I go, I daresay.'

They went to the door together and Emma shut her eyes and when she opened them again he was on the point of sitting on the bed.

'Not so well?' he inquired kindly.

'I feel very well, thank you,' said Emma in a stiff little voice.

He gave her a considered glance and smiled faintly, and his voice was bland. 'What a lovely girl your friend is – so lovely that I'm frightened of her.'

Emma considered this piece of nonsense before replying; for nonsense it was. 'Brenda's quite beautiful.'

'I couldn't agree with you more. And now tell me, how do you feel?'

Emma stole a look at him. He was examining his well-kept hands and had his head lowered; he looked up at that moment and she said hurriedly:

'I told you – I feel simply marvellous.'

'That's better. Do you suppose that the magnificent Brenda will allow me to come again this evening and bring two more visitors with me?'

Her eyes flew to his placid face. 'Two? Who are they – when will they come?'

'Yes, two, and I don't intend to tell you who, so don't ask.' He got up, smiling at her. 'I'll be back, Emma.'

After he had gone she sat back amongst the welter of magazines, going over their brief conversation. It was a little difficult to know if he had been teasing about Brenda. Apparently he hadn't, for Brenda, coming in an hour later, sat down comfortably on the end of the bed, observing goodnaturedly, 'Well, my technique failed, didn't it? Your professor's charming, but I didn't make much impression on that bland mask of his.'

Emma felt a warm glow of satisfaction at these words, but because she liked Brenda she remarked placatingly:

'Well, if you failed I can't see anyone else succeeding.'

Brenda gave her an amused look. 'Care to have a try yourself?'

Emma shook her head. 'I wouldn't know how,' she said, and meant it.

'Maybe that's the answer,' Brenda murmured. 'Lend me that *Vogue*, Emma.'

She went away presently, the magazine under one arm, and left Emma to her supper.

It was eight o'clock when the professor returned, bringing Little Willy and Kitty with him. Her sister looked radiant, Emma observed as Kitty darted across the room to hug her, dropping a paper parcel and some flowers on the bed as she did so.

'Emma – you poor dear! Fancy you with an appendix and Justin says you were ever so brave about it.' She caught sight of the roses and asked, 'Who's the boyfriend? Just look at those, anyone would think you were a film star. I'll put mine in a vase, shall I – there's a spray in the parcel – Chantilly, darling, so's you can sit in a cloud of fragrance.'

Emma decided to ignore the remark about the boyfriend. The men were talking together, but the professor had sharp ears. She went red in the face, hoping he hadn't heard, and asked, 'But Kitty – your exams – I thought . . .'

'One today, darling, and another tomorrow, but Will's taking me back. I'll be home at the end of the week, though, and Mother and I'll cosset you. How long will they give you to recover?' She didn't wait for an answer but repeated her question to Justin, who had come to lean against the end of the bed, watching her.

'Three weeks,' he answered casually as Will approached the bed and said awkwardly, 'Hullo, Emma. Hard luck, old girl – nice to see you better, though.'

Emma thanked him nicely and when it became obvious that he had no more to say on the subject, asked, 'Been busy, Will?'

'Lord, yes, Staff's pretty good, though, and now there's someone called Sister Luce. She keeps asking Justin if he's got the right instruments. It's a bit wearing, if you don't come back quickly we shall be old men before our time. Where did they dredge the creature up from anyway?'

Emma giggled. 'She was theatre sister for a week or two while I was still a staff nurse – long before your time,' she added severely, 'but they decided that she was unsuitable – but if there is no one else they'd have put her back in theatre; after all, she is trained for it. Perhaps you frighten her.'

Will cast her an indignant look and Justin roared with laughter. 'You're mistaken, Emma. We are frightened of her, aren't we, Will? But don't worry, dear girl, we shall hold up the tricky cases until you're back again.'

'You're not!' Emma sat up too quickly and winced. She looked quite pretty by reason of the splash of colour in her still pale cheeks. 'How very mean – supposing I still feel poorly? I might not be able to stand for hours on end, you know.'

'In which case,' interposed Justin smoothly, 'we shall just have to go on waiting, shan't we?'

He walked over to the door and picked up a parcel he had dropped on a chair and brought it back to the bed. 'Maybe these will help you to hasten your recovery, Emma.'

There were four books, of a sort to keep Emma amused and interested for hours. She examined them with delight and said happily,

'Thank you, Justin. The days are rather long, you know. You're very kind—' She bit her lip because each time she saw him she seemed to have said that, and he was looking amused now. But he didn't say anything, merely turned to Kitty and reminded her that if Will was to get her back to hospital in time for a good night's sleep she had better be going, whereupon she hugged Emma once more, besought her to take care of herself, signified her readiness to leave with Will immediately and then darted across the room to fling her arms round Justin's neck and kiss him soundly. 'Keep an eye on our Emma,' she commanded him as she went.

There was a little silence when they had gone and Emma, after a darting glance at the professor, began to leaf through the books with an almost painful interest. When he spoke his voice held the hint of a laugh.

'How fortunate,' he said, 'that I am sufficiently Kitty's slave to do exactly as she wishes.'

'Do what?' asked Emma, pretending not to know.

'Why, keep an eye on you, Emma, what else? How did the day go?'

She told him, although there wasn't much to tell. 'It seems strange with nothing to do – but I shall be getting up longer tomorrow and the next day I'm to dress.'

'And then three weeks' holiday – I may be gone before you return, Emma.'

She hadn't thought of that. 'No – you can't. I mean,' she amended hastily, 'it isn't as soon as that, is it? How time flies!' She paused, aware that he had no intention of answering this foolish remark. 'Will you go back to Holland?'

She stared at his passive face, feeling sick at the thought of it.

'Why, yes, for it is my home and my work is there.'

'I'll not take any more of your cases, then?'

'Probably not.' He sounded far too cheerful about it. 'I don't expect to return to this hospital in the immediate future, and in the meantime much could happen, Emma.'

He was staring hard at her and all she could think of to say was, 'Yes?'

'I intend to marry, Emma.'

She felt the colour leave her face, which didn't matter overmuch, for she was still pale from the operation, but it was important to keep a politely interested expression on her face at all costs. Inside her was desolation, to be ignored until she was alone and could weep in a decent solitude. She said now in a bright voice, 'That'll be nice for you. I hope you'll be happy.' And then because she couldn't help herself, 'Do I know her?'

He hadn't stopped staring, but now he smiled. 'Very well, Emma,' he began, and was interrupted by Mr. Phillips, who wandered in with an absent-minded air of not quite knowing why he had come, but when he caught sight of the professor he said at once, 'The very man I want – there's a case ...' He broke off and turned his attention upon Emma, sitting like a small statue against her pillows, willing him to go away again because Justin had been on the point of telling her something and now probably the opportunity would never occur again.

'Emma Hastings,' said Mr. Phillips, 'how are you?' He wandered over to the bed and peered at her in a kindly fashion. 'I must say you're not a very good colour. I'd better get the Path. Lab. people to see about your haemoglobin – a trifle anaemic, perhaps. I'll see Matron in the morning. Three weeks' sick leave, I said, didn't I? You may go home the day after your stitches come out. When's that?'

Emma told him.

'Yes, well – you'll do, have to take care of one of our best Sisters, won't we? A lifetime of work ahead of you, I fancy.'

He smiled at her kindly, patted her shoulder and said to Justin:

'Ah, yes, there's a woman – the X-rays show something in her chest. I'm not sure – I'd like you to take a look.'

Emma sat and watched the professor, without any apparent disappointment at having to leave her, agree to accompany Mr. Phillips. His casual goodnight to her as they went through the door held no hidden meaning, nor did he give her any but the briefest of glances. When the door had closed behind them, she burst into tears.

Justin didn't come at all the next day, although he sent a message via Brenda expressing the hope that she was improving. But Staff came, full of cheerful and amusing gossip and some rather touching messages from the theatre staff. It was only as she was on the point of leaving that she mentioned that the professor had finished his list at three o'clock that afternoon.

'Oh?' said Emma sharply. 'Why was that?'

'Don't know, Sister, and I'd never dare to ask him. He's a dear, isn't he? but very – you know, he's not the sort of person you'd . . .' She stopped again and Emma, helping her out, said, 'I know just what you mean, Staff. What's on for tomorrow?'

Staff told her. An all-day list, it seemed. Emma decided he wouldn't be coming to see her tomorrow either, and really, she told herself sternly, why should he? He had brought books and magazines and flowers and made sure that she was recovering; there was no need for him to see her again. Probably he had forgotten that she would be going home in three days and that he would be gone before she got back to work, and that might be a good thing, because then they wouldn't have to say goodbye.

She pecked at her supper, her temper not improved by the appearance of the night staff nurse at eight o'clock – a thin nervous young woman with a small frustrated face peering through a wild hair arrangement. She asked Emma fussy questions in a nervous way and Emma answered politely, refused a sleeping tablet and then listened with mounting irritation to a series of grumbles encompassing the nursing profession in general, night duty in particular, the patients, the food and the rudeness of an anaesthetist who had hauled her over the coals because a drip had gone into the tissues. 'As though I could help it, Sister,' moaned the girl.

Emma bit back the retort she longed to make and set about soothing her instead, for there were twenty odd patients in the main ward; if Night Nurse was upset she might possibly pass on her feelings to them, which would mean a night when bells pinged every few minutes and the junior nurse would be run off her feet shaking up pillows and warming milk. It was all wrong, but Emma knew from experience that it could happen; she set about calming her visitor and presently had the satisfaction of seeing her look more cheerful.

She was almost asleep when Brenda came in and chuckled hazily at her friend's observations on Staff Nurse Foster. 'Poor girl,' said Brenda, 'everything's a major disaster to her and everyone's in league against her, especially me. How's the boy-friend?'

The question was asked briskly and Emma, who was only half awake, looked bewildered. 'I haven't got one.'

'The professor, silly.'

'He's not – I work for him.'

'My mistake, ducky. As I said, he must prize your services very highly.'

'Very likely,' said Emma a little tartly, 'I work hard.'

'Which reminds me,' said Brenda, 'so do I. I'd better show my face in the ward. 'Bye, Emma – see you in the morning.'

The next day was long, dull and despite the books, magazines and visits from various of her friends, boring. Even the visit of the Principal Nursing Officer with the confirmation of three weeks' sick leave failed to excite Emma. By six o'clock she was quite peevish and decided that supper in bed with one of the books would be preferable to sitting in a chair hoping for Justin to come in. She kicked off her shoes pettishly because undressing was a wearisome business, and tugged at the zip at the back of her dress. It ran smoothly for several inches and then stuck, and however hard she pulled, it stayed stuck; for Emma this, to come at the end of a day she hadn't in the least enjoyed, was the last straw. Her usual even temper, already badly frayed, dissolved into childish tantrums so that when there was a brief knock on the door as it opened, she snapped, 'Oh, for heaven's sake come in and get me out of this wretched dress – the zip's caught.'

She didn't bother to look round but went on fumbling at the back of her dress, aware that added to everything else, her stitches were pulling, but her fingers froze as Justin said cheerfully, 'Take your fingers away, girl, I can't see unless you do – and stand still.'

She stood still while he worked the zip free, undid it to its length, inquired at his most placid, 'Is this your dressing-gown – this pink thing? Get out of that dress and put it on,' and when she hesitated: 'I can never understand why a girl can appear on a beach in next to nothing and yet be horrified at the idea of being seen in her undies. I should have thought that a bikini – er – exposed a good deal more of her person. Now be quick, Emma, for I want to talk to you.'

His voice was calm and reassuringly matter-of-fact. She did as she was told and slipped her arms into the dressing-gown he was holding out to her.

'Jump into bed,' he advised. 'You can finish undressing later.'

So she got into bed, still without words, but he didn't appear to have noticed her silence, for he made himself comfortable in the chair she had vacated, remarking, 'You seemed low-spirited yesterday. I've brought some champagne for you. Brenda has it – she'll see that you get a glass with your lunch. It will cheer you up.'

She looked at him then, her temper quite evaporated and smiled a little shyly. 'That's very . . .' she began, and then stopped because she was about to tell him that he was kind again and it really would not do. 'What a lovely surprise,' she amended. 'Thank you.'

He settled more comfortably in his chair, gave her a sharp glance and asked carelessly, 'Have you any plans?'

Emma shook her head, aware that instead of making plans like any sensible girl would, she wasted her days thinking about him.

'I shall go home,' she replied. 'I–I can potter in the garden, you know, and Kitty will be there, so it won't be too hard on Mother.'

The professor crossed one long leg over the other. 'I'm going over to Holland very shortly – just for a couple of days; I have some business to see to. Will you and Kitty travel with me and spend two or three weeks at my home? My aunt will be delighted to have you, she loves company and has frequently spoken of you.'

Emma opened her mouth and then prudently closed it again before she said something rash. Her instant desire had been to say yes; her pulse rate had jumped alarmingly at the mere idea. She said slowly, 'How kind,' and watched him smile. 'Kitty?' she began again.

'Kitty thinks it to be a splendid idea and so does your mother.' He answered casually, just as though, thought Emma crossly, it was of no importance to him what her own opinion of his plans would be. She frowned and he got to his feet and made his leisurely way to the door, saying:

'There's plenty of time to decide if you like the idea or not; I don't plan to go before Friday.' His hand was on the door when Emma found her voice.

'It sounds lovely,' she began, 'and I'm sorry I didn't – wasn't more . . . I've had a beastly day,' she added by way of explanation, an explanation which seemed to satisfy him, for he came back and sat down on the bed and said pleasantly:

'It will at least make a change for you and it is so quiet there you won't tire yourself out dashing around. The garden is most pleasant to sit in and there are some delightful walks when you feel like it, and we have many friends, you won't lack for company.'

Only yours, thought Emma. If she stayed away for three weeks he would be on the point of leaving the hospital; he might even be gone. She refused to think of it – three weeks was a long time, miracles happened still; one might happen for her. She smiled suddenly. 'I think I'd like to come very much, Justin, if you're sure your aunt . . .?'

He said briefly, 'I'm sure. We'll go on Friday evening,

there's a night ferry to Zeebrugge. You'll be able to get some sleep on board and we can be home shortly after breakfast. That gives me the rest of the day to settle my affairs and a few hours of leisure on Sunday before I return.'

'That's not very long.'

He turned away from her and looked out of the window at the view of Southampton's rooftops. 'I shall have time enough to do what I wish to do. You think you like the idea, then?'

Emma could think of nothing she would like better. She said so, her tongue rather more guarded than her thoughts. 'Do you want us to come here and meet you on Friday evening?' she wanted to know.

'I'm afraid you'll have to, Emma. We're not operating until the afternoon and it's quite a heavy list. I doubt if I'm free before five. Could Kitty drive you back in your car?'

'Of course – she's going to fetch me on Wednesday anyway. That gives us a day to get packed.'

He nodded and got to his feet once more. 'I must go, I'm due in theatre in a few minutes.'

Emma sat up in bed. 'An emergency?' and when he nodded again, 'Who's taking? Mary Worth?' Mary was another friend and Night Theatre Sister.

'Yes. I hadn't met her before. A very attractive girl,' a remark which was softened by, 'I miss you, Emma,' as he went through the door.

She said quickly before he could close it behind him, 'That's only because you've got used to me. Mary is super at her job, so is Staff . . .'

He didn't allow her to finish but cut through her observations with placid firmness, 'Your mistake, Emma. I shall never get used to you.'

The door shut quietly behind him.

Kitty, when she came to fetch Emma home, was surprisingly matter-of-fact about Justin's invitation, to Emma's tentative opinion that he seemed to be going to unnecessary lengths, inviting them both at a moment's notice, she replied rather dampingly, 'But why ever shouldn't he, Emma? He's only returning hospitality, after

145

all, and he knows you'll be better for a holiday and I suppose he wants you back in the theatre as soon as possible for everyone's benefit. And what more natural than asking me along too so that you won't be lonely? He's not going to be there, you know.'

Which seemed an argument Emma had no ready answer for.

She spent the short stay at home in packing, rather languidly because she still felt surprisingly fragile. In the end Kitty did it for her, adding quite a few clothes she had never intended to take with her, but as Kitty explained, they never knew; they might be asked to a party or something similar and feel utter fools if they hadn't anything to wear. 'I've put in your brown and white,' she continued, 'and that orange crêpe with the apron top and the white blouse, and I've put in another cotton dress. Really, Emma, we're going for almost three weeks and you don't have to wear the same old thing every day – supposing Justin were to come over and take us out?'

'That's most unlikely,' said Emma rather woodenly. 'He won't have time.'

'No? Well, perhaps Will could pop over.'

'Will? Why on earth should Will want to see us? We're not going for ever.'

'Not us – me,' said Kitty in a satisfied voice. 'He likes me – and I like him.' She snapped the case she had packed closed. 'There, now we're ready, we can have a lazy morning and leave after lunch.'

They arrived at William and Mary's with ten minutes to spare and Justin and Will came out of the Cardiac Thoracic Unit as Kitty parked untidily between Home Sister's elderly, well-cared-for Morris and the hospital secretary's dignified Rover.

Kitty bounced out of the car to meet them. 'You see we're on time,' she cried. 'Hullo, both of you. The luggage is in the boot.'

'And before we take it out give me the keys,' said Will, 'and I'll park this jalopy of yours in a straight line – Women!' he added scornfully.

'Yes, but aren't we nice?' Kitty remarked with engaging self-confidence. 'Besides, it's Emma's car and she drives very well.' And Emma, getting out, caught Justin's eye and had the grace to blush.

It was Kitty who decided airily that she would travel in front with Justin so that Emma could have the whole of the back seat to herself in case she wanted to sleep or put her feet up. Emma had no wish to put her feet up and would have said so if Justin hadn't so readily agreed that it seemed a capital idea. So she declared that she would be marvellously comfortable in the Rolls' luxurious back and would very likely go to sleep, and was in fact so quiet that she might well have been sleeping, while in fact she was wide awake, stifling a tendency to ill-humour, a fact which didn't prevent her, when they stopped for a meal, from declaring that she was perfectly happy where she was and refusing, quite emphatically, Justin's offer for her to sit in front with him for the remainder of the journey. It was a pity that he didn't seem to mind in the least, merely remarking, 'Just as you like, Emma,' and then turning to make some laughing remark to Kitty. Emma stared out of the window and decided that she hated him.

They were first in the queue of cars for the ferry and as the late evening was clear and warm, they got out and strolled round until it was time to embark, and under the influence of the professor's gentle conversation, Emma recovered her good temper and went off cheerfully enough with Kitty to their cabin with the injunction from Justin to meet him in ten minutes in the ship's bar. The cabin was decidedly more comfortable than the one Emma and her mother had occupied when they had returned from their holiday and she looked around with something like suspicion.

'Kitty, who booked the cabins? I mean, this one must have cost a lot more . . .'

'It's all right, Emma,' said Kitty. She tossed her handbag on the upper berth and studied her face in the little mirror. 'Mother said not to worry, she had some dividends she hadn't expected and we're to settle with her later on.'

It sounded reasonable enough. Emma poked at her hair. She looked pale and dull, she thought, staring at her reflection. Even the blue dress which suited her so well looked all wrong; not that it mattered, Justin wouldn't notice.

He was waiting for them at a table by a window so that they could see the lighted quayside. They drank Campari while he entertained them with a gentle flow of conversation which she found so soothing even though she suspected that he used it as a means to prevent anyone else taking the conversation into their own hands and probably asking too many questions.

She sipped her drink, frowning a little. She had a number of questions she would dearly love to ask him – about his home, and his aunt and Saskia – and how were they returning at the end of their stay? The information he had offered with his invitation had been scant and it seemed he had no wish to enlarge upon it. Emboldened by the Campari, she waited until there was pause in the conversation and asked:

'Why have you asked us to stay at your home, Justin?'

She was aware of the keen look he gave her, but his voice was casual and friendly. 'Why not?' he countered. 'It all fits in so well – I happen to be going over to Holland, you have a week or so to spare, my aunt enjoys guests and Saskia will be delighted to improve her English.'

He gave her a bland smile and she gave up and when, a minute later, he suggested that they might like to get some sleep, she got obediently to her feet, wished him good night, and followed Kitty down to their cabin.

It was barely half past four in the morning when Justin eased the Rolls over the cobbled streets of Zeebrugge towards the Dutch border. Emma, wide awake after several hours' sleep and refreshed with the tea and toast the stewardess had brought them, found herself sitting beside Justin looking out on to a pale grey morning which threatened rain.

Justin, she observed from a quick sidelong glance, looked as though he had slept the clock round; he also was as impeccably turned out as he always was. She wondered how he did it. 'Did you sleep?' she asked him.

'Soundly. And you?'

'Oh yes, though it was a short night. It's nice now, though, isn't it?' She gazed out at the sleeping houses lining the road, so quiet and the sun not quite up and almost no traffic and no people. 'There's such a lot to see, Kitty should be sitting here.'

The car sped through Blankenbugge and then past its suburbs and villas.

'No,' said Justin, 'you should be here, Emma. Where you belong.'

She stared ahead at the road unwinding before the car's speed. What exactly did he mean? She stole a look at him and he looked at her briefly and smiled. 'What – no answer to that, Emma?'

She shook her head. 'I'm not sure what you meant.'

'No? I'll explain later. Here's the turning to Sluis,' he glanced at his watch. 'I think we may reach Breskens in time to have coffee before the ferry is due.'

They had almost twenty minutes to spare, time enough to drink their coffee and eat long soft rolls stuffed with thinly cut cheese while Justin patiently answered Kitty's endless questions about their journey, and once on the ferry he continued to do so, apologizing to Emma because she had been that way before and it might be a little boring for her to hear it all again. She smiled and nodded and looked the other way to his pointing finger while he addressed himself to Kitty, but when they went down to the car once more and she offered to sit in the back he said instantly, 'No, Emma – stay in front, for I can see that Kitty is already half asleep and I should hate to keep her awake while I prosed on about churches and bridges.'

They took the big dyke road, avoiding Zierikzee as they crossed to Bruinesse and so to the island of Overflakkee. One more sea dyke and they were on the motorway to Rotterdam and presently weaving in and out of the complexity of morning traffic in that city, to turn away from it at length on to the Gouda road and then, finally, turn off once more to Oudewater.

They entered the little town from its opposite end this time and Justin drove slowly so that Emma could point out to Kitty where she and their mother had stayed and the little hall where they had been weighed to prove that they weren't witches. The small place was cheerful and bustling under the still grey sky and Kitty declared that she would have to visit it at the earliest possible opportunity. 'And where's your house, Justin?' she wanted to know.

'A mile or so outside the town,' he told her. They were outside the town now, driving down the country road Emma remembered so well, with its trees and its villas and the farms set well back in the fields, and at last Justin's house, standing solidly behind its ornamental iron gates, open to receive them.

'Has it a name?' asked Emma as Justin guided the Rolls up the short drive.

He pulled up before the double steps leading to the front door.

'Welcome to Huize den Linden, Emma,' said Justin softly.

# CHAPTER EIGHT

THE door was opened to them as they reached it by a plump middle-aged woman with a pleasant round face which broke into smiles as they entered. An old and valued member of the household, Emma supposed, watching the warm handshake Justin gave her and listening to the unintelligible exchange of greetings.

'This is Janeke,' Justin explained. 'She has been with us since I was a very small boy and we should be lost without her.' His smile was as warm as his handshake had been and Janeke transferred her smile to Emma and Kitty and offered a large capable hand, then waved it towards the hall in a welcoming gesture just as Emma caught sight of Mevrouw Teylingen coming towards them across the hall from a door on the left. Her greeting was friendly and her smile, if not as broad as Janeke's, was certainly gracious; she appeared to be really glad to see them and after greeting her nephew with every sign of pleasure, she made them welcome with a warmth and charm which Emma was secretly relieved to see. After all, their hostess hardly knew her and Kitty not at all; even though it was Justin's house, Mevrouw Teylingen might have been excused if she had shown some slight coolness towards them. On the contrary, she led the way, talking quite animatedly, into a sitting-room of some size, very comfortably furnished with a nicely wedded combination of antiques and modern armchairs, covered in a prussian blue velvet which exactly matched the lavishly draped curtains at the two long windows. The walls of the room were hung with a corn-coloured striped silk and partly covered with a variety of paintings and Emma was a little surprised to see an open fireplace with a plain marble surround in place of something more modern. The ceiling was high, as she had come to expect in the older Dutch houses which would make it cold in winter unless, as she suspected, there was hidden central heating.

She took the seat Justin offered her and embarked on a

polite, somewhat stilted conversation with their hostess while they drank the coffee Janeke had brought them, feeling a little envious of Kitty and Justin, sitting together on an enormous sofa and judging from Kitty's laughter, amusing themselves a good deal more than she was. But presently Justin broke off their talk to ask his aunt:

'Where are Bess and Caesar? Out with Saskia?'

Mevrouw Teylingen smiled with faint apology. 'Did I not tell you, Justin? Saskia's away – I'm afraid I forgot. I told Wim to shut the dogs in the stable, they were so excited.'

Justin got to his feet, frowning slightly. 'I'll fetch them,' he said curtly, and left the room to return in a very short time with the two dogs at his heels.

'Gordon setters!' exclaimed Emma as she saw them. 'You don't see many of those around – and they're beauties.'

Justin looked pleased. 'You know the breed? It's not very popular at present; a great many people can't put a name to them.'

He snapped a finger at them and they advanced daintily to where Emma was sitting and stood while she fondled them, and then, obediently to his signal, did the same for Kitty before dropping at his feet as he sat down again beside her.

They sat for perhaps half an hour, talking, Mevrouw Teylingen with a charm which, if Emma had had any remaining doubts about their welcome at Huize den Linden, calmed them completely. She was charming to Justin too so that Emma began to wonder if she had fancied his annoyance at the dogs being shut up. She dismissed the idea as fanciful on her part and followed Mevrouw Teylingen out of the room and across the hall with its tiled floor and plastered walls to the stairs at its back. It was quite a small staircase, hugging the wall before it opened out on to a landing above, but it had elaborately curved banisters; swags of fruit, wreaths of flowers and birds rioted on either side of the shallow uncarpeted steps. Emma stopped to peer at them on their way, resolving to examine them more closely later. Now she hurried to catch up with the others, already waiting for her at the top of the staircase.

They had a bedroom each with a bathroom between. The rooms were not over large, but they were lofty and a great deal bigger than their own rooms at home and furnished handsomely with somewhat heavy furniture of the Second Empire period, beautifully cared for and set off to perfection by the glazed chintz curtains, thick cream bedspread and cream carpeting. She went through the bathroom to find that Kitty's room was very similar and her sister busy unpacking, something she made haste to do herself before tidying her hair for lunch and changing out of the dress and coat she had travelled in and putting on a cotton dress, quite plain but for the double frill of its own pale green material running from neck to hem. It was a pretty dress and one which Justin hadn't seen before. Emma, viewing herself in the mirror before she joined Kitty in her room, hoped that he would notice it.

He didn't. Or if he did, he found it unworthy of comment, instead he inquired of her if she felt tired in such a tone that she instantly felt that she must look a fright despite the care with which she had done her face and hair, but she answered him nicely, if a little briefly, and when they went into lunch confined her replies to any remarks he directed to her to monosyllables, causing him to lift his eyebrows in a faint mockery which vexed her excessively. But Kitty filled any silences there might have been with a lively chatter which more than covered her own silence, and presently she left her sister to do most of the talking and looked around her.

The dining-room was of a fair size, furnished rather grandly with the oval Hepplewhite table around which they were seated and a side table of majestic proportions against one wall. There was a lacquered cabinet between the windows and on the further red damasked wall was a hooded fireplace. There were brass sconces at intervals around the walls and a number of paintings she was unable to see properly without craning her neck, although a flower painting opposite her caught her eye. She was studying it covertly when Julian said:

'I see you have noticed our van Huysum – it's an original and we're very proud of it. An ancestor of mine received it in payment of a debt – quite unaware of its future value, of course. You like paintings?'

It was a question, but he wasn't going to allow her time to answer it.

'In that case I'll take you round after lunch, we have one or two rather interesting portraits.' He smiled at her in a wholly friendly way so that she felt her childish ill-humour oozing away and felt ashamed of it too. She smiled back, 'I'd like that, but will you have the time?'

'I can always spare time for you, Emma.' His voice was casual, but there was a gleam in his eyes which made her colour faintly.

She found herself, ten minutes later, walking beside him across the hall, leaving Kitty and his aunt to chat in the sitting-room, and she wondered as she went why she should have the absurd idea that Mevrouw Teylingen was annoyed. Perhaps she had wanted half an hour to herself to rest – or to talk to Justin. Emma paused outside the double doors Justin was just about to open and asked, 'Do you suppose that Kitty . . . ?'

'No, I suppose nothing of the sort.' He laughed as he said it and when she asked him why he was so amused he raised his brows in that selfsame mockery again. 'Do you forget that old English saying, "One's too few, three's too many"?'

Emma, aware of a galloping pulse, said Oh! rather breathlessly, staring fixedly before her, and after a moment he said, his hand on the door handle, 'This is the finest room in the house, so you shall inspect it first.'

He was right; the room was indeed fine. It took up almost all of one side of the house, with windows overlooking the trim garden in front, and three more, floor-length, opening out on to a patio gay with flowers in tubs. The floor was almost entirely covered with a silky carpet of Persian design and the curtains were of a rich mulberry brocade, exactly matching the chair coverings. A pair of wall tables faced each other across the breadth of the carpet, bearing what Emma privately considered to be some truly hideous vases of gilt and enamel, and in one corner was a china display cabinet of walnut. There were a number of tables too and a dainty little worktable with a faded green silk bag, Emma went nearer to examine it and then stood looking around her with interest, and Justin said nothing at all, allowing her to look her fill. Presently she looked at him and smiled and he said, 'We don't use this room a great deal now – family gatherings, dinner parties and so on, but when I was a small boy we spent each evening here – the whole family. There were almost always guests too – aunts and uncles and cousins and friends.'

'Your mother didn't mind – I mean you being in here?' Emma waved an expressive arm at the lovely things surrounding them.

'No, we were expected to take care, of course; I think we all loved it so much we wouldn't have dreamed of doing otherwise.'

Emma said softly, 'You were happy.'

'As a small boy? Yes, very.'

'Aren't you happy now?' She didn't look at him as she asked.

'Yes.' She thought he was going to say something more, but instead he caught her by the arm and walked her over to the fireplace, above which was a large dark painting. It was a family portrait of the early nineteenth century, with the head of the family sitting beside his wife, while a number of children were grouped a little selfconsciously around them. Emma counted the little boys in their long trousers and short jackets, and the little girls in straight high-waisted dresses, their hair in stiff ringlets. 'Eight,' she said out loud, and looked with respect at the little painted lady sitting in the middle of them in her silken gown and ornate jewellery, her hand in her husband's. Unless the painter's brush had lied, she looked not only happy but supremely content as well – as well she might, Emma decided, for the man at her side was Justin – a Justin of earlier times and in different clothes, but still Justin. 'You're exactly like him,' she added, half under her breath.

'My great-great-grandparents,' explained Justin, ignoring her remark. 'A devoted couple, but then happy marriages run in the family.'

'And a great many children, it seems. Eight! – She must have found them a handful.'

'With nursemaids and servants? Of course not.'

'But there aren't nursemaids and servants nowadays.'

He looked at her with unconscious arrogance. 'Perhaps we are lucky not to have that problem. As for a nurse, my old nanny has a daughter who waits patiently for me to marry so that she can move in. . . .'

He grinned at her so wickedly that she coloured faintly and moved away so that he shouldn't see her face, and went to examine the vases on the side tables.

'Hideous, are they not?' he offered. 'Late Louis Seize – Gouthère. The clock on the mantelpiece is part of the set. We are used to them, but people seeing them for the first time are rather taken aback.'

'I like the candelabra,' said Emma, anxious not to embark on the subject of the vases, about which she knew nothing.

'Louis Quinze – Are you bored?'

Emma turned in astonishment, and not knowing that he had come to stand behind her, bumped her head into his waistcoat. And: 'Too good an opportunity to miss,' he murmured, and bent to kiss her. She was still mastering her breathing when he said in a perfectly ordinary voice, 'Come and see the little sitting-room, it's my favourite,' and led her out of the open french windows on to the patio and in through another door opening into a room which, although not small, could be so described if compared with the apartment which they had just left. It was comfortably furnished, with dog baskets thrust against two of its corners and a thick, bright brown carpet covering its wooden floor. The furniture was dark and solid and the chair covers and curtains were of a rich amber which glowed against the plain white walls. There was a great bookcase taking up the whole of one wall too, filled to capacity. Emma sighed blissfully; it was exactly her idea of homely comfort and when Justin asked, 'You like it, don't you?' she nodded.

'I like the whole house, how could I not? but how I should love to come home to this room and sit here and sew while . . . .' She stopped and went a slow, painful scar-

156

let, but he didn't seem to have noticed, for he was looking out of the window. He said without looking round, 'Yes, I feel that too. Come and look at the garden.'

It was very Dutch; formal and full of colour – there was no weed to be seen and Emma, thinking of the untidy small garden at the cottage observed, 'Oh, dear! It's perfect – when I think of our own garden. . . .'

'One of the nicest I have ever been in,' declared the professor positively, 'but you can see that a house like this one couldn't have anything else but a formal garden, and old Jan who looks after it for me would be hurt if I suggested otherwise. He's a great one for tradition.'

'So are you,' declared Emma before she could stop herself.

He eyed her coolly. 'Yes. Now I am going to take you back to the others – I have to go to Utrecht. I believe you heard my aunt explaining why Saskia was not here to welcome you – she is staying the night there and I want to see her.'

The glowing room lost its glow, just as the glow in Emma's heart was swallowed up by cold common sense. She had, just for a brief time, been living in a foolish make-believe world of her own, just because Justin had wanted to show her his home – he had kissed her too, but that, she told herself bleakly, had been on the spur of the moment. She said in a voice she was relieved to hear sounded cheerful, 'Oh, yes, of course. I hope I haven't made you late, you have so little time. You go again tomorrow, don't you?'

'Yes – but I shall be back within the next few weeks, when I intend to stay in Holland.'

She had nothing to say to this and his tone hardly invited comment. They walked back the way they had come and crossed the hall once more and entered the sitting-room where his aunt and Kitty, deep in some interesting conversation of their own, looked up in surprise. 'Back so soon?' queried Mevrouw Teylingen.

Justin said briefly, 'Saskia – had you forgotten?' and Emma saw the little satisfied smile playing around his aunt's mouth.

'She has been so impatient – !' She smiled at all three of

her companions as if to invite them to share her pleasure in her daughter's impatience, but Justin's face had no expression and Kitty and Emma, knowing of no reason to smile, merely sustained expressions of polite interest.

After the professor had gone, Mevrouw Teylingen suggested that they might like to take a short stroll, telling them at the same time that tea would be at half past three. 'Just a cup, you know,' she explained smilingly. 'Not your English afternoon tea, but you have only to ask if you would like toast or cake – Janeke is very good.'

They assured her that a cup of tea was all they could possibly want, and armed with their hostess's gentle instructions as to the best way to go, set off.

They returned an hour later, to find Mevrouw Teylingen in the sitting-room, the tea tray beside her and obviously ready for their company. The rest of the afternoon passed pleasantly enough, though Emma, while bearing her part in the talk, was wholly occupied in speculation as to whether Justin would be back that evening. Probably he would remain in Utrecht for dinner, even for the night; he hadn't seen Saskia for some time, they would have a lot to say to each other. She went upstairs presently to change her dress, for, as Mevrouw Teylingen had delicately indicated, she was in the habit of changing even when she was on her own. There was still no sign of the professor. Emma bathed, put on the first dress she laid her hands on and started, without much enthusiasm, to do things to her hair and face. 'So pointless,' she muttered to herself, 'just the three of us . . . .' She broke off because her quick ear had caught the whisper of the Rolls' engine as it turned in at the gate. By the time she had got to the window, all she saw of it was its elegant back sliding behind the screen of shrubs and trees which hid the garage from the house. Hardly had it disappeared than she was at the wardrobe, searching for the brown and white dress Justin liked.

If she had hoped that he would mention Saskia she was doomed to disappointment. He talked amusingly of everything under the sun; he even remarked upon the state of the traffic in Utrecht that afternoon and the fact that he had met some old friends. Emma, eating a delicious dinner with little or no appetite, commented brightly upon his remarks as he made them, her face stiff with the smile she was determined to keep there.

In the sitting-room once more, drinking coffee from tiny fragile cups, Mevrouw Teylingen remarked, 'How quiet it is without Saskia. What a pity there is no one to give you a game of billiards, Justin.'

Emma put down her cup with care. She had resented the remark about it being quiet; it implied that she and Kitty were complete nonentities.

'I play billiards,' she stated clearly, 'and I should enjoy a game.' She looked at Justin as she spoke, watching his slow, speculative smile.

'Excellent – and unexpected. You'll not mind if I give Emma a game?' He spoke to his aunt as he got to his feet and Kitty laughed and said:

'Don't look so amused, Justin, Emma's good,' and although Mevrouw Teylingen smiled, she did it reluctantly.

He beat her soundly, of course, although he told her with some surprise that he counted her a worthy opponent. 'Who taught you?' he wanted to know. They were standing at the open window of the billiard room at the back of the house, looking out on to the stretch of lawn and its surrounding flower beds.

'My father, when I was a little girl. We all played, and when my brother went away to school I took his place during term time, and then he went to medical school, so I still went on with it. I played in Oudewater.'

'You did?' he flung an arm around her shoulders. 'Tell me about it.'

She told and he laughed; kind, friendly laughter. 'I hope you know what a singular honour it was that they should have asked you.'

'Oh? I didn't know. I thought they were just being polite and friendly because we were strangers.'

He didn't remove his arm. 'It's a clear evening,' he observed. 'We'll go into the garden.'

'The others. . . .' ventured Emma, trying not to be aware of the arm, and was not answered, only propelled

159

gently forward on to the terrace and down its shallow steps on to the grass. It was indeed pleasant outside, with a muted evening sky and the garden's many colours already paling. She sniffed the fragrance of the rose bed in the lawn's centre and said impulsively, 'Oh, Justin, how can you bear to leave all this tomorrow – don't you want to stay?'

'More than anything in the world.' His voice was quiet. 'But I shall come back as I said, and live happily ever after, I hope. I've waited so long, I can wait a little longer.'

They had reached the end of the lawn and were walking along a path between shrubs, the trees behind marking the boundary of the garden. Emma noted their variety, forcing her mind to think of mundane things. It was astonishing how physical the pain of thinking of Justin and Saskia together in his house, perhaps walking this very path together, could be; certainly it was something she didn't want to talk about. After a moment she asked, 'Do roses grow well here?' and was aware of his hidden amusement as he embarked on a placidly meandering conversation about those flowers. It seemed he knew a great deal about them, and Emma, whose knowledge of them was sketchy, was reduced to murmurs of agreement at suitable intervals. They regained the terrace presently and rejoined the others and for the rest of that evening the only conversation she had with Justin was of the most casual sort.

It was beautiful weather the next morning and after breakfast Justin offered to take them for a drive round the immediate countryside. 'Otherwise,' he explained, 'Kitty won't see a great deal. We could go to Schoonhoven and have coffee there.'

Which they did; Kitty sitting in front, asking questions at each turn of the road and making Justin laugh a great deal. They stopped for coffee at the Bevedere and then went the long way home, past the castle of Ijsselstein and so back in time for lunch. Afterwards they went into the garden where garden chairs – super-comfortable ones; the kind Emma had admired in the glossy magazines – were grouped around a wrought iron, white-painted table, and after a little while Justin left them to fetch Saskia from Utrecht. He didn't offer to take anyone with him, and when he had gone Mevrouw Teylingen murmured that she would have a little rest in her room and would they be happy by themselves for a little while?

They sat in the sunshine, writing letters, not saying much until Janeke brought out the tea tray and their hostess joined them once more. It was an hour or so later when Emma's ever-listening ears heard the car return and ten minutes more before Justin and Saskia came down the garden towards them. Saskia, Emma saw in one lightning glance, was even prettier than she had remembered.

She greeted them both with charming friendliness and then, without any effort at all, made herself the focal point of the conversation. Emma, watching Justin's frequent slow smile, thought that he must surely be comparing Saskia's gaiety with her own rather ordinary person; it was something of a relief when visitors came and, naturally enough, stopped for a drink. Emma, annexed by an elderly man with a masterly command of the English language and an overwhelming interest in astronomy, allowed her attention to wander from time to time to peep at Justin, playing the host to perfection. He looked placid and cheerful and she supposed it was her imagination which caused her to find him thoughtful behind his smile. Presently he went over to his aunt and after a few words with her, started moving among his guests, pausing for a few moments to make some smiling remark to each of them, and Emma realized with a sinking heart that he was wishing them goodbye. He stayed some time with Kitty and then kissed her and left her laughing, to stroll across the grass to where Emma was still coping rather wildly with the stars. He spoke to her companion and then turned to her.

'I'm leaving now, Emma. Enjoy your holiday, and I think you will for Saskia will be here to keep you and Kitty company. I'm not quite sure when I shall be back.'

Emma glanced briefly at him and away again. 'No,' she answered too quickly, 'I'm sure you don't. I'll – I'll say goodbye, for I daresay we shall be back at work and maybe you will have left William and Mary's. Thank you very much for inviting us. It was good of you ... we do appreciate ....'

She came to a halt, aware that the last thing she wanted to do was to say goodbye to him, here in front of a lot of strangers. But perhaps it was a good thing. She said abruptly, 'Goodbye, Justin,' and put out her hand, and when she looked up into his face it was to find his green eyes very intent on hers, and although he was smiling, they were thoughtful.

He took her hand and bent his head and kissed her lightly on her cheek. His voice was so quiet that only she could hear. 'Dear Emma, surely you know by now that I never say goodbye?'

She knew no such thing, but there was no time to say so, for he spoke briefly to her companion in his own language and strolled away. A minute later she saw him walking unhurriedly across the lawn towards the house. He didn't look back, but he had barely disappeared when Saskia followed him and Emma, with a heart leaden with misery, turned her attention once more to her companion's discourse on stellar motions, asterism, chromesphere and solar flares; she knew nothing whatever about any of them, but at least they kept her mind from dwelling on other things.

The days passed pleasantly enough; they walked, drove and sat about in the garden, and Saskia was never without visitors. They came in a constant stream and usually stayed for lunch or dinner, and Saskia took care that Emma and Kitty met them all, for she was a perfect hostess even though Emma had the feeling that she had no desire to become more than a passing acquaintance to either of them. But she had little or no interest in their opinions or lives, merely begging them with casual friendliness to join any outing she had planned and making sure that they had everything they required for their comfort. Her mother was, however, rather more curious about them and asked a great many questions which both Kitty and Emma did their best to answer. Kitty rather resented them, but Emma was quick to excuse their hostess's curiosity. 'I dare say she's lonely,' she said. 'Saskia must be away from home quite a lot, and after all, she's very kind.'

'So she should be,' said Kitty sharply. 'After all, she lives here at Justin's expense.'

And would continue to do so, thought Emma silently, if he married Saskia.

Of the professor there was no word. Neither Mevrouw Teylingen nor Saskia mentioned him, and Emma, who longed to ask, found herself too shy to do so. The faint hope that he might write, if not to her, perhaps to Kitty, died slowly with the passing days and she began to wish that she had never come, for everything about the house reminded her of Justin and common sense told her that the quicker she put him out of her mind the better. She did her best; visiting the museums recommended by Mevrouw Teylingen when they went to Utrecht, walking round the open-air museum at Arnhem, inspecting the castle at Doorn where the German Kaiser had lived. They drove in Saskia's scarlet Mini through the Hoge Veluwe, one of the National Parks, to visit the Kroller-Muller Museum, although they didn't stay long because Saskia was bored long before they were halfway through the paintings, let alone the sculpture and the porcelain and hurried them away to Ede to visit more friends with whom they spent the rest of the day. On their way home that evening she disclosed that she was having a party the next day and plans were afoot for an expedition to No-ordwijk-aan-zee and what did they think of a trip to Amsterdam to sample the night life?

Kitty responded enthusiastically to these suggestions and Emma, who hated to hurt people's feelings anyway and didn't care what she did now that Justin had gone, agreed with more politeness than truth that she would find it great fun. But it wasn't – somehow the young men she met seemed too young and the talk a little vapid, a viewpoint for which she was quite prepared to blame herself; perhaps she was getting too old . . . She mentioned it to Kitty the day following the outing to Amsterdam.

'We go back in a couple of days,' she began carefully. 'Will you miss all this, Kitty?' She walked over to the window and looked out on to the bright garden. 'We haven't been as gay as this for years.'

Kitty got up off her bed and came to peer over her

sister's shoulder.

'It's been great. I've loved it – all that tearing around with Saskia and the restaurants and the people we've met,' she went on shrewdly, 'but you've not liked it very much, have you, darling? You're a home bird, aren't you? Fancy being able to spend the rest of your life looking at that garden and living in this lovely old house. How I'd love it – just with Justin, of course. Mevrouw Teylingen and Saskia would have to go somewhere else.'

Emma stared fixedly at the view. 'Oh, would you like to live here with Justin? I thought it was Will . . . he's written to you almost every day.'

'Silly,' said Kitty, 'of course it's Will – that's why I was so keen to come here. Absence makes the heart grow fonder and all that.' She looked at her sister. 'Funny he never mentions Justin – not once.' She added obscurely, 'I despair of you, Emma darling – you're so efficient in theatre, too.' Which remark she didn't attempt to elucidate, and even if Emma had asked her to do so there was no chance because there was a knock on the door and Saskia came in to tell them that some friends had called and would they like to come down and meet them?

The friends went just before dinner and Emma, changing into the pink shirtwaister, heaved a sigh of relief that Saskia had decided against a proposed plan to go to Utrecht and join those same friends at the Jaarbeurs restaurant for the evening. They had been out almost every night during the last week; it would be pleasant to have a quiet one at home, although she was aware that Saskia didn't like her overmuch, but perhaps she would be able to go along to the billiard room and knock a few billiard balls about. As it turned out, after half an hour or so in the sitting-room after dinner where the other three ladies had become engrossed in discussing Saskia's winter wardrobe, she was able to wander off unnoticed. She switched on the powerful light over the table in the billiard room, got herself a cue and began making aimless shots, her mind busy with the all-pervading thought that in two days' time they would be gone. There had been no message from the professor; possibly he had telephoned or wirtten to Saskia – he must have done one or the other –

but naturally Saskia wouldn't think it necessary to tell them about it. He would arrive back home after they had left – or at best, meet again for a fleeting moment at William and Mary's. Emma hit the ball blindly because she had closed her eyes in a stern endeavour to hold back tears, so that when Justin said from the doorway behind her: 'Hullo, Emma,' she dropped her cue, opened her eyes and saw that she had made a quite beautiful shot. She picked up the cue and turned round to face him, glad that the rest of the room outside the circle of light over the table was dim, but before she could say anything he had strolled over to the table, saying, 'That was a magnificent shot – I can see I shall have to look to my game or you'll be beating me.'

'I'm going home the day after tomorrow,' said Emma, and frowned at the stupidity of the remark. He stood in front of her, smiling. 'Yes – I hadn't forgotten – did you think I had? That's why I'm here.'

Her eyes searched his face and her heart did a double knock against her ribs, only to slide into her shoes as he went on, 'I've brought Will with me – he couldn't wait to see Kitty again. I only hope she feels the same about him.'

So that was why he had come back. 'She does,' said Emma faintly. 'I suppose she'll go back with him.'

'Naturally.' He had caught her two hands in his and was idly swinging them to and fro. 'He drove his own car.'

She allowed herself the pleasure of the feel of his hands on hers.

'Oh, did you travel with him?'

'God forbid! I drove myself.'

That had been another silly remark on her part; of course he would need his own car now he was back in Holland for good. She stood quietly, very conscious of him, wishing she had put on a prettier dress, aware of his own impeccable elegance and unshakable calm, aware too that she loved him more than ever. She essayed, 'Of course you'll need it here, won't you?' and heard the laugh in his voice as he echoed, 'Of course, I can't very well go to work without a car, can I?'

She longed to ask why he hadn't written but said instead, 'You aren't going back to William and Mary's?'

'Probably not. Have you forgotten that I intend to settle down – did I not tell you that I should marry?' He was still holding her hands and looking down at her with a smile to melt her very bones. 'Emma, can't you guess whom I shall marry?'

She stared up into the green eyes and the gleam in them made her suddenly reckless. She was about to answer him when the door was flung open and Saskia danced in. She ran across the room, flung her arms around his neck and kissed him, crying, 'Justin, how lovely! I've been longing for you to come,' and somehow he wasn't holding Emma's hands any more, for Saskia's arms were around his neck and she was laughing and talking at the same time, and presently he was laughing with her as though it hadn't really mattered that he and Emma had been interrupted.

Emma stood a little apart, not looking at them and feeling cold inside and rather sick because she had so nearly given herself away. Her relief at not having done so was so great that for the time being at least, it overshadowed every other feeling, so that presently she was able to walk arm-in-arm with Justin, laughing and talking to them both as though seeing them reunited was the one thing she had wished for most. Once in the sitting-room it was easier, for Will was there. She flung herself at him, very much to his surprise, exclaiming how delighted she was to see him again and begging to hear all the news of the hospital.

He said a little awkwardly, 'Hullo, Emma. Good lord, you do sound keen – anyone would think you wanted to get back to work. I must say you look as fit as a flea, old lady – you've been having a smashing time, so I'm told.'

Emma caught at this conversational straw and embarked on a detailed account of their holiday, very conscious of Justin and Saskia deep in conversation by a window and conscious too that Will was longing to get back to Kitty. It was Mevrouw Teylingen who separated them at last, gently urging Will to take his bag up to his room and then come down for a drink before bedtime. 'You must be tired,' she urged, 'and I'm sure you will want to make the most of Kitty's last day – I daresay you have already made plans to go out.'

It seemed he had, Kitty had already said that she would show him the surrounding countryside he explained to his hostess and then, rather red in the face, said hastily to Emma, 'You must come too, Emma.'

She improvised hastily, 'Thanks, Willy, but I can't possibly. I must go into Oudewater – I've an appointment at the hairdresser and there are one or two things I want to get, and it's my last chance.'

She smiled at him quite naturally, confident that he wouldn't stop to wonder why the possessor of long brown hair, done in a neat bun on top of her head without the aid of waves or curls, should suddenly wish to visit the hairdresser's. His relief was so patent that she almost laughed out loud.

She was ready for bed, sitting aimlessly before her mirror staring at her reflection when Kitty came in. Kitty glowed; she said at once:

'Isn't it marvellous that he came? He never said a word in his letters . . . he's going again the day after tomorrow. You don't mind if I go with him, darling?' She added belatedly, 'You can come too, if you like.'

Emma turned round on her stool and studied her sister. 'No, darling, I'll go back as we arranged, only you'll have to see about your ticket. I shall be back a bit after you – Will said something about taking the day boat, but that won't matter at all. Are you going to marry him?'

Kitty smiled dreamily. 'However did you guess?' she asked. 'Of course I am, just as soon as we can get everything planned.' She looked apologetic. 'I know we haven't known each other long and you've been friends with him for ages, but somehow we just knew, and you don't need to know each other, do you?'

Emma didn't answer this purely rhetorical question. 'I'm so glad, darling. Will's a dear and just right for you and you're exactly what he needs. Mother will be so pleased.'

'Yes. Emma, I thought that you and Justin – I mean, it seemed as if. . . .'

Emma examined a non-existent spot on her chin in the mirror. 'Oh, we're great friends,' she said airily, 'but you know how it is, people come and go.' She yawned and got to her feet. 'I'm tired, Kitty, time for bed . . . all this excitement. Won't it be fun, planning the wedding and where you'll live? Will you finish your training?'

Kitty nodded. 'Yes, that's one thing we're sure about, though it's all a bit vague.' She strolled to the door. 'Good night, darling.' At the door she paused. 'Do you suppose Justin's going to marry Saskia?'

'I should think it very likely.' Emma's voice wasn't quite steady because she had been taken unawares. She jumped into bed and pulled the bedclothes up very high so that her voice, when she said good night, was muffled.

Emma wakened at six o'clock after a night of sleeping and waking and thinking which had got her nowhere at all. She lay and watched the morning sky brighten and then got up, because to lie there in bed any longer would have been quite intolerable. She dressed quickly and slipped on quiet feet down the staircase, across the hall and out of the small sitting-room's window on to the terrace. The garden looked lovely under the gentle warmth of the sun. She paused for a minute to look around her and then hurried across the grass to its furthest end where there was a door in the wall leading on to a narrow country lane. The lane wound through flat meadows, occasionally with a small canal for company, on the other side of which the cows clustered. It was all very peaceful and secure and although it wasn't as beautiful as the Dorset countryside, Emma had come to like it very much. She walked fast, trying to outstrip misery and failing so singularly that she began to cry, not caring in the least because there was no one to see; every now and then she wiped away the tears with the back of her hand, but fresh ones fell and after a while she didn't bother any more.

She slowed her walk to an amble presently, not looking at all where she was going and stumbling a good deal, sniffling miserably. She heard the first whistle only vaguely and the second one made no impression either. It was only when Bess and Caesar came bounding up to leap joyfully at her that she came to a halt and because there was no alternative, turned round. Justin was only a few yards away and she turned round again quickly because her face looked so awful, and began to walk on at a great rate, but he caught up with her and turned her round to face him again. His voice was very kind. 'Emma, dear Emma, crying – why?'

She sniffed and mumbled grumpily without looking at him, and then because she had to make the best of a bad job, 'I suppose it's because the holiday's over.'

'But yesterday you were all agog to hear all the hospital news. I thought you were so anxious to get back to work.'

She cast him a smouldering look and sniffed. 'Well, of course I am,' she declared, and then burst into tears again.

His arms were very comforting. He held her close until her sobs quietened and then he lifted her chin with a gentle compelling hand and kissed her; she kissed him back, powerless it seemed to do otherwise, and then stood silent within the circle of his arms, looking at him. He smiled at her and it seemed strange, because she was filled with such a wild excitement, that his face was so calm, only his eyes gleamed beneath their lids and a small muscle twitched at the corner of his mouth. When he spoke his voice was as calm as his face.

'Emma, I have to go to Utrecht this morning – in a few minutes. I shan't be back until the day after tomorrow; I don't know when. Will you wait for me? Never mind your plans, we can alter those quickly enough, only be here, at my home when I get back. I must talk to you.'

Emma smiled soggily. 'Very well, Justin,' she said meekly, 'only won't Kitty and Will mind?'

His eyebrows arched. 'Why should they mind? You weren't going with them – besides, I imagine they have other things to think about.'

He laughed suddenly and released her, catching her by the arm and swinging her along beside him as they walked briskly back along the little lane, the two dogs racing ahead. At the door of the house he paused at the bottom of the double steps and lightly kissed her hair. 'Till I see you again, Emma,' he said, and walked away in the direction of the stables, leaving her to drift up the steps and indoors, her head in enchanted clouds.

She was a little late for breakfast because it took her a few minutes to erase the havoc of her tear-stained face. She slipped into her place beside Kitty and wished everyone good morning in a happy voice and got on with her meal, hoping that someone would say something about Justin so that she could tell them that she wouldn't be going until he returned, but no one did, at least not until the meal was almost over and they were dispersing from the table. It was then that Saskia said:

'I'll say goodbye. I'm off to Utrecht in half an hour or so and I shall be there a couple of days, I expect – it depends on . . .' she laughed, 'well, it depends. Have a good journey, won't you?' As she left the room Emma heard her voice, very clear in the lofty hall, calling to her mother. 'Have you any message for Justin?' she asked.

Emma found the day long; she went to Oudewater because she had told Will she was going, but once there, she merely roamed the streets of the little town, doing nothing, trying to puzzle out why Justin hadn't told her that he was going to meet Saskia in Utrecht. In the end she forced herself to stop thinking about it, he would be back the following day with some simple explanation she hadn't thought of. She loved him and trusted him and he had asked her to stay because he wanted to see her, surely that fact alone should be sufficient.

She had lunch after that, in De Witte Engel, and carried on some sort of conversation with the landlord who remembered her very well, and afterwards, because there was still the afternoon to get through, she walked slowly back to Huize den Linden and spent the empty hours sitting in the garden until the others returned. It was easier when they were there and presently she went indoors to pack and change her dress for dinner, cheering herself with the thought that the evening couldn't last for ever and it would soon be tomorrow and Justin would return.

# CHAPTER NINE

WILL and Kitty left quite early the following morning and Emma, coming back into the house after having seen them off, found Mevrouw Teylingen waiting for her in the hall.

'There you are, Emma,' she said kindly. 'Come and keep me company over breakfast, you must feel a little lonely without your sister and Mr. Lunn.' She tucked an arm under Emma's and led her to the dining-room where the meal was lying ready on the table. Mevrouw Teylingen seated herself and bade Emma do the same.

'You will be leaving soon, my dear?' she inquired gently. 'I rather gathered from what Kitty told me that you will be going some time today.'

Emma accepted a cup of coffee and found herself, to her annoyance, colouring under Mevrouw Teylingen's bright gaze. 'Well,' she began, 'Justin has asked me to stay until he . . . I'm not sure when I'm going.'

Her hostess gave a little laugh. 'How like Justin! He can't bear to see you go, Emma, and how well I understand him. You see, he has had many girl-friends, but you are different because, forgive me – you are not pretty, my dear, but you are a pleasant companion and charming and above all, you understand his work so that he can talk about it to you. You must have helped him a great deal during these last few months. He has had to wait so long for his dream to come true and he has been so patient; to have had a friend such as you, an older woman who has outgrown a young girl's silly dreams, must have helped him so much, for it has been hard for him – harder for him than for Saskia.'

'For Saskia?' repeated Emma. It was like being toppled into a bad dream. She wondered what she was going to hear next, and she didn't have long to wait.

'Did he not tell you? Perhaps he felt it to be unnecessary, for you are such a sensible girl.'

Emma didn't feel in the least sensible. She asked in a

voice which, she was surprised to hear, sounded quite normal, 'Justin and Saskia? Are they– do they love each other?'

Her hostess smiled at her. She at any rate, thought poor Emma, was enjoying the conversation. 'Of course, my dear. Isn't it charming?'

'But Justin is seventeen years older than Saskia. . . .'

'What are a few years? He has known and loved her since she was a baby. When she was a child we lived in The Hague, but even then they saw a great deal of each other, and when Justin's father died ten years ago and his mother two years later and I was myself a widow, we came to make our home with him – someone had to run the house, and I have always loved this place so much. Saskia was fifteen then and in all these years they have remained devoted.'

'Why haven't they married?' asked Emma, the question almost choking her. But she had to wait 'for her answer, for Mevrouw Teylingen didn't reply at once but offered her more coffee and Emma was forced to pass her cup. Only when it had been returned to her did her companion answer.

'This will seem extraordinary to you, perhaps, Emma, but when Saskia's father was dying he asked her to promise not to marry before she was twenty-four – so odd, don't you think? but there it is. So she has waited, but now, within a very short time, it will be her birthday.'

Mevrouw Teylingen nodded and beamed at Emma as if to invite her to join in her pleasure at the prospect, but Emma didn't answer because she couldn't trust her voice any more and because she was remembering. Hadn't Justin told her – and how happy he had looked when he had done so – that he was going to take a wife? He had even asked her to guess who it was and she, poor fool, had thought it was herself and would have said so if Saskia hadn't come in at that moment. She thanked heaven for that now, swallowing humiliation and wretchedness and, keeping her voice calm with a great effort, remarked, 'Well, I think I might be in the way if I stay on, don't you, Mevrouw Teylingen? What do you suggest that I do?'

Her hostess answered her without hesitation. 'Why, my dear, there is no reason for you to go – nothing is altered, is it? Saskia has always understood – unless,' she paused and went on delicately, 'am I right in supposing that you have lost your heart a little, after all? If that is so, then surely for your own sake it would be best to go.' She looked at her watch. 'I daresay there is a plane . . . Justin won't be back until tomorrow, though I don't know when.'

Emma sat back in her chair. 'I'm not running away, Mevrouw Teylingen,' she said steadily. 'If I leave tomorrow, that will be time enough. I won't go before I have seen Justin and wished him good-bye – I said that I would wait for him to return, and after all, we are good friends. Besides, that gives me time to cancel my ticket and arrange for a flight.'

She thought that Mevrouw Teylingen looked annoyed, but the expression was so fleeting on her handsome face that Emma told herself that she had been mistaken. 'Will Saskia be back before I go?' she asked.

'No – she isn't returning until tomorrow evening. What a pity, she will be sorry to have missed you, but I daresay you two girls will write to each other.'

Emma thought it unlikely; Saskia had never shown any preference for her company, although they had got on well enough, and for her part, she could think of no reason for writing to Justin's future wife. She got to her feet. 'I think I'll go for a walk,' she said quietly, 'it's such a lovely day after the rain.'

Mevrouw Teylingen beamed at her. 'That's right, Emma, but take care not to tire yourself. Justin invited you here so that you should have a good rest before you started work again. He's such a good man, you know, always doing a kindness to anyone who needs it.'

Emma thought about that remark too while she strolled along the lanes behind the house. Had Justin just been doing her a kindness? Had she been blinded by her own feelings for him so that she had imagined that he was beginning to love her? She tried to recall any occasion when he and Saskia had behaved like two people in love and could think of none – possibly, she told herself with her usual good sense, because Justin wasn't the kind of man to show his feelings in public. She wondered about the other girls Mevrouw Teylingen had talked about too. Had they been trivial affairs, to while away the time until he could claim his Saskia, and in any case surely he and Saskia could have become engaged even if Saskia was bound by her promise. Emma frowned and stopped to think with greater ease. Saskia didn't strike her as the sort of girl who would bother about keeping a promise if it interfered with her own inclinations. She walked on again slowly thinking about herself and Justin; it hadn't been an affair; it had gone deeper than that, with her at any rate and, she had thought, with him too. But she had so obviously thought wrongly; Mevrouw Teylingen's words made sense. She came to a crossroads and sat down on the grass verge, staring at the flat country around her and longing suddenly to be away from it all, back in theatre, working so hard that she had no time to think. Tears which she had been holding in check suddenly got the better of her; they trickled slowly down her cheeks and at first she wiped them angrily away, and then didn't bother any more but let them fall as they pleased.

It was when she got back to the house for lunch, calm but still puffy-eyed, that Mevrouw Teylingen told her that Justin would arrive early the following morning, and added kindly that she had taken it upon herself to book a seat for Emma on a plane leaving about midday. Emma, touched by her hostess's thoughtfulness, and not caring how she went as long as it was soon, thanked her gratefully.

She was ready to leave when Justin arrived back the next day, although there was still half an hour to wait for the taxi. He came striding through the door and when he saw her standing rather aimlessly in the middle of the hall, came straight towards her, smiling, only to check his stride as his quick glance took in the suitcase beside her. The smile slid from his face, leaving it without expression, and when he spoke his voice was harsh. 'Emma, what is the matter? Where are you going?' He stopped before her, staring unsmilingly into her face, his eyebrows raised. 'Escaping before I could get home?' His voice was silky.

'No,' said Emma quickly, appalled at his perceptiveness, and truthful even while she was brokenhearted. 'I wouldn't do that, Justin. I stayed so that I could say good-bye.'

'Indeed? So you are leaving us – leaving me, Emma, my dear Emma.'

Emma nodded. 'Yes, and I don't have to explain, do I? I mean you must know without me having to tell you, and I'd rather not talk about it, if you don't mind.' She gave him a rather shaky smile, proud of her self-control when what she really longed to do was to scream at him at the top of her voice that she loved him to distraction and had been foolish enough to imagine that he was beginning to love her when all the time he had merely been seeking solace – safe solace with an older woman – against his longing for Saskia. She choked on the thought, seeing herself as a kind of stopgap for him, and because she hadn't been demanding or asked questions, he had taken it for granted that she looked upon the whole thing as an episode to be forgotten once she was back in hospital. She scowled at him, causing his eyebrows to soar once more.

'My dear Emma, what have I done?' He moved a little nearer. 'I must insist upon being told.'

She moved a little away and then stopped because the stairs were behind her and that way she was cut off from retreat. She sidled sideways instead and he laughed. There was the beginning of anger in his laugh, though, and his snapped 'Well?' did nothing to invite her confidence.

She said quietly, 'Look, I was going back very soon anyway, wasn't I? It surely doesn't matter if I go a day or two earlier. I didn't think you would mind – not now Saskia's birthday is in less than a week.'

'What the devil has Saskia's birthday got to do with it?' he demanded, and then smiled suddenly at her, a tender, mocking smile which tore her heart in ribbons. She drew breath with difficulty. 'Please let me go, Justin, without a fuss,' she said in a cold little voice which quenched the smile and had the instant effect she had wanted.

'Of course, dear girl – I would be the last person to hold you.' His voice was light, it was also impersonal; it was as though he had gone a long way away in a matter of seconds. 'How are you going?' He spoke pleasantly, the perfect, well-mannered host.

'By plane – the taxi's coming. . . .'

He frowned. 'Taxi? When there's a car in the garage – you only had to ask Piet.'

'Mevrouw Teylingen thought that a taxi would be better.'

He said nothing to that, but, 'I'll drive you myself,' he began when there was the sound of someone coming along the upper landing and down the stairs and he turned to see who it was, saying to her over one shoulder in a careless voice, 'Don't argue, please. When does your plane leave?'

When she told him he said, 'Good – I've time for some coffee.' He turned back again to the stairs and observed pleasantly, 'Good morning, Tante Wilhelmina. I've just told Emma that I will take her to Schipol, I've nothing to do for a few hours. How is it that you ordered a taxi when Piet could have taken the car?'

Mevrouw Teylingen came down the staircase at her usual stately pace although she was breathing rapidly. 'Justin dear, you're a little earlier than I had expected, but how nice. Did I do wrong? It seemed a good idea – I'm sorry. Did I hear you say that you would drive Emma yourself? Then may I come too? I should enjoy the drive and I want to see the dear child safely on to her plane.' She smiled at Emma as she spoke and Emma returned the smile warmly because she really was a kind and thoughtful hostess and she had tried so hard to help.

Mevrouw Teylingen swept past Justin now and tucked Emma's hand under her arm. 'Shall we all have coffee? I'm sure it's ready and I want to hear about your plans, Justin.'

He nodded carelessly and said with his usual courtesy, 'Just as you like, Tante Wilhelmina. I'll cancel that taxi and join you.'

They drank their coffee in the little sitting-room while they carried on an uneasy conversation, largely sustained by Mevrouw Teylingen, who didn't appear to notice her nephew's absent-mindedness, or that Emma hardly spoke at all. Presently she got up, saying, 'If you like to go out to the car, Justin, we will join you in a minute or so. There is something I wish to give to Emma before she leaves.' She bore Emma away upstairs to the big bedroom Emma had never seen, and told her to sit down while her hostess put on her hat and coat. Emma, undecided as to whether she was relieved not to be left alone with Justin or disappointed at not having the chance to talk to him again, did as she was asked and when Mevrouw Teylingen presented her with a little package and a charming little speech in which she stressed how much she would miss Emma, accepted it with gratitude and followed her companion downstairs again with an air of composure which successfully concealed her chaotic thoughts.

Her bags were already in the car and so was Justin, sitting behind the wheel, looking thoughtful. He got out, however, when he saw them at the door and ushered his aunt into the back seat, then opened the door for Emma to sit beside him. As she got in Mevrouw Teylingen said a little plaintively, 'Oh, dear – I had hoped that Emma would sit with me,' a remark which fell upon apparently deaf ears, for Justin didn't answer her but got into his own seat and drove away in silence – a silence, Emma realized, he had no intention of breaking.

'It's a pleasant morning,' she began. Her voice sounded a little high-pitched and wooden to her ears, but on the whole it wasn't too bad. She tried again. 'I shall get a splendid view of Holland from the air.'

She had no success with this unoriginal remark and there was a nasty little pause while she cudgelled her tired brain to think of some topic in which he would be forced to take an interest. How dreadfully English she was, she thought without humour, to fall back on the weather. 'It rained in the night,' she said finally.

When he did speak his voice was pleasant and casual. 'So you were awake in the night to hear the rain.'

She undid the clasp of her handbag and then did it up again and when she spoke, addressed her fidgeting fingers. 'Well – yes.'

'Making up your mind to leave me?' His voice was still casual, but when she peeped at him she saw that his lips were curved in a smile – not a very nice smile.

'No – I'd already done that.'

'Oh, before you went to bed, perhaps?'

She replied without thinking, 'Oh, yes – long before then.'

His voice held mild interest, nothing more. 'Ah, and when was that, I wonder? When I kissed you before I went away?'

She cried out in sudden pain, 'No, oh, no, Justin! You weren't there, it was after you had gone, after Kitty and Will had gone, when. . . .'

Perhaps her voice had been too loud, for Mevrouw Teylingen interrupted her, her own voice a little louder than usual.

'Emma dear, there is the windmill about which I told you – you remember? The one which is supposed to be haunted. Such a pity we never managed to visit it.' She went on at some length about the mill. It was surprising what a great deal of information she had to offer Emma about it, and when she at length stopped, Justin gave no sign of wishing to continue their own conversation, but talked instead, in the impersonal tones of a casual acquaintance, of the various landmarks they were passing, nor did he attempt to do anything else for the remainder of the journey.

When they arrived at Schipol he saw to her luggage, bought her an armful of magazines, observed that the flight should be a good one and then went on to talk easily about a number of subjects which, to Emma at least, didn't matter in the least. She, agreeing politely that the weather, on the whole, was better in England than it was in Holland, and that the new enclosing dykes along the coast were a remarkable feat of engineering, longed to shout 'Stop!' so that she could have a chance to say all the things she wished to say and now would never have the chance to tell.

Her flight was called and she submitted to Mevrouw Teylingen's kiss and clasp of the hand with a kind of numb resignation before she turned to Justin. Since she had to say good-bye, she would get it over quickly – a sentiment it seemed he shared, for he gave her the briefest of handclasps and said nothing at all, and as he had allowed the lids to droop over his eyes, it was impossible to tell, looking up into his impassive face, what he was thinking. She said briefly, 'Good-bye, Justin,' and turned away to the escalator. At its top she looked back. Mevrouw Teylingen waved, but Justin wasn't even looking.

She had obediently fastened her seat belt, sucked her barley sugar, accepted the daily newspaper and unfastened her seat belt again, all without being aware of what she was doing. It was only as she craned her neck to see Holland's coastline slide away beneath her that she remembered that Justin hadn't said good-bye, which was strangely comforting even though she would never see him again.

Her hospital bedroom, after her room at Huize den Linden, was bare and poky and unwelcoming. She unpacked, reported to the office for duty on the following morning and went down to the tea she didn't want.

In the Sisters' sitting-room she was welcomed back by her friends and colleagues, who according to their various natures asked a variety of questions about her holiday, ranging from the sort of weather she had had, from Sister Cox, who wasn't romantic, to an inquiry as to how many times Professor Teylingen had taken her out and where, from Madge, who was. She answered their questions in a serene voice which successfully hid her true feelings and the fact that her thoughts were far away; even while she discussed the weather with the thoroughness Sister Cox expected of her, she was wondering, with a sense of loss almost too great to be borne, what Justin was doing.

Professor Teylingen wasn't drinking tea, nor was he answering questions; he was asking them. He had just returned to his home after an exacting afternoon in the theatre and now, in his study, he was facing his aunt who, bidden to join him there, was sitting with a very straight back in the chair before him. Unlike Emma, he had a great many questions to ask, lounging back against his desk with his hands in his pockets, he said quite pleasantly, yet with a hint of steel in his voice.

'And now, Tante Wilhelmina, that I have the time to put my own affairs in order, I should like to know exactly what it was that you said to Emma while I was away.'

He smiled at her as he spoke, but his eyes were hard and glittering. Her own dropped before them and after a moment she began to tell him.

The strict theatre routine was strangely comforting to Emma, for it gave her no time to think, and because Sister Cox was only working for an hour or two each day, Emma took most of the lists, going off duty each day too tired to do much more than eat and sleep. Little Willy, now that he was to be her brother-in-law, lectured her severely on overworking and lack of social life and she listened to him obediently, looking meek, and went her own way. She had driven home in the Ford on her first days off, and her mother, in the instinctive way that mothers have, had asked few questions, and those of only superficial interest concerning her stay with Mevrouw Teylingen, and once or twice, lulled by her mother's silence, Emma had been tempted to tell her all about it. Perhaps, she decided, she would in a little while, when she could speak of it without feeling the urgent need to burst into tears.

Instead, they talked about Kitty's wedding and future. She was to finish her training as a doctor, Will had been adamant about that; he would pay her fees, and he had already applied for a post at her hospital, which, if he was successful, would entitle him to a flat, so that he and Kitty could set up house and live there until she had qualified. Then, Will had said firmly, they would look around for a practice and go into partnership, and Emma had been secretly amused to see how meekly Kitty had agreed with him. He might be a shy man, but he had a will of his own – like someone else she knew. She sighed, and her mother, sitting at the table totting up the egg money, heard her and without appearing to do, gave her an anxious look. That something had happened in Holland was only too evident. Emma's face had got thin even in the few days in which she had been back at work and she ate almost nothing. Mrs. Hastings shut her various little notebooks although she hadn't finished her sums and said brightly:

'I long for a glass of sherry – let's have one, shall we? And then how about running across to the vicarage and fetching that book I promised to take to Mrs. Coffin next time I go?'

Emma fetched the sherry and as her mother had known she would, expressed her willingness to fetch the book too and take it to Mrs. Coffin while she was about it; it was a pleasant evening, the walk would do her good.

Mrs. Coffin was glad to see her. Emma sat down when bidden to do so and listened to Mrs. Coffin's experiences in hospital and how she had returned home and how very kind everyone in the village had been. Having exhausted this interesting topic she wanted to know, rather archly, how Emma's young man was getting on, and when Emma said she was mistaken, it was Kitty who had the young man, Mrs. Coffin had smiled and said that that was all fiddlesticks. It had been obvious to her, ill though she had been at the time, that the handsome doctor who had rescued her from the well had fancied Emma. 'I'm an old woman,' she went on, 'and you can't tell me, Emma – never a word did he say, nor did he do more than glance at you, but certainly he fancied you.'

Not any more, thought Emma, and plunged into further inquiries concerning Mrs. Coffin's state of health without answering any more of her questions. That good lady said no more on the subject of young men; she gave Emma a knowing look from her faded blue eyes, mentally storing up a few inquiries of her own about dear Emma, next time her mother should call.

There was a terrific list when Emma went back on duty on the Wednesday. She frowned over it in the office, wondering what Mr. Soames had been at to allow so many cases, but when she queried them with Sister Cox, that lady had tossed her severely capped head and remarked acidly that it was about time they did some work now that the foreigner had gone and she herself was on duty again. It was a pity that an hour later, just as she was preparing to scrub, she decided that the ache in her toes justified her going off duty. She went back to the office where Emma was frowning over the replacements list and said briskly:

'You'll have to manage, Sister Hastings. Staff's off at five, isn't she? Well, she'll have to stay on – you've got an evening, haven't you? Mr. Soames should be through by then.' She didn't mention the work which would have to be done after the last case had gone back to the ward – nor did Emma. She knew better than to argue with Mad Minnie when she was in one of her mean moods, but of one thing she was certain, Staff should go off at four o'clock, not five – the poor girl had hours of time due to her. She had been working like a slave and deserved it. Emma got up from the desk and took off her cuffs, preparatory to scrubbing. She said, 'Very well, Sister Cox,' in a quiet, non-committal voice, while she mentally juggled with the day's off-duty for the nurses. With luck they would manage and it wouldn't be the first time.

She broke the news to Mr. Bone as she went through the anaesthetic room and he gave the thumbs-up sign and muttered, 'Thank God, girl, I'm not in a mood for Minnie today,' and smiled at her broadly, and Mr. Soames and Little Willy, while not using Mr. Bone's exact words, obviously shared his opinion, adding that they hoped she would be able to manage.

'Yes, thanks, just about,' said Emma, and now she came to think about it she was quite glad, for she would have no leisure to think all day and she had half promised to go to the housemen's party that evening. With any luck she would be so tired that she would sleep all night, something she hadn't been doing lately.

The day went well despite the rush of work. Emma and Staff gobbled sandwiches and drank a jug of coffee between them while the nurses went to their dinner, sitting in the office with the tray between them and their shoes off. They both looked hot and tired and pale and neither of them had any make-up on any more.

'That was a piece of luck,' commented Staff, 'those two cases going so well.' She bit hugely into a ham sandwich. 'I thought the second one was going to take longer, didn't you?'

Emma nodded. 'Yes, I did, at least we're up to time so

far. You scrub for the lobectomy, will you? I'll dish for the aortic aneurysm and take it, it'll take some time, and you're to go at four whether it's finished or not, but before you do, dish for the stricture of oesophagus, will you? Cully's off at five, too, isn't she – and the technicians and Mrs. . . .' she brightened. 'There's Staff Nichols on at eight. If we're not cleared up she'll give a hand, she always does.'

Staff puckered her forehead in a frown. 'Yes, but Sister, what about you? You'll not get off at all. Suppose I stay?'

'No need,' said Emma decisively. 'I've not got anything planned for this evening, only the party, and that won't brighten up until ten o'clock.'

Staff nodded in agreement. 'True, if you're not too tired. You don't look – that is, Sister, you haven't looked very well since you've been off, kind of pale and unhappy.'

Emma poured the last of the coffee. Collins was a nice girl, she was probably only repeating what everyone else was saying. 'That's an appendix for you,' said Emma serenely. 'Takes the stuffing out of a body, I can tell you.'

Collins eyed her thoughtfully. 'Did you have a lovely time at the professor's house?' she asked at length.

Emma had been thankful that until now they had been too busy to chat about anything. She had imagined erroneously, she now realized, that after a week or so it would be easier for her to answer that sort of question should she be asked it, but all the pain and misery she had kept damped down inside her since she had left Holland came surging back so that she had difficulty in speaking. With an effort she replied lightly:

'Oh, absolutely gorgeous – I must tell you all about it some time, but we'd better get cracking now, hadn't we?'

The afternoon went as well as the morning had done – Emma sent the nurses to tea one by one, snatched a cup herself with the surgeons between cases, chivvied Staff off duty and returned to the theatre. There were two more cases, the aneurysm and an emergency – a lung abscess, and that would mean a lobectomy. As the patient was wheeled in Mr. Soames looked at the clock and said, 'The last one, I hope – if they spring anything else on me I shall put my foot down.'

Everyone knew that he didn't mean that; if a dozen such cases were to come in one after the other, Mr. Soames would grumble luridly at each of them and perform brilliantly as he always did, and Little Willy would stand opposite him assisting, without a word of complaint.

Emma nodded to those fortunate enough to be going off duty and watched them slip quietly away. They were already late, she would have to make it up to them when she could – when next Mad Minnie was off duty. She was left with Jessop, doing her best, and the two technicians who had offered to work overtime. Emma gave them each an encouraging nod from behind her mask and bent to her trolleys.

It was well after seven when the case was wheeled away and the men had gone. Emma, not bothering to take off her mask or gown, left Jessop to clear up and wash down and started on the instruments. There were more than usual to do because Jessop hadn't had the chance to take away those which had been finished with. Emma collected them into a bowl and went over to the sinks. Each one would have to be scrubbed, rinsed, inspected and bunched on rings according to its kind and autoclaved.

The evening was warm, the close warmth of an approaching storm. Emma pushed her theatre cap back from her forehead and set to work. She was almost through as Jessop put the finishing touches to the now spotless theatre. Emma looked round with a trained, eagle eye. The girl was shaping very well and was entirely trustworthy, something every nurse, and even more so in theatre, needed to be. Emma made a mental note to persuade Mad Minnie to give Jessop a glowing report at the end of the month and said cheerfully, 'Finished, Nurse? Off you go then. You're over your time, I'm afraid, but I'll see that you get it back. You've done very well.'

Jessop beamed. 'Oh, Sister, have I? Thank you. I don't mind when you're here, you know. Shall I ask them to save your supper?'

'Supper?' Emma's thoughts had been miles away, with Justin. 'No, thank you, Jessop. I'll have a cup of tea or something, I'm too tired to eat.'

She looked up as she spoke and surprised a look of excited amazement on Jessop's face. She was staring at the door so that Emma, naturally enough, turned to look too.

Justin was standing there. 'A pity you're not hungry, Emma,' he said with the casual calm of someone who had only just left them and had returned on an afterthought. 'I thought we might dine together, unless of course you prefer the party downstairs.'

He walked slowly into the theatre, paused in front of Jessop and said with a smile, 'I've just been talking to Peter Moore – he was hoping you had finished, he's waiting to take you to the party, I believe.' At which remark Jessop went a bright pink and smiled widely. 'I should run if I were you,' he suggested mildly, 'that is if Sister has finished with you.'

He lifted an inquiring eyebrow at Emma who said, breathless, 'Yes, no – yes, of course, Nurse Jessop. I hope you have a lovely evening.'

Jessop fled to the door. Before she went through it, however, she paused and looked back. 'And you, Sister, I hope you have a lovely evening too.'

'A discerning girl,' observed the professor, strolling a little further. 'What have you still to do? The sharps and needles? Good, get on with them, dear girl. I want to talk to you and if you're occupied it will be easier for me.'

'Why?' asked Emma in a whisper.

He went to lean against one of Sister Cox's white-painted glass-fronted cabinets, where the more out-of-the-way instruments were kept.

'My darling, think. If you are cleaning knives and so forth it rather discourages me from taking you in my arms, which is what I want to do, but before I do that we have to understand one another, do we not? I think I shall talk better if there is the width of the theatre between us.'

He smiled tenderly at her and she dropped a string of forceps back into the sink with a little clang. 'Be sure and warn me when you are finished,' he urged her gently.

Emma nodded, picked up the last of the instruments and walked across to the shutter in the wall which opened into the sterilizing room, pushed it up, placed the rings of instruments in the basket waiting for them, then crossed the theatre, out through its door and into the sterilizing room to screw down the lid of the autoclave and turn on the steam. She went through this exercise without knowing in the least what she was doing – luckily she had done it so many times that there was no fear of her doing it wrong – and then walked back into the theatre again. Justin was still there; for one awful moment she had thought that it might all be a dream, brought on by too much work and nothing much to eat for most of the day, but he was there all right. He walked towards her as she made her way to the operating table where the sharps and needles were drawn up in orderly fashion, awaiting her attention. She came to a halt by them, looking at him inquiringly. When he was near enough he stretched out a hand and pulled her mask down under her chin and then went back again to where he had been standing, saying in a quiet voice:

'That's better. I must see your dear face, it seems a long time, though it's barely ten days. I missed you, Emma. Did you miss me?'

'Yes,' said Emma, not looking at him. Her hands shook a little as she picked up the curved stitch scissors. There were a lot of sharps and a great many needles; she wondered what Justin would do when she had finished them.

'I should have known,' he began. 'It wasn't until I got home from the afternoon list at the hospital that my brain began to work – you numbed it, my sweet darling, going off like that; I couldn't think and I didn't dare until I'd finished my work, then on the way home I began to see a glimmer of sense in it all, for you said, if you remember, that you had come to a decision to leave while I was away and after Will and Kitty had gone, so I knew that it must have been when you were alone with Tante Wilhelmina. I didn't know what she had said to you, I could only guess that it was something she didn't want me to know about, otherwise why was she so careful to prevent us from talking to each other? I had almost made sense of it by the time I reached home, and when I asked her, she told me.'

He paused and in the silence Emma sniffed, because the hard lump of unhappiness she had been carrying around with her for days was melting fast and she was going to cry at any moment. 'Did you believe her, dear love?' His voice was very loving, and Emma, busy with her sharps, sniffed again and said in a damp voice, 'Well, yes – you see, it all made sense to me too and I thought your aunt liked me, and Saskia's so pretty . . .'

'And I have never told you that I love you, have I?'

Emma was arranging her variety of scissors in the thick glass container which housed them. 'No,' she said soberly while her heart sang, 'you never have.' She snapped the lid of the container on securely and turned her attention to the needles.

The professor crossed one leg over the other and thrust his hands into his pockets. He could have been discussing the weather, so calm was his face, only his eyes glinted greenly.

'I had some ridiculous old-fashioned notion about not rushing you, my darling. Kindly remember that I am middle-aged and therefore a little out-of date in such matters.'

'How could you be – all those girls!' declared Emma quite viciously. 'Your aunt told me,' she went on, stabbing some cutting needles into their square of lint with extraordinary violence.

'None of it is true,' said Justin, watching her – reading her thoughts. 'It is simple when you know; Tante Wilhelmina would have liked to live in my house for the rest of her life – all that nonsense about Saskia marrying me was pure fiction so that you would go away. You see she guessed how I felt about you, Emma. As for Saskia, I've never thought of the girl other than as a young cousin, and she looks upon me in the light of an older brother.'

'Indeed?' Emma's voice was cool, 'and the – the girls – Mevrouw Teylingen told me that you have had a great many girl-friends.'

'Naturally,' he agreed genially, and she took her eyes off her work just long enough to see the amusement on his face. 'I'm forty, Emma – surely a bachelor of that age is allowed girl-friends?' He saw the look on her face. 'Only girl-friends, my dearest Emma, never one special one, not until I met you, sitting in that ridiculous car of yours, spitting with rage because the door wouldn't open. I should have kissed you then and there and married you out of hand. As it is, you have been my constant distraction ever since. The only cure is to marry you and never let you out of my sight again.'

Emma had finished the needles. She folded the lint carefully, aware that Justin had come across the tiled floor, to stand, tall and large and solid, beside her. She turned her back on him and heard him say,

'If you will turn round, my dearest girl, I will ask you to marry me.' She felt his fingers at the back of her neck, untying the strings of her mask. He pulled her cap off too, so that her hair, already untidy, was worse than ever, but he didn't touch her and she stayed as she was.

'Before I do I want to know what will happen to Mevrouw Teylingen and Saskia – will they go on living at Huize den Linden?'

'Saskia is going to live in Utrecht. She is going to marry someone who lives there – that was why I went there, to meet him. Her mother knew nothing of it – it was a little shock for her, I'm afraid, but I have bought a house for her in The Hague. She will be happy there, I think, and in time we shall become friends again and she will come to visit us, I daresay, but I want no one in my home but you, my darling, and me and the children you will doubtless see fit to present me with.'

She hadn't quite finished. 'You've been ten days – I never thought I'd see you again.'

She felt his hands on her shoulders as he turned her round at last.

'I have a job like any other man – I couldn't get away sooner, and I wasn't going to write and risk any more misunderstandings. And now have you finished asking questions, because I have one to ask you, my love.' Emma smiled at him then. 'Will you marry me, Emma darling?'

he asked.

He gave her no chance to answer him, but bent and kissed her mouth with slow gentleness and then again, very hard so that she was left without breath.

'You haven't answered,' said the professor, and kissed her again, this time with ruthlessness.

'Well,' said Emma, still very much out of breath, 'you give me no chance.' She smiled at him and her mouth had never curved so sweetly. 'Of course I will, my dearest.'

She reached up to put her arms around his neck. 'What did you wish when we blew out the candles?' she wanted to know.

Justin smiled. 'That is my secret, my love, although it is only fair to tell you that my wish came true.'

'So did mine,' said Emma, and reached up to kiss him.

# Have You Missed Any of These
# *Harlequin Romances?*

# Other 'Medical' Harlequin Romances
## you may enjoy

Over the years when Harlequin Romances have been published, many of our most popular titles have been stories revolving around life and romance in medical fields throughout the world.

An assortment of some of these titles, available through the Harlequin Reader Service, is listed on the back of this page.

Should you wish to obtain any, simply fill out the order coupon below.

# Other 'Medical'
# Harlequin Romances
## you may enjoy . . .

All books listed are 50c.   Please use the handy order co

E